C. L. DONLEY

Halcyon*

Second edition

This book was professionally typeset on Reedsy.
Find out more at reedsy.com

Contents

Prologue		v
1	Cliff	1
2	Bria	8
3	Felix	13
4	Cliff	23
5	Bria	37
6	Lyric	53
7	Luke	62
8	Bria	72
9	Cliff	90
10	Luke	101
11	Luke	116
12	Bria	128
13	Luke	142
14	Bria	155
15	Luke	173
16	Bria	186
17	Cliff	196
18	Chase	211
19	Bria	220
20	Cliff	232
21	Luke	241
22	Bria	253
23	Epilogue	264

Join the C.L. Donley Mailing List!   271

Books by C.L. Donley   272

About the Author   273

Prologue

Five Years Ago

Felix was on patrol when he got the call.

"We got a white male, mid-20's, on the edge of the Wester bridge, looking ready to jump."

"I see him," Felix responded, the closest patrol highwayman in the area.

He slowly pulled up to the median, nixing the flashing lights in case he spooked this guy.

For some odd reason, the first thing he noticed was that the dude wasn't all that bad looking. A solid five. Six on a real good day.

He just needed a chick, a remedy that only solidified its place in his mind as time wore on. And from the looks of it, that would be relatively easy. He was gonna be home in time for dinner.

"Hey bro," Felix said to the man who had his hands behind him backward on the railing, like a four-year-old ignoring the insistent warnings of his mom.

"Hey," the guy answered with a nervous laugh. The low tone of his voice took Felix aback. He was like the Barry White of bridge jumpers.

"Look, there's a better way to watch the ferries if that's what you're trying to do. We got a couple of phone calls. You're spookin' the motorists."

"I'm not trying to watch the ferries. I'm gonna jump."

"Jump? Like... to kill yourself?"

"Yeah."

"Well, are ya sure this is gonna do it?"

"Yeah. I saw a documentary about it."

Felix looked down at the water below that certainly looked intimidating, but not like it could kill a guy.

"Well, I hope you're right about that, chief. For your sake. You don't look like a guy that has a history of... being right about things."

The young man huffed a laugh that slowly turned into a lighthearted giggle, then a belly laugh, tears clinging to red eyes. Finally, he stopped.

"You got me, officer."

"What's got you ready to kill yourself, if you don't mind me asking."

"I do mind. I don't wanna talk about it," the man shook his head mournfully with his eyes shut, like it was making him sick.

"Look, bro, I'm not asking for a whole long story, trust me on that. Just trying to figure out your thought process here."

"Well, my thought process is that I'm a piece of shit. And I can't bear to spend another minute with myself."

"Well, I gotta level with you... uh... guy."

"Cliff."

"...You're hanging off a bridge and your name is Cliff?"

"Yeah."

"Well... Cliff... I gotta level with you, I think if you jump offa this bridge, the ambulance is gonna come scoop out your broken, but living, body, and you're gonna be spending even more time with yourself than you ever wanted to. Don't you have someone in your life that cares about you?"

At that, Cliff visibly comes apart, shaking, veins in his neck and forehead bulging. Now he wasn't looking so pretty.

Felix wanted to lunge, in case he made a mistake reading this guy, but he stays put, even when Cliff shakily shifts his weight to a more comfortable position, eyeing the water below.

Clearly the answer to this question was "yes." Felix was starting to worry if this guy had done something to him or her himself.

"I did something... horrible."

Shit.

"What'd you do, Cliff?"

"I hurt someone. Someone really fucking special."

Double shit.

"Wait, who are we talking about?"

"Her name's Lyric," he replied in a labored stutter, "or at least that's what she called herself. I don't know her real name."

"What does this 'Lyric' look like?"

"She's...you know... heavy set. Black. Er... African American. Got this real pretty face. You know, one of those big girls that you're sure would be a ten if they lost the fuckin' weight..."

Felix prepared himself to call in an 041A, but the way this guy was talking, he wasn't so confident he was dealing with a homicide.

"What'd you do to her, Cliff?"

"I broke her heart. I was her Match. And I fuckin'... I'm a piece of shit bro, just let me jump. Whatever happens to me, I deserve it."

"I don't understand, why can't you just... go get her."

"What part of 'I'm a piece of shit' do you not get!" Cliff spat, yelling. "I don't want her to be with me. She doesn't deserve me. And I don't deserve anyone."

"But if she's your 'match' or whatever you keep saying... I don't know, wouldn't it be easier to just... make yourself into the type a guy that deserves her? Then you can both be happy?"

Cliff stopped and listened to his words, a serene twinkle in his eye for a brief moment.

"That'd never work."

"Well, why not?"

"Because they make it so you can't track 'em down after you say 'no,' it's... this program thing we were a part of."

"Oh, you're not talking about that Halcyon thing? Where they guarantee you find your soulmate or whatever? You must be loaded."

"I live with my parents. They paid for it."

"Ah," Felix said, the picture getting the slightest bit clearer. "I thought it was guaranteed? They had 100% success, that's their whole thing."

"I guess I'm the first loser. Not surprising."

"Decent looking guy like you, wealthy family. What do you need with a program like that anyway?"

"I was engaged once before but she dumped me. I didn't wanna go at first, but I started to look forward to it. 'Halcyon's a sure thing' everyone told me. I couldn't lose."

"You should sue those fuckers "

"It's not their fault. I opted out," Cliff shook his head, calming down. "When the program's over, they separate you. They do this exit interview and rattle off a buncha shit, and they're required to tell you that you can opt-out, which means you're basically cut off from that person for the rest of your life," he continued with a sniff.

"You go in with fake names, you don't know anything about

them except for what they tell you, which they make sure is vague. It's basically like they're in witness protection."

"How do they make sure?"

"Make sure what?"

"That some chick doesn't just give you her home address? During the program?" Felix asked.

"You're monitored 24 hours a day. Plus, there's no reason to break the rules, really. Everyone's there to get a match, everybody follows the rules."

"What if you see someone in there you like more?"

Cliff's mind goes to Cherie and Dave.

"I saw something like that. But you're not allowed to talk about the program to anyone else, once you're gone or while you're there. They all become ghosts after you leave."

"So you could be in trouble for what you just told me?"

"...Not really. It's more like... if your grandma had a secret recipe. They don't want anyone knowing how the sausage gets made."

Felix saw the other squad car he'd called in a ways off. He needed to keep him talking just a bit longer.

"So... you're here about to kill yourself because they paired you up with a fat chick, and you reacted by... being a dude?"

Cliff closed his black eyes.

"We were together in there for six months. Day in, day out. It was like co-ed jail. She knew everything about me. Not the facts, but... me. She knew me. And I knew her. We fucked. We fucked a lot. She was a virgin when she got there, you know? But sexual. Real fuckin' sexual. Like... the kind I always dreamed about.

"She had these huge tits," he sniffed, snot trickling out of his nostrils. But he was still holding on to the railing with both hands and he didn't seem to notice. "Wasn't really my thing, but... it became my thing. She became my thing. She fuckin' loved me, bro. And I just... let her go."

Felix fully got the picture now. Poor bastard.

"You thought you could do better than her."

Cliff huffed a confirming laugh. "It's wierd because... I knew that I couldn't. But I still did it because... I had to. I just couldn't go through with it. Couldn't be with her," he marveled. "I'm a piece of shit, so... I did what pieces of shit do."

"I don't think piece of shit guys know that that's what they are."

"Of course they do," Cliff scoffed. "I'm just... spoiled, I guess. I'm so fucking tired of me bro..." Cliff mourned. The water works started up again and Felix watched him for sudden movements. Thankfully he had more to say.

"She was my fucking Match, dude!" Cliff spat. "My parents said I'd been on a waiting list for a year when they got the call. And then I waited a year to get matched," he heaved, full-on crying now. "I tried to move on. Immediately. I left there, and I got fucked up... some chick gave me crabs," he confessed, bawling and leaking water from every opening in his raw face.

He removed one of his arms to cover his face with his jacket sleeve and sob. It took everything in Felix not to rush out and grab him and give himself away. He stiffened and kept his eyes on Cliff while he signaled the other car. Cliff continued.

"I hadn't watched any porn in six months, and I got home. Jesus. It was like the situation room at the fuckin' pentagon. Fuckin' twelve windows open..."

"Well Cliff, I gotta tell ya, your 'piece of shit' assessment sounds pretty accurate," Felix sympathized.

Cliff just nodded.

"I say, before you make this decision, you run it by your

'match' first."

"I just told you, I have no way of tracking her down."

"Can't be that hard. I mean, I'm a cop, I got... resources. Fat chick, African American, got enough dough to afford this program..."

"She sings. Really good. Like a fucking angel."

"See? The haystack is getting smaller and smaller."

"Who are you, anyway?"

"Who am I? I'm Felix."

"Okay."

"Him over there, that's Officer Paul."

Cliff looked over his shoulder in the direction Felix is looking in and saw another officer closing in on him.

To his credit, Felix didn't gloat about how long he'd been able to stall and get Cliff talking. He just continued his conversation earnestly.

"Now we won't put the cuffs on you, you're not under arrest."

"I can't go home. I'm not going back to my parents' house."

"We'll take you wherever you want."

"Wherever I want?"

"Well, within reason. There's a couple of places—"

"I don't want to go to some hospital."

"Okay."

"I don't wanna talk to a shrink."

"Fine, I'll drop you off at my house. You can meet the wife, the kids. Put a little pallet on the couch for you."

"Really?"

"No, bro."

Cliff stared at him a bit and then snickered. Felix smiled. He looked over at Officer Paul, who was well within range to stop him from doing what he was thinking.

Calmly he sniffed, his blotchy face calm as he put one leg over the railing and then the other. A few onlooking cars honked as if in support as the trio made it back to Felix's squad car.

"So what do you wanna—"

Before Felix could finish his sentence, Cliff had already found his out.

The bus blared its hideous horn as Cliff quickly backed himself away from the officers and into the traffic.

Felix instinctively turns his head away from the carnage. He'd made the mistake of not looking away before, and it wasn't worth nightmares.

But he'll never forget the sound.

1

Cliff

I can't stop fiddling with the silverware that gleams on top of the clean white linen tablecloth. There's an empty plate staring back at me as I sit at the bistro just a block away from the live music venue boasting three acts from the modest marquee.

The name of the club is "The Lion's Den." Surrounded in lights below the club's name are three acts, one of which is A Band Named Lyric, also the headliner.

After spending a year in Houston, I'm about to come face to face with Bria Forrester, the lead singer and the woman I'm now 99.9% sure was my Match.

Now that I'm within a few feet of her, I'm a fucking mess.

I have so much less than what I started this with. The last six years have just been embarrassing. I don't feel worth the wait.

Moving to Houston was one thing, but now I feel like I'm going to start coming apart at the atomic level. So does Felix, who's flown in from Chicago especially as emotional support for this occasion.

"Dude, you're actually changing colors," he says. He speaks

again when I don't answer him. "You're really fucked up right now, aren't you?"

I can only nod my head and breathe through my nose, an old anxiety attack technique from my days in the hospital after I gained my memories back.

Part of me wants to go running back there. Part of me doesn't want to catch this carrot.

"Bro, you got this. If this is it, I mean... this is everything. Right?"

"I don't think I can do it."

"Hank, you always get to this point and start freaking out. You just gotta get over the wall."

"I don't think I can."

"You have to."

"I don't."

"Bro. I have listened to you moan, and bitch, and cry, for six... fucking... years. And in that time, I have molded you, and fashioned you, into a badass."

I look across the table at him after he stops.

"You need me to continue?" Felix asks. I nod.

"When I found you, you were a pile of *shit* and *feces*, in a drunken stupor. About to kill yourself. Not about to, you did. You stepped in front of a fucking bus. It was Cliff versus the bus, and you know who fucking won? Well, the bus did. The bus definitely won that one but *you*... also won. Because you met me."

"This pep talk has taken a turn."

"And when you decided you didn't want to quit, that you wanted to live, you transformed yourself. From the lowest pile of shit to one of the greatest highway patrolman in the tri-state area."

"I did most of that."

"You look good, you smell good. You fuck girls and never call them."

"Not a good time to bring that up."

"What I mean is, you *both* consent to *not call* each other afterward. Because they know you can't be tied down. They don't even try. They just want a taste of the Cliff bar, so they can go through life and be satisfied."

My breathing slows. Felix is completely ridiculous, but that's why he's helping. It's true, mostly. I've come a long way. Dragged myself all the way down from whatever is below the bottom.

"Now you're gonna walk into that seedy-looking club, and you're gonna look that bitch... sorry, that girl... *woman,* in the face, and say, 'Lyric, it's me, "Luke." I was so miserable without you that I jumped in front of a bus. I've come to take you home.'"

I hang my head and let out another sigh. If he only knew how far away that ship has sailed for me.

"You guys ready to order yet?"

"We still need a minute, I'm so sorry," I raised my head up.

"Look, if you guys aren't gonna use the table—"

"Here's twenty," Felix offered. "Just give me and my friend some time to get it together here."

The waitress quietly put the bill in her front apron. "Take all the time you need."

My attention remained on Felix. "There's still a chance that it's not her."

"Is there, though?" Felix wrinkles his face.

"There's always a chance, you know. I could walk up to her and she could just look at me like I'm insane."

"Is that what this weird back and forth is all about? The fear

3

this is just some broken unreliable flashback? All of this and she doesn't even remember it?"

I try not to get emotional and mostly succeed. "It's worse than the thought of rejection. I can't explain it."

Felix just rolls his eyes at me. "C'mon dude. To know a girl named Lyric who sings in A Band Name *Lyric*??"

"Right?"

"If this isn't her, then she's simply not out there. And then... maybe let's make this the last time we do this."

His words give me a panicky feeling, but I nod.

"...Maybe you're right."

"You know what? I wouldn't be surprised if the part that's freaking you out the most is you not being able to do this to yourself anymore. Part of you has become comfortable with the search. You're afraid of it being anything other than a drill."

"...No, I'm pretty sure I'm just scared that she's going to reject me the same way I rejected her. And since I totally have it coming, the odds are slim that this will go in my favor."

"....Potato, po*tah*to."

I watch Felix order and finish a burger while all I can do is nurse a glass of water and push a salad around my plate.

I can hear faint music playing up and down the downtown strip. It's probably another hour or so before it's time for A Band Named Lyric to go on.

The name Lyric was an alias. We all had one. Mine was Luke, chosen for my love of all things Star Wars, and the distaste for my real name, the name of my father.

No one was allowed to share their real names in the program, or much of their lives beyond what's experienced in the program. Everything was heavily monitored, and the rules were taken seriously, especially since the program cost a shitload of time and money, and no one wanted to risk leaving there without a Match.

The Halcyon program is still a thing. They like to boast their residual longevity rates, with none of the Halcyon couples reporting divorce or separation by anything other than death. Now, their slogan boasts 99% success. I can't help but think I'm responsible for that 1%.

There's no blueprint for what I'm doing. I signed over the rights to know anything about her when I opted out. So I can only follow my gut.

The first time I saw Bria I thought, *no way is that her.* She should've been a needle in the entire barn, forget the haystack. No way do I deserve to be that lucky.

But as soon as I moved here, my anxiety all but went away. Like I knew I was breathing the same air as her and I was okay. Every once in a while I'd panic a little, wondering what the hell I was even doing, but I kept on. Still too afraid to show up at one of her gigs and force myself to get it over with.

For six months I was looking over my shoulder, waiting to run into Lyric at any moment. After a year, though, the band's profile keeps rising, and an extra lap around the grocery store is not enough to force this encounter anymore. I was going to have to rip the band-aid off. I had to go to a show.

I stand at the back of the venue with Felix, watching the young 20-somethings continue to crowd in as the night wears on and the band prepares to go on. The feeling of adrenaline has intensified and I don't know whether I wanted to catch a glimpse of her or not, if I want the night to be over as soon as possible or to never end.

My head involuntarily whips in every direction, anticipating a glimpse of her. Even though rationally I know all I have to do is wait for her to emerge onto the stage.

Suddenly the lights dim and the crowd begins whooping and hollering as the spotlight comes on and the MC announced the next band.

"Ladies and gentlemen, without further ado, A Band Named Lyric."

The crowd instantly goes wild as the lights go out again and the stage turns blood red like a darkroom.

Three guys and three girls come and slowly take their places at instruments set up on the stage. Bria, clearly the lead, comes out in a sparkling gold mini skirt, a black blazer with a t-shirt underneath. Her hair's in a messy bun with strands falling careless across her flawlessly made-up face.

My heart revs and revs like it's trying to leave the jail of my body, my mind tries to stay steady and objective. Trying to make her out in the darkness.

She has the same average height, the same proportions as I remember but of course smaller. Much smaller. Still what some men would consider plus size, but barely.

I knew she lost the weight, but being in the same room with her makes it harder for me to reconcile for some reason. My memories fight what I'm seeing and almost win out. There's no way this could be Lyric, I think every other second.

But between those seconds I'm sure, heart-breakingly sure that I'm in the right place.

The spotlight returns and I look into the rockstar's face.

Her big eyes are dramatized by her shimmery dark eyeshadow, her sharp cheekbones pronounced and contoured. Her full gorgeous lips the deep red color of arousal. Beautiful. Arresting. Stunning.

I just need to hear her sing, I think. The voice would cinch it.

Even though I listened to a few tracks before I had to stop. It was too slick. Unsettling. I didn't want to listen to any more unless I could be sure I was hearing my *prasice*, Lyric.

Bria launches into an acapella cover of an old 90's song like she's read my mind, her and her backup singer behind her.

And it's like my memory's come back to me all over again, transporting me against my will, back to those hourless days we spent holed up in our quarters. Lyric singing absent-mindedly, not knowing or believing her own talent.

The voice that lulled me to sleep, made me believe in miracles, and eventually grated on me. The voice I was meant to hear until I died.

The band swells behind her and her voice is swept along the rapid of the drums and guitars until finally, her voice bursts forth like a supernova, confident and full of life on the wings of the chorus. Everyone in the audience can feel it— they're witnessing something special.

But none of them really knew how special it was. None of them heard it in its infant stage. Not like I had. I stand transfixed, her image blurred behind my gathering tears.

"Dude, this chick is *amazing*!" Felix shouts into my ear halfway into the performance. I don't say anything as Felix looks over at me wide-eyed like a child.

Me, I'm as calm and quieted as an old tree, knowing this is the last time I'd have to wonder if I'm batshit crazy or not, or if I would have to go on another wild goose chase for a girl.

I know I've found the one.

2

Bria

"This one wasn't on the setlist," I announce halfway through the set, "But there's a special person in the house tonight. At least, I think there is," I giggle, sweaty and shaking, adrenaline pouring through me, more than usual.

The familiar silhouette of a man I've only ever known as Luke stands stoically in the back of the club, head and shoulders above everyone else here.

"If he isn't, then my mistake. I'm gonna do this one anyway because it's one of my favorites that's gotten me through... many a night. If he is, then this is for you."

I give Braxton the signal. He starts a meager kick while the piano begins climbing the ladder of a melody familiar to many in the audience.

Most know the original, but I can see some of the regulars. The die-hards, the ones there from the beginning— well, my beginning— that drive out of town to every show. Instantly they are "whoo!"ing before the first line quickly begins.

"Tough girl/in the fast lane/No time for love/No time for hate..."

I'm so damn lucky to be doing this. So grateful.

I don't want to cry as soon as the fucking song begins. Not if the one I think is here really is.

He doesn't get to see me cry. Ever.

But he needs to know a little bit of what he missed when he was gone, what he did. And this is my chance to convey it the best way I know how.

The song gets to the vamp and I can't resist closing my eyes and leaning into it as I grasp the empty mic stand, giving it a bitter bite so that I'm gritting my teeth as the words come out:

"*I come home/on my own/ check my phone/ nothin' though/act busy/ order in/ paid TV/ it's agony...*"

I don't mean to do it to 'em. The whole room didn't leave me there at check-out alone, waiting on my Match for hours like a doofus. Because he said he would be there. He said he was going to choose me...

"*I may cry ruining my make-up /wash away all the things you've taken/ I don't care if I don't look pretty/ big girls cry when their hearts are breaking...*"

I feel the energy in the room. Everyone's with me.

Everyone's felt it, whatever I'm singing about, even the boys. And they are all united in disdain for this fuckface, whoever *he* is— and they know it's a guy. It always fuckin' is.

I swear I can feel the energy of one, who is very uncomfortable.

He really *is* here. But I can't look at him now. Or I'll totally lose it.

The audience sings along by the second verse and now I might cry for a totally different reason.

When he left me, I was 86 pounds heavier.

He didn't see the other 86 I gained after I went home.

Nor did he see me claw myself out of that hell one pound at a time. Or give myself the skin removal surgery as a gift after a year of keeping the weight off. Or get on the stage for the first time ever at my heaviest.

And now the stage is by far the most comfortable place I can be. Now I have an army, and they're helping me humiliate this dirtbag.

He should probably not stick around after the show if he knows what's good for him.

"*I wake up/I wake up/I wake up/I wake up...*"

Jesus. The days stack up in my mind as I sing, flashes of the lowest lows that no one else would ever know. So many days...

I turn away from the crowd, but I don't want to look at my band either or I will fall all over them weeping. They don't know anything about my life before I wandered into the Astrose with Skye and saw them perform for the first time.

I let the audience fill in for a while, but I've only got a few seconds to pull it together.

I'm not gonna make it. The music is driving, the audience encouraging me to crowd surf my emotions right here, as though they know full well what they're asking for.

There's no place to hide, which is usually a good thing. I've got no choice but to use it.

I squeeze out tears with my eyes shut tight, scream-singing:

"*I wake up/I wake up/I wake up/aloooooooone...*"

I'm on my knees before I know what's happening as I riff off the background vocal, prostrate in front of the hot lights, pounding at my chest with a conviction that would have Celine on her feet.

Braxton is playing steady and strong, holding me up as I put a hand out, willing myself to deliver the last line as pretty and haunting as I can:

"*Big girls cry when their heart is breaking.*"

The stage instantly goes dark, a stroke of genius by the lighting guy and I think, *we're definitely playing this place again.*

The crowd is going bananas, which is good, because I need a moment to recover, and so do they.

Damn. Now the finale is gonna seem like a throwaway compared to this moment, but oh well.

It needed to happen.

I imagined a couple of scenarios over the years, if, by some miracle, we ever ran into each other on the outside.

At first, they were almost always tearful and rant-filled. In front of a crowd. Later they became full of sweet and syrupy revenge, smiley and cold.

"Luke? Is that you?" I'd say as though he were a distant memory, while I'm a size six.

It was the image I was walking to on the treadmill, and eventually running to. Running to the moment when he was simply a footnote, the impetus to become the person I was always meant to be. No more important than the head of a match.

Then I would say, "Well... I gotta go. But it was good to see you!"

I haven't thought about that fantasy in a long time, I realize, as we complete the set.

I was always accompanied by a man in those fantasies. Some-one to come and wrap his arms around my shoulders while he looked on at the devastation in the face of my "Match."

But like the fantasies, the phantom man who never had a speaking line also faded away. I can't even imagine being tied down right now. I simply don't want it.

Chase and I got our tryst out of the way pretty early and now we're great friends, great songwriters. Connected in a way now that means more to us both.

"Thank you, San Antonio," I say in a husky, seasoned singer voice. "My name's Bria, we're A Band Named Lyric, good night!"

3

Felix

Gotta be honest, part of me always wondered if Cliff was a little touched in the head and/or making all this Halcyon shit up.

I mean, can you blame me? First time I meet the guy he's on the side of a bridge ranting and raving about his "long-distance girlfriend," or whatever. That he conveniently couldn't find and didn't know her name. Because he was in this confidential program. Then he loses his memory, gets it back and suddenly sees her on TV, I mean it reeked of bullshit. Even when the parents came around and corroborated the story.

In a way, it justified his grandiose, attention-seeking behavior and his need to be obsessed with someone and be their knight in shining armor. Maybe he would snap out of it if we hung long enough.

Or maybe, just maybe, he wasn't bullshitting.

I'll be damned if he wasn't telling the complete truth this whole time.

I look over at Cliff who is nervously biting his nail as this Lyric chick begins the song dedicated to him. I shake my head as I listen.

Yep. He was telling the truth and this is the girl. Holy hell, is this the girl.

The fact that she spotted him in a crowded dark room full of strangers tells me all I need to know about this Halcyon thing being no fucking joke. Cliff didn't even seem fazed.

Sheezus. I've never heard the song before, but it's about big girls crying, the double meaning my only clue that this girl had ever been a fatty.

She's still pretty curvy. All the good stuff on her there was plenty of. A gorgeous face, just like he was always going on about. If she was ever shy and insecure, no one in this room would believe it.

I take back every cynical thought I ever had about this situation. This is a girl worth moving across the country for.

He undersold her talent, though. The girl has golden pipes. And she's currently using one of those pipes to beat Clifford to a pulp with it.

She's whipping him gooood with this one. Which he deserves, for sure. Listening to her side of it on the stage, it's making me wonder for the first time if Cliff even deserves a happy ending.

But then I remember Cliff clinging to life in the hospital, Cliff on the back of a bridge, ranting and raving about what a terrible piece of shit he is and how he doesn't deserve to live.

When he was in rehab, I promised to answer the phone whenever he called, no matter what time of day or night. Because I was so bowled over that the man had survived, I figured it was the least I could do. I'd regretted it within days.

"I was just thinkin' about sniff... you know how you stare at someone sniff sniff... and you're so close to 'em that your eyes start to cross? That's what we used to do. Just lay in bed. Looking at

each other until we had three eyes. No talking just sniff... *looking at each other until we couldn't see each other anymore. And I just* sniff sniff... *gave her away. The thought of even doing that with someone else just* sniff sniff... *makes me sick now* sniff...."

He's suffered enough, I think. We both have.

She and the guitarist seem to have quite the chemistry.

She keeps getting right in his face as she sings certain parts. Or just looking at him like there's no one else in the room, rocking the mic stand as she serenades him. Meanwhile, he pays her no mind, strumming away. Like a true fucking rock star.

He's gotta be the boyfriend. This is gonna be messy as shit.

The applause goes on and on as the band retreats backstage. Some people stay put in hopes for an encore, but when the lights come up to reveal a duller-than-average room, the die-hards give up. A soft level of reggae music starts wafting through the air and the crowd begins filing out and milling around.

A few tipsy couples brush by us on the way to the door. Cliff still hasn't moved. His arms are stiffly folded as they have been the entire show. Finally, I speak up.

"I can't believe, after all this waiting, you're fucking waiting."

"I'm not waiting. I'm leaving."

"Is that so?" I chuckle. This dude can't be fucking serious.

"I'm just... I need a minute to recover."

No way did I fly all the way from Chicago for him to walk out right now. I need to see some kissing. With tongue.

"Bro, I came all this way—"

"And I appreciate it. She saw me. She knows I'm here. It's more than I could've asked for."

"You ever think about the fact that she might actually want to talk to you just as much? Maybe she looked for you too."

Cliff takes in a big breath and hangs his head as he exhales.

He's been doing that a lot tonight.

"You gotta man up. You owe her that. Right?"

Cliff doesn't answer.

"There seem to be quite a few gentlemen in the band. Looks like the guitarist might have a thing for her," I warn him.

"Good for him," Cliff answers.

"I can't fuckin' believe my ears right now, dude," I scoff.

"You heard the song. She hates my fucking guts."

"What'd you expect? She thinks you abandoned her."

"I did abandon her."

"But she doesn't know what you've been through," I argue. Was he really going to not tell her about the bridge?

"A very expensive and proven program paired you up through a biological and psychological evaluation. You think guitar guy can possibly top that?"

"Since when did you become team Halcyon?" Cliff scoffs.

"Since tonight. This program paired your dumb ass up with a hot rock star."

"You don't know the half."

"Was this chick really fat once?"

"She was."

"Don't you want to put your arms around that new and improved chassis?" I rib him.

"She's not gonna let me touch her."

"Bro, enough speculation. That's what damn near killed you. Let's play a game of 'find out for sure.'"

"And what if *that* kills me?"

"Then let's stop prolonging the inevitable."

Cliff's quiet because he knows he can't argue with that. I extend my arm in front of us both.

"Shall we?"

16

Just as he's about to make a move, the band members started filing out into the general population that's left.

Out comes Lyric. Some stop to talk to her, some take selfies.

I watch Cliff watch Lyric comfortably interacting with her public. She has sweet, approachable energy, looking everyone in the eyes and listening with animated expressions as they tell her how much they loved the show, where they traveled from, and who she reminded them of.

When I turn back to see Cliff behind me, he's nowhere.

I manage to spot his back as he's heading toward the front door. I quickly turn to follow him.

"You're not that guy on Wester bridge anymore, Hank," I say when we're outside.

"You can stop calling me that now."

"You can't put this off," I say, my feet rushing to keep up with his as we head outside onto the cold wet sidewalk.

"Sure I can."

"What, you're just gonna keep popping up at every show now?"

"Maybe. Maybe she'll—"

"Hey!"

A forceful female voice cuts him off. Cliff and I whirl around at the same time.

There's Lyric, her feet apart in an angry stance just outside the club. I can't see inside but I can hear a beer bottle drop.

Cliff doesn't say a word as Lyric's eyes burn through him.

"Is this you, walking out on me *again*??" she shouts.

Cliff stands there, the loaded silence of years blowing between them like tumbleweeds in a desert showdown.

"I want you," he shouts back. *My* man!

"Is that right?"

"Yeah."

"Since when?"

"Since... now."

"Really!" she answers in a loud, sarcastic laugh.

"Yes."

"Why? Because I'm 100 pounds lighter and I'm more con-fident without you and I'm doing what you said I could never do?"

"Yep."

Uy. I can hear the groans from inside the bar.

"Wow. I can't believe you'd actually admit that."

"I owe you the truth, Lyric."

"That's not my name."

"I owe you the truth, Bria."

Her eyes narrow at the sound of her real name.

"What's yours?" she asks.

"Cliff."

"Seriously?"

"Yeah."

"Okay... Cliff. Since you owe me the truth, tell me something," Bria shouts. There's a little waver in her voice as she broaches the question.

"Did you *ever* love me? At all?"

Fuck. You could still hear that naive girl who signed up for a soul mate. Cliff closes his eyes with a sigh.

"No."

But I really wanted to and I'm sorry, I tried to will him to say, but he didn't elaborate. Like he couldn't make a single excuse come out of his mouth without barfing.

I don't know why he's so fucking hard on himself, but that's the thing about Cliff. It's like he wants punishment.

18

Bria stands stone faced for a bit before she nods slowly, silently. I can see her mouth tremble as tears fall down her cheeks. She retreats back inside the club like a shellshocked soldier. Fucking yikes.

"Sooo... that went well, I think," I say.

Cliff just stands there, looking in the direction of the closed door of the club, like he can't believe what just happened. Hell, I can't believe what just happened.

"Cliff, you alright buddy?"

"I can't believe I survived that."

"Don't celebrate yet. The night's still young."

"Wasn't so bad."

"See? Six years of anxiety gone in an instant. How's it feel?"

"I think I'm having a moment of clarity," Cliff answered in a guru's voice.

"That's just the trauma of being made to look like an ass hat outside of a nightclub talking."

Cliff's confession is drawing a lot of eyes, so we try to turn ourselves invisible as we head back to the parking lot like the rest of the faceless show goers.

We parked in a small gravelly parking lot a block away, a massive overpass looming above us.

"So what happens now?" I ask on the way back to his car. Which is my old one.

"What happens now is that we're going to go get some food because I'm starving. Then I'm dropping you off at the airport tomorrow morning."

"I meant after that."

"After that, I'm headed to Dallas."

"What's in Dallas?"

"She is," he answers resolutely.

And again: *My* man!

"What's the plan?"

"For now, just showing up. No matter what. They're playing in Dallas tomorrow. Then Austin.

"A road trip, huh? Gonna follow her like a groupie?"

"More or less," he replies, compulsively looking around. "They're driving the cargo van with the trailer. She drives a Versa, of all things. I got the license plate."

"Anything you need, let me know," I assure him. I pat his back. "You're on your way, bro. You ready?"

He runs a hand through his hair, really thinking about it.

"Yeah. She may not hear me out, but I need to try."

"Bro, why didn't you tell her the truth?" I ask him as I make my way to the passenger side door.

"What's the truth?"

"That you've been chasing after her all this time and every-thing you've done has been for her?"

He leans on the open door with his shoe on the foot step, the open door chiming monotonous and slow.

"Because I fucked her over. And that's what page she left this on. We needed to get that part out of the way first."

Funny, because if I was him I would choose the part where I jumped in front of a bus and played Harrison Ford in Regarding Henry for about a year, then I fuckin' regained all my motor functions like a boss, joined the highway patrol and got a lateral transfer to Houston, Texas after a year of re-certification and waiting, but...

I guess that's just me.

I shake my head. "Damn. I mean I get it but... if she knew what you've been through—"

"What I've been through I brought on myself. But what she's

been through, what I put her through *again* even showing back up tonight... it's not about me."

"Well, she needs to know. If you don't tell her, I will," I say, climbing inside. Cliff follows suit and our doors slam shut in unison.

"You're my best friend, Felix, you know that?" he says.

"Pretty sure I'm your only friend, Cliff," I answer back.

I see a figure out of the corner of my eye. Looks like a woman coming towards us on foot. One that has to be Lyric.

I lean forward, pointing to get his attention. "Heads up."

He doesn't bother shutting the door when he jumps back out of my old Suburban and walks across the dirty gravel, meeting her halfway under the overpass.

"You shouldn't walk around here alone," I hear him say.

She's still walking full speed towards him even after he stops and I think, maybe she's about to beat the shit out of him. Either that or walk right up to him and start making out.

I hope that's what happens. I spent $300 bucks on this plane ticket and I got a great view from where I'm sitting.

She's changed out of the skirt into a pair of skin-tight jeans. Sweet Jesus.

Her leather jacket hangs off her shoulders and she looks like a black Marilyn Monroe with that wistful look on her face. The fact that Cliff was ever dating this chick is telling me more about him than six years of friendship. She's the type of girl he would never pick on his own. The type of girl he probably needs.

Abruptly she begins slowing down once they're not even a foot away.

They freeze, just staring at each other.

She looks like she's about to launch into a big speech, or maybe some bad news. I hear him say something, take a step towards her, and she steps back with a flinch.

Holy high school drama, Batman. He should just kiss her already.

Suddenly the whole parking lot is engulfed in the headlights of a cargo van behind her. The horn honks and it's as if she suddenly comes to herself.

She backs up without a word, turns and heads for the passenger door of the van.

Cliff just stands there watching as the cargo van reverses the way it came. Which is impressive, considering the trailer attached to it in the back.

Cliff helplessly watches it make its way out of the parking lot, back onto the street and drive away out of sight. Then he just fuckin' stands there.

I honk the horn and he turns around like I startled him out of a trance. The suspense is killing me.

I yell out of the driver side door that he left open, "So what'd she say?"

"Bro," he shouts, standing there with a puzzled look, "I think I'm gonna get her back."

4

Cliff

Seven Years Ago

6pm. I returned home from completing my first week of "work." My parents would be at a party until late. That gave me enough time to jerk myself silly, take a shower, eat dinner, check the messageboard, and find a few of my InCel gamer brothers to play a couple hours of Halo before bed. All in that order.

Ever since my fiancée broke up with me, I've been living at home.

It was a humbling experience to say the least, coming back home after the woman they didn't approve of dumped me. The folks went easy on me when I got home last year, but this year my dad let his agitation show big time.

"If you don't want to be cut off, son, you'll make yourself useful."

Getting "cut off" was the quintessential threat used in every Chicago Novak household. It stopped misbehaving, tom foolery, questionable life decisions and socially unacceptable behavior.

It never had much of an effect on me, but I let everyone think

23

it did. Didn't want to play a decent hand over nothing.

Maybe I'm just spoiled beyond a sense of danger, but I sincerely don't see what's so frightening about not have a constant stream of income.

My life's just as aimless and meandering as anyone who lives on the street. In college, I sometimes spent the night on benches outside to see if I could do it. Campus security never said anything to me. And yet, somehow my parents got wind of it. That was before I flunked out.

I've grown up in a fifth-generation, family-owned empire. Power. The electric kind to be precise. Renewable energy, as well.

So far I'd been forced to work in three different departments of the Chicago headquarters of Novak Electric where my father is a regional director.

He hates it, but he's not doing it for the money, obviously. He's doing it because he can't be seen not doing his part in the family business. Spending the fortune without contributing to it was considered "unpatriotic" and therefore notoriously frowned upon.

My generation has it a little easier, but not by much— especially if you're connected by blood like my father, rather than marriage. My cousin became a playwright, and everyone wished her well. To her face, anyway.

First, I was shipped off to Finance, since that's what I had been studying.

Headquarters is crawling with Novaks, so I worked under one of my uncles. I hated it. But I stuck it out for a year because I had my own office and could spend most of the day watching porn.

Then I tried my hand at Sales, which I wasn't bad at, but I never seemed to meet the quotas and I didn't have an office, so

I had to go to the bathrooms to watch porn. Thus, I spent a lot of time in the bathroom.

Now I'm in Marketing. Why anyone needs to market electricity is beyond me. But my immediate boss is an attractive older woman, no relation. And I have my own office again.

If a woman is asking you if you're gay, it's obviously a shit test. Why would anyone take that seriously? She was just messing with you. She knows you're not gay. Shame on you for taking the bait.

After work, I spend a few hours a day counseling my fellow InCels via the messageboard on which I'm a moderator. It was a community I'd been part of for ten years— anonymously, of course.

A few of our numbers had given it a bad name after they made national headlines, usually by killing themselves or others. Actually, it didn't even really have a name at all until then.

I was going to an all boys high school when I joined, and besides a random distant cousin who took pity on me and gave me some pointers beyond "be yourself," I'd managed to gain experience with a few women in my 25 years. Once I met Stacey at Harvard, I lost interest and stayed away from the board for a few years.

Now I was more of a mentor. I had far more experience than most of these poor bastards had, and I have a lot of wisdom to pass on. Mainly stemming from what I'd done wrong. And as well-meaning as most women seem to be with their advice, only a man could coach another man.

Stacey had unfortunately been my teacher. She had issues. More issues than I did.

But she was beautiful. And she had no idea. She used to be a cutter, tried to hide an eating disorder from me.

I ran my money, my grades, my fragile relationships all into the ground in the pursuit of rescuing Stacey, as much as one can run a fortune into the ground.

No one supported us as a couple, and I gladly walked away from everyone in return.

Eventually, I succeeded. Stacey did a complete 180 and we were happy. She got used to being loved. She was grateful to me and I got to see it every day.

That is, until one day.

One day it just...faded.

I eventually found out she'd cheated on me with one of my... socialite connections, let's say.

And now they were engaged, which is why I hadn't left my room in nearly two years.

I always felt alienated in this little tight-knit elitist world I was born into. And now I can't even recognize my tiny corner of it.

She left me with nothing. She left me with depression. And addictions and a futility about life.

And I was back on the messageboard, licking my wounds and asking forgiveness.

Honestly, Western women are spoiled and at this point not worth the effort. Too much prosperity, too many choices. My suggestion: ditch the West. It's scorched earth. Asian women are cool if you can deal with little to no T&A. Slavic countries are probably your best bet. They dress conservative and are brought up with conservative values. They cook, clean. Basically, if you can keep a job, they're in love.

My mother was basically a mail order bride from Croatia. Back before eHarmony or Tinder.

My dad's a lot like me. He likes to be efficient with his time. He needed a wife. But I have a feeling he never anticipated my mother completing him. I credit her subservience to him as the corner stone to their relationship.

Everyone says that you're not supposed to rely on another person to make you happy. I get it.

But deep down, for as long as I can remember, I've done just that. And the truth is, so has everyone else.

I can't just ignore such a compelling intuition. Somehow I just know, that if I had a woman, I would be happy.

I know it because it's the one thing I don't have. And the one thing money can't get me.

And by woman I mean, a genuine relationship where we're both getting what we want. And by getting what we want, I mean lots of sex. Love. Mutual admiration.

You would think that it would be easy for me to get a woman. But it's been notoriously difficult.

For one thing, I've always been awkward, socially or otherwise. Unnervingly blunt and ill-mannered and well, you know, awkward.

Not the best looking guy. My mom would call it "unconventionally handsome."

I tend to agree. Expensive suits bump every man up three points at least.

I never understood how the guys I grew up with felt comfortable pretending to be some kind of prince. Especially since we all grew up believing our lives were common.

Or at least, I did. It's hard to feign the confidence my name commands beyond an exchange or two. Especially with the girls who've known me essentially from birth and are just as driven as the men that head the families they marry into.

Even normies are notoriously unreliable. Dazzle them for a date or two, but be prepared to keep them away from every male member of your family for the rest of your life.

Women of my caliber these days like a self-made man.

I want to be self made. But how the fuck do I do that?

Never chase. Never, ever chase. Stick every girl you meet in the friend zone. I do this to pretty girls all the time. It drives them insane. Focus on your own goals and let women come to you.

This I knew from personal experience.

I went to college with no friends aside from the Hewitts and most of the East Coast families in our social circle, who are insufferable.

I approached a few women and threw money at them, but soon grew tired of that. So far, it's been no luck for me.

At least, not when it comes to quality. I always manage to organically get the attention of self-involved, low-hanging fruit for some reason. Like I have some kind of sign on my forehead.

My room's the only one on the bottom floor, and with my gaming headset on, the whole place could be getting robbed and I wouldn't know it. So I didn't hear my parents come home.

And I also didn't hear my mom knocking on my door that I usually kept locked.

My mother's sudden presence in my room gave my heart a start. What if I'd decided to reverse my daily routine?

"Jesus, Mom."

"Sorry, dear. Do you have a minute?"

"Not really."

"Something came in the mail for you." My mother held up a large manila envelope. I couldn't think for the life of me what it was.

"I don't think I ordered anything."

"You didn't, *dragi*. It's from your father and I."

I used my game controller to duck my online avatar in the

corner of the live battle I was in the middle of, took the envelope from my mother's outstretched hand and opened it.

"What's this?"

"It's your admission form. To Halcyon."

"Halcyon? That matchmaking thing?"

"They say they've got an opening."

I opened the manila envelop and perused the cover of the catalog: a silhouetted couple watching the sunset from a mountain. *Find your forever match* it read.

"I don't want to go."

"*Dragi*, why not?"

"Honestly, you should be glad that I'm not angry," I flopped the packet down on my desk. "I know Dad probably put you up to this. You know how expensive that place is."

"We're just worried about you, Clifford," mother revved up the guilt machine, "that Stacey has broken your heart. She's stolen our son from us!"

"Hate to break it to you mom, but I'm kind of a loser. Stacey was just the only one around here nice enough to show me."

"It's not true, Clifford. You're a smart, sensitive boy. So adventurous. We used to have the groundskeeper search the property to find you and bring you home. Now you barely leave your room."

"Mom, you're glorifying my childhood again. Just like Dr. Woodrow said," I replied. Dr. Woodrow was the therapist my mother made me see in high school, after she'd snooped through my belongings at school and found the suicidal/homicidal scribblings in my journal. "If I were still that same boy today, it would just get me arrested."

"You know what I mean, Clifford. You overwhelm yourself. You need to be a man, but you are too depressed," she coaxed, her small gentle hand in my black hair, attempting to tame it. "You need to find a woman, like your father did me. Someone worthy to receive your love."

No wonder I was so shit with women. Even my own mother was convinced that I wasn't a man.

I couldn't deny, I did find her words persuasive, however.

Halcyon had a 100% success rate.

It was one thing to deign to waste my valuable time picking up vain whores on the weekends, it was another to spare no expense to cull the herd and find someone truly valuable to me.

If I was certain to find the woman I was destined to be with, that would adore and serve me for life, I could allow myself to be hopeful.

Though, how would I keep her once I got her?

"Mom, you and Dad wasted your money. I'm not even in the position to *date*, let alone find a soulmate. What would we do, move in here?"

"You would move out, of course. We would help you. She wouldn't have to know."

I thought for a moment. Being at home is a bit like purgatory, but living alone is hell.

Much too isolating. Obviously a relationship would change all that. Specifically a wife. Maybe give me incentive to really find my place in the world.

But I really fucking hate the world.

Besides, what if I failed? Again?

"No, mom. I can't do it. I mean, I appreciate the gesture and everything—"

"This is not optional, Clifford. You will do this."

There's that hard eastern-European ethic she'd been hiding.

"...And what if I refuse?"

"It's time for you to survive on your own. I suggested that you do so with love, like I had. But either way, you will have to leave the nest."

My mother's from Yugoslavia, the part which became Croatia once she found my father and moved to the U.S.

Her life had been hard growing up and it made me look at her in almost a reverent light. Every respectful word to my father, every undeserved extravagance my parents bestowed upon me, every stern rebuke against ungratefulness was the evidence that those grim, toned-down stories were still a part of her.

But this was the first time she was dealing with me, not as a son but as an adult. And I knew not to question her resolve.

Her demeanor was alarmingly devoid of sentimentality, and I knew then that she was willing to cut me off.

Because sometimes you spend your whole life raising a child, and that child goes to shit.

It was a reality that would be painful to her, but she could endure and everyone knew it.

I, however, knew I could not.

"What do I have to do?" I sighed.

"There's an orientation next month."

"I suppose there's no harm in checking it out. I've heard it takes months to hear back from this place."

Mom gave me a kiss on the top of my head while I picked the Halcyon pamphlet back up, perusing it. Quietly she made her way out of my room.

"Good night, *dragi*."

"Close the door behind you, please."

When I got back to the game, my entire squad had already died and I was bumped from the match. I was distracted enough already that it didn't matter.

A guaranteed mate. The unspoken etiquette in our circles dictated that Halcyon was for losers, but I have long suspected that a handful of our friends' sudden nuptials in the last few years could be attributed to it.

I really needed to get myself in the best shape possible in the short time I had before this program started, and I didn't just mean physically.

Even if I found my calling in the marketing department of Novak Electric tomorrow, I'd have to up and quit just to go into the program.

The whole thing was daunting, but already it was starting to let an unfamiliar emotion sink in: hope.

* * *

The day Halcyon called me and told me that they'd found a match I was at the end of my rope.

It was over a year later. I was at home in my room, thinking about flying to some remote part of the world and never coming back.

My InCel group voted me out after ten years, which really fucking hurt.

They all assumed I was lying about the experience I had, apparently. And then someone did some digging.

They called me a "Chad" who was only pretending to be an InCel. I argued that after ten years, people grow and change. But the new blood put it to a vote.

Only two of the guys still play online matches with me: sloshingfat and bigbertha2477. I only know them by their screen names.

I left the job I'd kept for nearly a year.

Human resources, of all departments. I worked in a cubicle handling unemployment claims for former employees. Still boring, but something about it kept my attention.

I spent a lot of time on the phone, which I quite liked. It was the only place I'd worked thus far where there was actually an argument that it had to be done.

I seemed to garner this reputation where people were handing things off to me that they were too chicken shit to do. I'd been working there since March, was making actual money and much of my porn habit had waned on its own.

I was down to an hour a day, roughly— my lunch was an hour long and lent me plenty of time to get in a fix and scarf down a sandwich.

A decent looking girl named Megan worked there that I instantly began ignoring, and within a week she was needlessly informing me that she already had a boyfriend.

She at least had some flirt about her. As soon as a normie found out my last name they were instantly shameless, usually.

But this time felt different, because while I was intentionally ignoring Megan, the dream girl I'd been forming in my head ever since I'd finished orientation with Halcyon had practically taken over my brain.

I couldn't believe I was going to get to have sex for six months straight with someone that was psychologically and biologically inclined to be in love with me. And then that was just gonna be my life.

I imagined myself introducing my new gorgeous wife to all my family. Hacking the InCel messageboard, complete with links to my wedding invitation. Recommending the Halcyon program to literally *everyone*. Paying my father back for as long as it took for pushing me into the best life ever.

I knew it wasn't a good idea to imagine a girl before seeing her, especially having to wait as long as I would have to. Girls who needed a program like this probably didn't look like Beyonce anyway.

I didn't want her to see any disappointment on my face on the day we meet. She would probably be a little to a lot homely. Maybe even ugly.

I wasn't too worried about that. All women are essentially beautiful.

Most attractive women were bad news anyway. As long as she wasn't a shallow mindless female version of a bro, I could absolutely deal.

I would have be the one to show her how beautiful she was.

I found myself masturbating, more often than not, to my own imaginings rather than porn, something I hadn't done since I was a teenager.

I started to fall off the wagon about nine months in. Megan, the cute girl at work, broke up with her boyfriend and we had sex after work.

"Listen, Megan, I hope you understand that this doesn't mean anything. We're not in a relationship. And we're never going to be."

"Relax, Cliff. I'd never be in a relationship with a guy at work."

"Then... why'd you fuck me?"

"Judgy much? Why did you?"

We continued our illicit affair for some weeks during which I felt conscience-stricken. As though I were already cheating on my Match.

Why was it always like this? The moment something good enters your life, here comes some sloppy bullshit that's desperate for your attention.

I had to break it off. Halcyon could call me any minute. I

needed to get clean, in more ways than one. Megan was a skank, apparently. I'd used protection with her, but we were going down on each other. What if I'd contracted something?

I couldn't stop being an idiot, and I couldn't stop my fearful paranoia that my idiot actions were causing. I rid myself of the temptation the best way that I could, and that was to quit coming to work.

I left and came home at the same time every day, but somehow Dad found out.

I have a suspicion Megan was bad-mouthing me around the office once I was gone and no longer returning her texts.

Suddenly I was back at home, doing nothing and losing hope I'd ever hear back from Halcyon.

Six months later I was practically living in my room, jobless, ambitionless, and my parents essentially uninterested in talking to me.

I had nothing to say to them. It was days until Halcyon would have to tell me that there was nobody on Earth that matched me, and I would have to come back in.

I was resolved to tell them "no thanks" and ask for a refund. Maybe I could go somewhere overseas. We didn't have many holdings outside of the U.S. Puerto Rico, perhaps.

I was playing Roblox, of all things, when I got the call.

"Mr. Novak. Congratulations, we've found a match for you."

"What?!" I scoffed with my brow furrowed.

I thought for sure they were going to tell me I would need to re-apply.

"Check-in will be at 8am tomorrow."

"Tomorrow?"

"Yes, sir. We'll need you to contact Tiffany with the one-name alias that you've chosen so that we can use it for all your contact information, meal information, security codes and passes and your assigned therapist."

They'd discussed the aliases at orientation, urging us to pick something thoughtful that we would want to be called by our match and others for six months, not to mention memorable enough to answer to.

I had mine picked out within minutes. And had fantasized being called by that name for over a year.

"...Okay."

"Your plane ticket will arrive today at 3pm. Will someone be there to sign for it?"

"I'll be here."

"Very good. Your match will be at check-in as well where you will go through processing together."

I swallowed.

"She'll be there?" I asked nervously.

"Yes, sir."

"I... okay. I- thank you."

"No, thank you," I heard the plastic smile in her voice that somehow also seemed sincere. "Congratulations and welcome to Halcyon."

5

Bria

We could've gotten up early tomorrow to head to Dallas, first for our radio interview and then for the gig later that night, but the gear was all packed and so were we. Taking the three-hour trek to Dallas and paying to use two hotel rooms for about eight hours was preferable to doing this all again tomorrow.

In the front seat all the way to Dallas, I'm lost in thought. The yellow and white lines further entrance me as they go by. All is quiet in the cramped quarters of the cargo van turned tour bus, the hitched trailer swaying a bit due to Chase's lead foot.

I'm a million miles away because I'm stuck reliving the moment that Luke suddenly appeared in the audience of my show tonight like a hallucination. I would've been half-convinced he was one if he wasn't wearing facial hair, a t-shirt and jeans instead of a Halcyon jumpsuit.

Strange. I hadn't thought of him in ages and yet he's never not with me. He walked in and jarred me for a moment, like being pulled through time. His hair was shorter as if his lifestyle somehow required it. It was 90's-heartthrob-shoulder-length

37

when we met and he always stayed clean-shaven.

At the time, I thought he was weird-looking, as most of society probably did. He's got this big face, no chin and a wide mouth that gets even wider when he smiles, his laugh lines like two massive parentheses. Oddly prominent features that he doesn't seem in a rush to reconcile. Photogenic as fuck. The kind of exotic look that would cause natives to speak to him in their language without hesitation if you traveled together, no matter what country you went to.

He was my weird-looking hottie, with his jet black hair, towering, lanky frame, and long hands. The way he could devour me with his black eyes that were a bit too close together. He was as emotionally unstable as he looked. But darkly fierce and sensitive. And his deep voice like a pur that made panties drop, children fall in line and men not want to fight him.

He looks the exact opposite of emotionally unstable now. His air is steady and absurdly masculine. I'm positive I had almost nothing to do with that and it makes me sad. After all these years he's perfect. And I'm... nearly there.

I tried to play coy even though I was desperate to go right up to him and slap him. Kiss him. Shove his hand right down the front of my pants and make myself feel the way I haven't been able to replicate in six years. And then, who knows. Maybe bite that big schnoz of his right off his face. He's even more beautiful now than he was then.

Just when he and his friend began to walk out of the club I abruptly ended whatever surface conversation I was having. A panicked feeling came over me and my breath seized.

I couldn't believe it. He was actually gonna do it again. He was going to walk out.

That motherfucker. He owed it to me to wait a million years.

The fact that he didn't seem to know that had me seeing red.

"You said San Antonio," Chase in the driver seat breaks through my flashback.

"What?" I say, distracted. I harmlessly let my eyes drift to his perfectly pointed jawline, my favorite pasttime up until a few years ago. It's still not the worst way to pass the time.

"Tonight. On stage. You said, 'thank you San Antonio,'" he sighs.

"Did I??"

"Yes."

"Jesus."

"That can't happen again," Chase reprimands me.

"Come on, Chase. Bands tour, they get turned around. It happens all the time."

"In their own hometown??"

"Houston understands."

"They're the only ones. You better not do that shit again on this tour."

Ugh. I hate it when Chase gets all snippy with me.

"Chase, it's not a big deal."

"Sorry, but the correct response is, 'It won't happen again.'"

"You wanna just get into what this is really about?" I ask, looking for a fight. Turns out so was he.

"Depends. Are we gonna talk about whatever the hell happened tonight?"

"What happened?" I play dumb.

"I guess not," Chase says, his eyes alertly on the dark road. "I gotta say, this guy seems like quite the douchebag."

"Ancient history," I reply. Chase scoffs a laugh.

"I'll say. And from what I could tell it looked pretty serious. More than you ever let on."

I may have eluded to a "bad break up" once or twice while we dated. Ultimately, it was the excuse I used to end it with Chase. It wasn't a lie. But it wasn't the whole truth.

"You were the one that assumed it wasn't serious."

"No, I figured it was serious. You never brought this guy up more than once. For most people, that means it's not worth talking about."

"It isn't," I insist, but my short tone conveys the opposite.

"For most people, maybe. But not for you."

I hope he isn't expecting me to respond to that. I look out at the flat farmland in the pitch black that goes on for miles.

"Is he the reason we never worked out?" he wonders. I roll my eyes and scoff. I don't know why I'm so determined to make Luke out to be nothing. It's not necessary. Especially since I've moved on.

"Chase, you're being ridiculous."

"*Wow*," Chase marvels with a shake of his head. Briefly, he glances over at me with one hand on the wheel. "So many revelations tonight."

"We're better as friends, Chase. Obviously."

"Which is what you decided."

"And you conceded."

"What choice do I have? Look, I'm not trying to pry myself back into your heart, I just want to know. Otherwise, it doesn't make sense."

It made perfect sense to me. There's no spark between Chase and me outside of a studio.

It broke my heart to find out that I simply couldn't love him. He was so kind. He got me through the hardest time of my life with just his guitar.

He confessed his feelings when the weight loss plateaued and

I was at my lowest. Well, my second lowest.

I was convinced that Chase was my true match. That Halcyon was all smoke and mirrors.

I still believe Halcyon is smoke and mirrors. But Chase isn't my Match.

I've abandoned the premise of "matches" altogether, like re-wiring my brainwashed mind after leaving a cult. I appreciate the program for what it was, what it taught me, namely that people created their own destinies.

Though I have to give them credit for whatever their methods were. Luke —er, Cliff— could play my body like a symphony.

He was my first. He was absolutely my match in that way. When I discovered that sex could actually be terrible, it fucking shocked me. That alone was worth the price of admission.

"If there's one thing he taught me, it's that sometimes the things that don't make sense is what you're forced to deal with. We don't work, Chase. I don't know why. We work better as writing partners. We were chasing the wrong chemistry."

"And the complete and total vegetative state we found you in has nothing to do with this guy?"

"I was in a 'vegetative state'?"

"You were."

I scoff again, feeling offended but then think about what I must've been like carrying around the very raw feelings of Halcyon, not to mention the weight equivalent of an extra person.

"There was a time I would've answered 'yes.' But now I know it had nothing to do with him and everything to do with me."

"Thank you, Dr. Phil. At least I got you to admit that you dated the guy."

"We didn't date."

"Bri—"

"We were in Halcyon together."

Chase sits in silence as if stunned.

"Halcyon?? That... matchmaking cult?"

"Is it really that surprising?"

"Well, no I mean... it's not like you couldn't afford it, but... I just don't understand why you would work so hard to keep it secret."

"Wasn't really a secret, I was just embarrassed. To be the one that this program suddenly doesn't work for."

"I thought their whole thing was their 100% success rate?"

"I think it's 99% now. Pretty sure that's us. I should probably sue them or something, huh?"

"So, what it's all just... bullshit then?"

"No. As far as I know, we're the only ones that never stuck. But I sort of have no way of verifying that. No one was allowed to share any information that allowed for keeping in touch."

"So... how'd this guy find you?"

Chase's question resonates through my brain and causes a funny feeling in the pit of my stomach and my heart to suddenly jolt to attention.

What if he's been looking for me this whole time? What if he instantly regretted his decision and has been moving heaven and Earth to find some random black girl from six years ago whom he only knew by an alias?

Such a dumb fuck. That's *so* like him to do.

Nah. Anyone with internet access could probably find me if they wanted to. Years ago. So I don't know what he's after.

It's likely I'll never find love I can trust. Not the kind that gives me everything I want. And he's the reason why. I'm not willing to settle. Especially now that I don't have to.

"Bria?" Chase's voice snaps me out of my thoughts again.

"What?"

"I asked you how this guy found you if everything's anonymous."

"Don't know," I finally answer with a shrug, "Must've just... known where to look."

"He didn't know your mom's Minnie Forrester?"

"No. Not six years ago. A few people thought I looked familiar. But it wasn't hard to figure out, I'm sure. Once we were out. With my issues plastered all over the press."

"Well. However he did, I have a feeling we won't be seeing the last of him, unfortunately," he says.

I stifle a smile. *Don't you dare be happy about this... what is wrong with you??*

I give him a convincing groan.

"Yeah, well. Me too."

Seven Years Ago

"Happy Biiiiiirthdaaaaay.....toooooo yoooooou!"

I laughed as my entire immediate family gathered closely around me in a semi-circle, ending their boisterous happy birthday chorus like a gospel choir and then melted it into resounding cheers.

The penthouse view of the city was full of sky as the sun finished setting, and the stark white furniture of the hotel restaurant and bar glowed by the light of all 21 candles along the border of my big birthday cake.

"Make a wish!"

I sat uncomfortably amid my family and "friends," a white

sheet cake decorated further with frosty white flourishes sat directly in front of me. Cameras flashed intermittently during what was supposed to be a modest 21st birthday.

But my family didn't do modest. They were incapable. Sounds of nieces, cousins, nephews and uncles, not to mention staff, drowned out the sound of hip- hop music playing loudly in the background.

I debuted a brand new Gucci dress that my mother had custom made for me. I felt beautiful and my family never failed to surround me with confidence and support.

Perhaps if I'd grown up normal, and not the youngest in one of the most famous musical families on the planet, they would be more stern with me, less forgiving of my ballooning weight and disastrous yo-yo dieting.

But there was no need to teach me how cruel the world can be, or instill a healthy fear of botched first impressions. I'd learned it quicker than most.

No, the family was committed to being a well of positivity. A haven I could always come to. And while they had their failings, I couldn't deny the success of their strategy.

Still, I knew I'd be cut a modest slice of birthday cake. I'd pretend not to notice and spend the rest of the evening watching the remains like a hawk.

I gingerly leaned over the big cake, drew a big breath and blew out all my candles in one long gust and everyone whooped and clapped. I'd inherited the family's lung power, just not as much of the talent.

"We saved the best for first, baby girl," my father began, handing me a manila envelope.

"What's this?"

"Charles, don't give it to her now!"

"Why not?"

"Because!" my famous disco diva mother Minnie snatched the envelope from my father's hand. "This one's for later, baby. In private."

I forgot all about the incident until the next morning, when I emerged from my bedroom in a satin white robe and joined my mother at the dining room table.

The unapologetically blue day gleamed from the floor to ceiling windows in the living area. The beach was a thin yellow line below, the only separation between water and sky.

"Here, honey. Happy birthday," Mom handed me the familiar manila envelope.

I took a swig of orange juice and reached across the table. I opened the top flap and slowly read.

"...You got me into Halcyon??"

"It's not a done deal yet. You still have to go through the testing."

I'd been talking about Halcyon since I was eighteen. Now I was 21, and their flawless reputation had only grown.

"How did you ever convince dad?"

"I told him you were smart for wanting it," my gorgeous mother explained in her red kimono robe. Her full head of satiny ringlets were frizzy from going to bed without her headscarf. "We wanted you to go out and see the world but... you've been everywhere that we have. Seen what there is to see. And you know what you want. And it's love," she smiled that million dollar smile that made her a star, the one that made you feel like every song she sang was about you and to you. She reached out and gave my hand a motherly stroke of understanding.

"You wanna have that love that we can't give you. Can't nobody blame you for that. And I told him, if there was a program that could help you avoid all the mistakes we're scared you're gonna make, there wasn't much to lose."

"Oh my God, I can't believe you did it, Mom!"

"*Who* can't believe it?" Mom gave me an indignant look, snatching her hand back. "Besides, you should probably start early. The reputation is building and even with the high price tag, the waiting list is gettin' real. Might take a year or two to even find someone."

"Well I hope it does. Can't very well quit school at the drop of a hat to go play Big Brother for six months."

"You would love that, Bri, admit it."

"Not when I'm so close, Mom. One more year to go."

"Chile, you know your dad would have you up at the label tomorrow if you asked."

I grabbed the chilled crystal carafe and topped off my orange juice. "I gotta know what I'm doing when I get there, Mama."

"Nothing works better than experience for that, Bri."

I, of course, expected Mother to be Team Experience. She accomplished everything she has up to now by jumping in with both feet and learning the hard way as fast as she possibly could.

"So you're saying you wasted all your money sending me to college?"

"No, I'm just saying... if they call you in the middle of everything, you should just go. College ain't goin' nowhere. You'll regret it much more if you don't. Trust me."

"I will. 'Course I will. But honestly, what are the odds of that?" I said, absent-mindedly flipping through her Halcyon pamphlet. Suddenly I froze.

"Omigod, Mom... this thing says I gotta be there *tomorrow*."

"Tomorrow? For what?"

"Preliminary orientation, it says."

"Oh. My bad."

"'Your *bad*??'"

"Don't look at me like that Bri. I wanted to give it to you earlier, but your Daddy wanted to surprise you!"

"How long have y'all been holding onto this?"

Mom gave me a prolonged silence of guilt before she gave me a diva wave of her hand. "...Well, I can't imagine how that even matters right now."

That night, I couldn't sleep. Even with the extensive training video they'd sent via email, I didn't know what to expect for preliminary exams.

Would I have to lose weight by the time the program began? I'd planned to do it anyway. A quick cleanse was nothing. I just had to time it right, because I tend to gain the weight right back and with a vengeance.

I anticipated losing weight inside as well. Regular meals, cooked by a professional chef, a nutritionist, no snacking allowed. I wasn't going to try and reach my record low, 170. They were going to take extensive pictures of me and I didn't want to set a false expectation at the start in case I couldn't keep the weight off.

I just wanted a little confidence boost going in. If this guy was supposed to be my Match, he should love me the way I am. Right? Whether I stayed this weight or not. "Through thick and thin," as it were.

The program had 100% success. I had to trust the program. They wouldn't pair me with some weirdo with a BBW fetish. Would they?

Of course, I hadn't even thought about the fact that they might pair me with someone I wasn't attracted to. What if I'm *his* type, but there's no spark between us?

Trust the program, was my mind's refrain.

I clearly couldn't wrap it around how this whole thing worked. I was ahead of myself anyways. Tomorrow was just the preliminaries. And finding a match would take time.

I'd been unlucky in love. A hopeless romantic, and hopelessly awkward in front of any man I wasn't related to.

I made a habit of crushing on guys from afar. I told myself all the aggrandizing and heartache was good for my poetry.

I made the mistake of telling my famous child star sister Skye the object of my teenage obsession... and it did not go well.

A fellow co-star of my sister's, actor-turned-R&B-sensation, Marcus. Turns out he wasn't that great an actor.

He had stars in his eyes when we finally met, but it was only for the potential to become a Forrester by marriage. He seemed to like me as a person, but he couldn't hide his lack of physical attraction to me.

It took me forever to see it. He was 25 and I'd just turned 18. It was slightly scandalous and I just wanted to be Jane Eyre so badly, completely ignoring 3/4 of that book.

Overall, it was hard enough on my self-esteem, being both the biggest and least talented person in an entertainment family. The last thing I needed to worry about was the ulterior motives of the people around me.

For me, this program was a Godsend.

The next morning, I felt like I was back at school, taking my SAT's. I got there bright and early at Halcyon Headquarters, a Silicon Valley-esque building with a campus as big and green as a college. Halcyon was tall as a skyscraper and as long as a football field. If it wasn't also housing carefully matched couples on top of being the administrative headquarters, it would've seemed gratuitous.

"Ms. Forrester, join the other candidates in the waiting area, we'll take you all at once," said the smiling receptionist behind a low desk, an intimidating wall of glass elevators, staircases and balconies in the background.

Other than school, I wasn't used to not being recognized. Every time I walked out of my house, I was on my way somewhere I would either know someone or be known. I wasn't famous for anything but being the "fat Forrester."

I only had to see it once in a magazine when I was young to know that's what I was, no matter how many accounts their people blocked or tabloids they kept away from me.

I walked over to the group of a dozen or so candidates, enjoying this new dose of anonymity. A few minorities, but mostly white, diverse in age and gender. After a few seconds of testing eye contact, no one committed. They were likely wondering the same thing I was— is my match somewhere in this group?

What they probably *weren't* wondering is why a girl like me was there. If anyone needed to pay a conglomerate to find me a date it was this one. I imagined they resented me for showing up and skewing their odds.

"I think that's everyone. If you all will just follow me." The receptionist was blonde and impeccably dressed in a black suit jacket and skirt and high black heels.

They click-clacked a short distance to a mirrored wall which turned out to be an entrance to a softly lit conference room lined with long tables and comfortable chairs. Each seat had a set of writing utensils and notebook paper for each candidate.

The receptionist left us with instructions: "Please sit at one of the prepared seats, and please watch the monitor. Dr. Wynchell will be with you in just a moment."

"Welcome, candidates to the Halcyon Project. This afternoon, you will begin your orientation into the program, in which your eligibility with our existing pool of candidates will be determined. You will be given your MBTI assessment, enneagram, our own psychological assessment devised by our Halcyon panel of medical professionals, dietary assessment, biological compatibility control, and your pictures will be taken. In your pamphlet, we recommended allotting at least four hours for this process, but please be advised that it could take longer."

While Halcyon presented an image of professional opulence, individual care and prestige, they also had a knack for appearing extremely busy, and that the busy-ness was always in service to efficacy.

This cattle-like approach lent Halcyon its credibility, beyond its results. Because of its high price tag, Halcyon tended to draw the kind that could afford to be treated like cattle and consider it exotic. On one hand, you were an individual, paying a lot of money to be delivered an individual experience. And yet on the other, you were a biological code, a series of impulses that had to be understood in order to create a product, and that product was, essentially, love.

And so, to this aim, I allowed myself to be poked, prodded, and subject to a battery of embarrassing tests with questions like, "do you feel shame when you masturbate?" or seemingly arbitrary ones like, "I believe in the fundamental kindness of human beings" and all its re-worded control variations.

I got to the dreaded photo portion, which also involved undressing down to my underwear, being weighed on a medical scale, and the biological compatibility control, which oddly just consisted of me sniffing smelly t-shirts and rating the pleasantness of each funk from least to greatest.

After five long hours it was over.

"You're all set."

"All set?"

"Yes, Ms. Forrester," the receptionist at the desk smiled to me once I was done. "We have all your information, and we'll keep you updated."

"Any chance you could give me a timeline?"

"After 18 months, we request any unpaired candidates re-take the written portion of the evaluation, but I don't think that will be necessary in your case."

"No? Why not?"

"You scored very well, Ms. Forrester."

I had no idea what that meant for a test that seemed in no way measurable, but I was glad to get some positive feedback. And I was surprised that the "scores," whatever they were, would be back so soon.

"Wow, that's great news," I sighed. "So, you think... even with my size..."

"We've had plenty of plus-sized candidates, and even a few who were morbidly obese."

"You're kidding."

"Not at all. We requested they shed the appropriate level of weight before entering, but that won't be an issue in your case, of course."

'Of course'? I eyed the scale just as well as the doctor did this afternoon. 270 was borderline obese at my height. Was I getting the Forrester treatment again?

"Okay. Well, I was thinking of shedding a few pounds before the program began. In case you find—"

"We'd rather you didn't, Ms. Forrester."

"Oh... well, I just wanted to, you know... for me. It gives me a bit of confidence—"

"I understand. Still. Something like that would be a pretty big variable and could skew your results."

"I see. Well, cheeseburgers it is, then."

"Conversely, try not to gain as well, Ms. Forrester."

"Of course. I just meant— nevermind. Okay, I'll... I guess I'm done! Thank you."

"Thank *you*, Ms. Forrester. And thank you for choosing Halcyon.

6

Lyric

"*Follow the intake staff through that corridor, Ms. Forrester.*" Directly behind the receptionist area was the Halcyon campus, where candidates resided for six months.

Once inside, there's a clear view of a courtyard and a beautiful view of the mountains. Just outside the courtyard that separated the business offices from the campus was a closed-off entrance with a long hallway like the jetbridge to an airplane.

I arrived Sunday morning with my one allotted bag to carry inside, loaded up with my hair products and tools, my favorite silk robe, custom lingerie that my sister and I went shopping for, and my iPad loaded up with my favorite romance novels in case I got bored. Though I hoped that I would never need them.

My heart was pounding something terrible, waiting in front for the man that was apparently my Match.

The receptionist had been right: I only waited three months before I got the call back saying I'd been chosen.

Fortunately, it was right after exams for the fall semester were over. I could simply pick up where I left off next fall. Or perhaps next winter, if we decided to marry quick.

My heart started again. I was talking crazy. But that was the thing. That was the point of Halcyon. It still seemed surreal. Like a high-priced, naughty virtual reality game.

But between the sharp appearance of the staff, procedures both mysterious and accommodating, and the commanding architecture of Halcyon, no one dared not take it seriously.

"Your uniforms are already in your room and today we will be calibrating the door to open with your fingerprints. You will be known in the system as Lyric, as well as to your assigned therapist, Dr. Payton, as well as to the other Halcyon candidates. Your Match's Halcyon name is Luke."

"Luke and Lyric," I smiled. Had a bit of a ring to it. "Do you know when he'll be arriving?"

"I'm told he's just outside at reception."

"He's here??"

"Yes, Lyric. Matches always arrive at the same time."

I took a deep breath and sat on one of the long benches that lined the hallway entrance. Through the glass windows on each side of the entranceway I could barely make out a tiny entourage of people headed to where I was waiting.

Finally, the great glass doors opened and in walked a tall, casually dressed white guy who had a gamer nerd vibe. At least I guessed he was white.

His features, were distinct and his skin was a little more tan as though the son of immigrants. His jet black hair was a bit thick, long in the front and fit securely behind one ear or both. He seemed shy as he looked this way and that around the high-heeled and clipboarded staff, likely looking for his Match— for me. Lyric.

Finally we made eye contact and I gave him a warm smile meant to calm him.

It did not seem to calm him, nor did he return it. His eyes shot to the ground.

I took a breath as I did a now common re-calibration of expectations.

You're fat. And he's not happy, I ruthlessly assessed.

Then I started doing what I always did when I was the big girl at school, at the party, on the double-date. I willed my most confident facade to the surface, stood and gave him a wicked blast of eye contact as we shook hands, eye contact that he seemed to return under duress, as if my gaze was a UFO beaming him up.

Eventually, he gave me a toothless smile with his wide mouth and pronounced, deep laugh lines around his eyes that were beady and dark.

I relaxed. I couldn't read him, but he seemed open to me, not as disappointed as he seemed walking in. I wasn't really paying attention when we touched. I was just trying to get through the moment.

"Luke, this is your designated Match, Lyric."

"Okay," was all he said. He faced the blonde in the suit and didn't look back at me again.

I heard ringing in my ears as though an explosion happened.

The edges of my vision blurred like I'd just experienced a teary-eyed pain. I had, just not the physical kind. And I couldn't let it show at the moment.

The woman at the desk gave him the same rundown she'd given me and I just stood there, as though I was internally bleeding and trying to hide.

"So as we laid out during orientation, you'll be required to attend hourly counseling sessions once a week after lunch, with one individual session being optional no more than twice a week for each candidate. Obviously, today will be the exception since today was your processing day. You'll be sent to counseling tomorrow. Your assigned therapist is Dr. Manuel Payton. You'll schedule your individual sessions with him. There are no clocks in your quarters, but outside timepieces are permitted. The main clock is located in the lobby and chimes at noon and 6pm only."

"Okay," I responded.

I stole a glance at Luke, who only seemed to be paying attention on the surface. His features were so dark and he had this brooding energy that made me want to drink him in, but I didn't dare.

"Your jumpsuits are already in your closets and tailored with your measurements. When you are in quarters, you're permitted to wear whatever you brought along in your carry-ons. But we ask that you wear your jumpsuits when going to meals, therapy, or walking the grounds so that staff can identify you. Lunch will be served from noon to 2pm, and dinner from 6 to 8pm. I'd advise you not to miss it, otherwise it will be another five hours until dinner service."

"Do we have our own food?"

"Not yet. The dining hall is only open Monday through Friday. On weekends you'll be given boxed meals to prepare. You'll be able to take doggy bags back to your room as well. Participants are free to sit anywhere, but of course we encourage you to eat with your respective Matches."

"Any idea what's on the menu today?" I continued to make small talk.

It was the wrong topic to expound on it seemed, and I felt it as soon as it left my mouth.

Luke abruptly left the conversation again and explored the back bedrooms.

"The kitchen staff is very guarded about their menu, but I assure you it will be one of the best meals you've ever had. It always is."

"Can't wait," I shamelessly smiled.

Because fuck it.

It looked like my love affair with food was about to become rekindled, more fiery and passionate than ever, because this dude was stabbing me right in the issues and we had a long six months ahead. God only knows what we would do with the two hours before lunch.

"Anyone have any questions?"

Can you please not leave?

"I don't have any."

"Luke?"

He quietly shook his head.

"Very good. Welcome to Halcyon, guys."

"Thanks," I say. I don't move as she goes out of the front door and the room is blanketed in silence. Since it can't get any worse, and he already seems pretty bad at bluffing, I decide to address the elephant in the room that was, well... me.

"So? Out with it," I sigh.

"Out with what?"

"You're not happy. Admit it," I point down at myself, determined to beat him to the punch of ruthlessness.

"Okay," his voice comes out in a low hum. "I'm not happy. Are you?"

"Well, I don't know how I could be. If you're not."

His mood softened, as if shared misery made him more comfortable.

"I tend to not be happy in general, so you shouldn't take it personally," he replied, unbiased.

"I see," I laugh a bit. Because, well you have to. "Great, well. At least you're honest."

He scoffed. "Yeah. I think I do remember circling 'honesty' on that uh...evaluation thing."

"To describe you, or your ideal?"

"Both."

"Don't suppose you remember circling BBW on that same evaluation?" I attempted a joke. He didn't find it funny.

"No, that wasn't one of the options."

"Damn. Sorry about that, I guess."

"It isn't your fault, *Jesus*," he scoffed, turning to head into the room directly behind him. He didn't say anything more.

Oooooookay...

"Well... I guess I'll go change," I said.

There was a large wardrobe in the master bedroom with several jumpsuits hanging up on either side. About a half dozen each, with our Halcyon names embroidered on them. I grabbed one off the hanger and headed into the bathroom, the most private non-private area there was.

The dining hall had a large, industrial feel that didn't seem conducive to enjoying a meal or conversation, continuing its prison-like vibe. The lighting was harsh and everyone wore jumpsuits— thankfully more akin to the space program than jail— with their chosen aliases embroidered and plainly visible over the breast pocket. Meals were uniform, albeit award-winning.

It was sparse when we got there for lunch. I spotted a couple laughing and talking at the end of one of the dining hall's very long tables that made up three separate columns of six rows. They looked like they were having an infinitely better time than we were, so I instantly made a beeline for them.

"Let's go make friends," I said, instantly walking over before Luke had a chance to respond.

"These seats taken?" I asked.

"Not at all. You guys must've just got here."

"We did. Today. I'm Lyric. That tree trunk over there's Luke."

"I'm Jem," the woman said, with a poised, genuine air. She pointed to her Match. "This is Darren. Nice to meet you guys."

"Jem, like the cartoon?"

"Oh my gosh, no way you're old as me," she grinned.

"Too young for the original, but I loved the movie and my mom bought me the show on DVD."

"I forced my family to call me Jem when I was a kid, so it seemed appropriate."

I looked around out of social compulsion, but noticed not a lot of people were in there. "Is it usually this empty in here?"

"Well... just on intake day. Happens about every three weeks."

"How long have you guys been here?"

"Four months today," Darren revealed as they gave each other a long glance.

"Aw, you guys are cute. I saw you when I first came in and I thought, those two look cool."

While I continued to chat, Luke walked over to the chow line where there wasn't any wait time. Once he was gone there was a moment of quiet before Jem began.

"So...he seems nice."

"Yeah, I don't think I'm what he expected," I wrinkled my nose.

"Oh no..." Jem gave me a moan of sympathy.

"Yeah."

"He'll come around," Darren confidently asserted, as if he knew something I didn't.

"Is he what *you* expected?"

I tossed my head this way and that. "Uh... no. I don't know, I guess. I'm just... trying to trust the program, you know?"

"Well, don't let it get you down. We've seen some weird shit in here."

"There was another black woman in here when we first got here. Violet," Jem dished. "She got paired with Han, who's from the Philipines, and she was *pissed*."

"Oh no!" My eyes were wide. "What happened?"

"Same thing that happens to everyone around here. They adapted."

"Dey and Samantha are around here somewhere. Samantha doesn't even speak English. But, you know, they made it work," Jem said.

"They're both hot," Darren interjected.

"I know, but Dey started learning Croatian right off the bat. I think he's fluent now."

Meanwhile I looked around the empty space again, in the midst of an epiphany.

"Um.... is the reason everyone skips lunch on intake day because they're..." I lowered my voice, "too busy having sex?"

The couple gave me a reluctant and simultaneous nod.

Holy shit.

Luke was on his way back to the table by then and the conversation abruptly ended.

I smelled his tray before I saw it. Wood-fired pizza, but I couldn't quite make out the toppings. Basil. Sausage. Possibly figs.

"Well, at least the food's good, right?" I tried to make light with a self-deprecating joke. But "Luke" gave me nothing, not even a grunt.

60

Oh boy. Yep. This was... definitely my worst nightmare.

7

Luke

When I got to the Halcyon entrance, everyone was rattling shit off, but I couldn't be expected to pay attention.

Another woman, one that I would've given any amount of money to be my Match instead of Lyric, walked up to us and we were on the move. I looked down at my feet that were somehow moving one in front of the other.

Of course. Of fucking course.

This is my life. A never-ending spiral of expectations shot down by reality.

People keep telling me to be grateful. That the world's been handed to me. My parents, my mother. Society.

Can someone point me in the direction of the things that've been handed to me, that *aren't* made of shit? And don't come with a punch to the fucking face?

An overweight black chick? Really Halcyon??

"Halcyon headquarters is as tall underneath the ground as it is above," the attendant rattled while the insides of my brain wrestled, "These north elevators are the only ones that will take you to either the fifteen floors above or below."

"Will we be... below ground? Like... in a bunker?" Lyric asked.

"No, you're assigned quarters are on the 5th floor."

"Oh thank goodness. If I had to live underground I would've died," Lyric scoffed.

"All of our underground floors have 11-foot ceilings and an ergonomic design that's medically proven to lower feelings of claustrophobia. But luckily you won't have to worry."

This has gotta be a mistake. A fucking mistake. They made me pick out physical pictures of women for an hour just to pair me with the exact opposite?

Is this like, the lightning round or something? Do I spin a wheel? Phone a friend?

After a quiet elevator ride, we're led to the room, a decent-sized rectangle, with a small "L" kitchen area, dining table with two chairs, living room and two bedrooms— one with a large king-sized bed and one with two twin beds.

"Luke, Lyric, this will be your quarters for the length of your stay with us."

"Kinda nice," Lyric volunteered shyly. I remained mute.

It was okay. Cement was all the rage these days as a building material, and though the program had made the most of it with its modern decor and polished surfaces, it wasn't shying away from its overall "fancy jail" vibe, which seemed intentional.

"As you know, there are no televisions at Halcyon, no wi-fi, no windows besides one long panel in the kitchen over the sink that faces the courtyard, and no doors save for the front door."

"Not even to the bathroom?"

"Not even to the bathroom. And it is the only unmonitored area in all the rooms, so be advised."

I walked to the bathroom as she spoke, which indeed had no door but had a bit of a maze entrance, like a locker room.

Once inside there was a very large bathtub and separate adjacent shower. So more than likely, I was going to see this chick naked??

Don't get me wrong, she seems nice. She's got a pretty face. But that's not gonna get my dick hard. And also, it's not what I want. She shouldn't be wasting her time trying to make me happy.

They need to find her a guy that's into this. I'm not into this. This isn't fair to either of us.

We went to lunch and Lyric took her turn in line as I sat at the table. The couple she randomly ambushed sparked a conversation with me.

"Hey, is she famous, your Match? She kinda looks familiar," Jem asked.

"I don't think so," I answered.

"We've seen a couple of famous people in here. Darren, who was the guy from that movie?"

"Chris Holt."

"Yeah, Chris Holt was in here, trying to feign anonymity. We all had to call him 'Reggie.'"

"Reggie?"

"Yeah, I think that was his dad's name, wasn't it, babe?"

"No, I think he said it was his first acting coach or something."

"She's not my Match," I said.

Jem and Darren looked at each other.

"Who, Lyric?"

"Yeah."

Jem and Darren did another double-take.

"Dude. I'm telling you. You'll get used to it," Darren offered.

"Easy for you to say," I said, pointing to Jem. "I don't wanna 'get used to it.' I didn't pay a bunch of money and wait a year and a half to get 'used' to someone. I could do that on the outside."

"Bro, I hear you. But you gotta trust the program."

I just scoffed and shook my head as Lyric made her way back to the now tense table. She didn't need a psychic to know just what the topic of conversation was while she was gone.

"Well, we were on our way back to the barracks. That's what we call 'em. What floor are you guys on?"

"Fifth."

"We're on the seventh. We're here just about the same time every day. You know, if you guys have questions or, just wanna hang out," Jem said.

"Thanks," Lyric smiled.

"No problem. We could've used a more knowledgeable couple or two when we first got here," Jem replied.

"Yeah. We've got Dr. Mayfield, but some shit you just wanna talk to anonymous strangers about who are going through the exact same thing," Darren said.

"We should really bring that up to them during the exit interview, huh babe?"

I looked at the relatively attractive and uniform couple, wondering what obstacles they could possibly have to navigate.

After lunch, we returned wordlessly to our quarters.

"You can have the biggest room," I told her.

The biggest room was the one with the king-sized bed, the one I presume we're supposed to share at some point.

If the room with the two twin beds were any indication, an adjustment period was normal. But it didn't make me feel any less terrible as I watched her wordlessly retreat to the larger room.

It seems like life keeps forcing me to be the jerk.

I decided to take a shower, because there was literally nothing else to do. I finished, dried off, and put on my sweatpants, one of only a handful of things I'd packed. I looked in on her listening to something between her headphones. She felt my presence near the door and startled, removing one of her ears.

"Look, I just wanna say that... I'm sorry if I'm being a dick to you and everything, I'm just a little... caught off guard by this... whole thing. Not exactly my finest moment."

Lyric huffed a little laugh. "Yeah, I get it. I mean... me too."

"Anyway, I'm sure all this'll be cleared up by tomorrow."

Lyric furrowed her brow. "Excuse me?"

"Whatever mix-up this is. It's just... not fair to either of us. I'll put in a word with the counselor tomorrow. I paid a lotta money to be here. I'm sure you did too."

She just looked at me, for a long time, like I was insane and she didn't know what to say, so she said nothing.

Not sure what was so weird about what I said, but eventually I walked away to the living room. I laid on the couch, alone with my thoughts which was kind of maddening, but the only entertainment I had.

I must've laid stewing in self-pity so long that I fell asleep. I woke up in pitch blackness, a sliver of moonlight coming through the glass panels in the kitchen.

I walked by Lyric's room on the way to mine, where she was passed out in relatively the same spot that I last left her, having fallen asleep with the sounds of an audiobook seeping through her headphones.

* * *

We sat in our first counseling session a day and a half after first laying eyes on each other, side by side in the tweed chairs, hands politely in our laps. Dr. Payton was our assigned therapist and

66

openly noted the body language as soon as he sat in the chair across from us.

"So?" Dr. Payton breathed, "first impressions? Anyone?"

"Seems awfully quiet around here," I started.

"Quiet?"

"Yeah, I mean... this place is huge. Cafeteria's huge, but it's like a ghost town everywhere."

"Well, that happens when there's a huge influx of candidates, in or out. Most of the new couples spend their first few weeks exploring their relationship."

I could see Lyric out of the corner of my eye with her hands in her lap, unconsciously fiddling with them, as if trying to will herself invisible.

"I see. So the first thing everyone does when they get here is just... jump into bed with each other?" I said with a bit of disgust. Hypocritical, since I'd planned on that very thing. Lyric squirmed in her chair.

"We encourage sexual attachment early. As early as possible," said Dr. Payton.

"Because sex is a great foundation for a relationship?"

"In a controlled setting, yes. It can be."

Now it was my turn to squirm.

"Forgive me, Luke, I think you misunderstood my line of questioning. When I asked about first impressions, I meant between the two of you, and not the program as a whole."

I looked over at Lyric briefly and cleared my throat, reluctant to take the lead.

"Well, yesterday, I expressed to Lyric that... there's a real possibility that we won't need to... that there might be a mixup so just, to stay packed and... yeah. Wait and see what happens."

Dr. Payton's eyes narrowed and I could tell he was hiding

shock.

"Luke, I'm sure you understand that Halcyon uses a meticulous process. I can assure you that Lyric here isn't going anywhere."

"Is there a way I can just, go home?" Lyric pleaded. "I mean... surely they can't keep me here against my will?"

"Unfortunately, Lyric, considering the paperwork you signed when orientation began, unless there's a danger to your life or health, or on my recommendation I've determined some significant threat to you or your match, you will be unable to leave the program without legal action."

Her composure started to crumble, but she kept it together. I gave her a sympathetic look.

"Now let me reassure you both, you're not the first couple to begin your first day with reservations, sometimes disappointment and even shock. And you won't be the last. Most people expect to be paired with their constructed ideals, which is understandable. And in rare instances, it does happen. But if it were the norm, there would be no need to be reminded to trust the program." Dr. Payton moved forward in his chair. "Let me also stress, that the odds of finding a second match in our Halcyon database is considered mathematically impossible, and would take considerably more than 18 months to find. So, try to see each other as the valuable treasure that you are to one another."

I briefly looked over at her again, feeling a bit scummy.

"Individual sessions are available twice a week in addition to your mandatory joint session. I recommend both of you schedule one as soon as possible."

"Are these sessions... confidential?" I asked.

"Of course."

"I'll go first, I guess. Tomorrow after lunch?"

"Very well."

Wordlessly we returned to our quarters. Since there were no doors to slam, I retreated to the smaller room while Lyric shut out the world with her headphones.

After dinner, I took a long hot shower in the bathroom's roomy, spa-like stall. We'd been allowed to bring one outside bag up to 20lbs full of whatever contraband was allowed in. They recommended favored items of clothing and any personal effects that could pose as conversation starters. I packed a sparse smattering of basics, including my lucky boxers and a pair of pajama bottoms that I felt I looked pretty good in. I thought I'd be spending six months naked and fucking, so I barely backed anything. And with all the women receiving Halcyon-patented birth control patches for the time being, I didn't even need to pack condoms. I did a piss poor job. I should've just caved and let my mom pack for me.

When I got to bed, I didn't know what time it was, because there were no clocks in the place. We weren't allowed to bring phones, but Lyric was smart enough to bring a tablet. Probably with tons of downloaded stuff on it. Maybe I could ask to borrow it, eventually. That is, if I haven't figured out a way out of this by now.

I sighed, looking at the ceiling from my bed as though I was doing hard time. I had the sinking feeling that this place was a fucking scam. Convincing, I couldn't deny. But the way everyone just went about the day like anything about this was normal... I felt like I was in a psych ward.

I was bored. Horny with nothing to look at, and feeling robbed. I should be locked in here with my dream girl and fucking her senseless. Not holed up in the world's worst co-ed summer camp. I sighed again. Now I was half chub.

"Lyric?" I called. To see if she was awake. No answer. The rooms shared a wall and I couldn't see her from where I lay facing the living room. I could've tiptoed around the corner and looked in, to be absolutely sure she was asleep or wearing her headphones, but then, what if I startled her? And what excuse could I give?

I'd much rather feign ignorance.

"Lyric!" I whispered this time, one hand already down my pants. I'd tried to jack off in the shower but was inexplicably unsuccessful.

It'd been a porn-free 36 hours. I certainly wouldn't be able to sleep without finding relief first.

My dick seemed to like this business of the doorless room. I felt kind of gross having to listen for Lyric in the next room over, for sudden movements. "Sudden" being relative, in her case. But I couldn't totally relax. Fat people had a way of being unusually stealthy.

Every time I thought of being caught, of Lyric coming around the corner while I masturbated, too far gone to stop, it gave my heart an unusual jolt, mostly of shame but just enough arousal to make me think this jackoff session would be more successful than the last. I pulled my dick out and began to stroke in earnest.

"Lyric," I whispered, my last ditch effort before all bets were off. The name she chose was kind of pretty. In a poignant, sad way. It suited her. But the way she blew me off after the counseling session made her seem kind of bitchy. Like she wasn't used to being treated the way she's being treated. Maybe she's from a wealthy family too. She'd have to be, to afford a place like this. But she was certainly new money if she was. Maybe the daughter of some famous rapper or something. If that was the case, then I couldn't conceive anything I had that she would even want. Besides a dick in the mouth.

"Oh shit," I whispered to no one. *Where'd that come from*, I distantly wondered. But only distantly, because it didn't matter. Right now I was locked onto the image of my dick going into Lyric's pouty, spoiled mouth. If I had to guess, she was probably a virgin too. She always had a little makeup on. Smokey eyes. Wine-colored lips. Holy cow, she was totally a rich chick, how had I not picked up on that?

I still didn't want to fuck her. I couldn't imagine it. But I could smear that burgundy lipstick all over my cock every single day of my life. Besides her lips, her eyes were definitely the best thing on her body. I wouldn't mind seeing those looking up at me from her knees...

"*Fuck*," I whispered, cum spilling into my own hand. Well that took an unexpected turn. I let out a breathy chuckle, too lazy to get up from my bed. I reached around the floor for my bathtowel. I sighed.

Whatever works, I said to myself.

8

Bria

The Halcyon dreams have started up again tonight.

I used to have them all the time when I first left Halcyon, as you can imagine. Usually involving Luke running or walking away, or pleasuring me while fading away, or being mute.

Then they tapered off. I always took their re-appearance as a sign of growth. But Luke's re-appearance is hitting my subconscious mind like an allergic reaction.

In this one we were at the fire pit, where we'd hang out on the weekends. The whole gang was there. Jem, Darren, Dey, Sam. Luke had his arm around me and I was singing, which would've never happened back then.

And I was big in the dream. Big. To the point of exaggeration.

Everyone was making out. I turned to him, urging him to do the same with me. He kept scooting further and further away from me on the bench, to a cartoonish degree. Until it became long and detached in the air and turned into piano keys as I woke up.

I wake in a rage, throwing a poor defenseless tumbler at a wall in my Dallas hotel room, cursing.

I haven't thought about this guy in ages. And suddenly out of nowhere...

"God*dammit*!" I scream into a pillow.

I don't care about this anymore, I'm not even that person anymore.

And he never wanted me.

Or he does now, apparently?

What the hell do these dreams even mean and what do they want from me?

I look at the clock. 3:07am.

I switch on a lamp and look at my reflection in the mirror across from my bed, next to the television.

A lyric swims by in the quiet. I grab the little writing pad with the hotel insignia at the top and begin to write.

"You came all this way/ To say you never loved me."

Hm. The muse has a point. Just where *had* he come from anyway?

I half expected a whole sob story and him begging for forgiveness, but he didn't.

And I probably would've fallen for it. That's how bad I wanted an explanation. Still.

Why didn't he know that? Why wouldn't he give me one? Any human person would have.

He was always a bit immature, but I don't remember him being so shallow. It would anger me if he hadn't been so bold about wanting me now.

And yet, if I hadn't stopped him he would've just walked out the door.

It was weird. The whole thing was weird. If anything, the Halcyon dreams should end for good now, as I thought they had.

I jot a few more ideas down to satisfy my mind. If I'm lucky I'll manage a few more hours of sleep. I humor the muse a little while longer.

It's a draw, of sorts. After about an hour my exhaustion returns. I quickly switch off all the lights and fall back into a dreamless sleep until morning.

The next day we go to this breakfast spot that we always have to stop in when we're in Dallas. Just a greasy spoon where the bacon is the kind of crispy I like and the food's so consistently, dependably the same it's like visiting a memory.

Me, Chase, April and Braxton share one booth. Chelsea and Jacob sit at a small table, the married couple of the group. We keep trying to make April and Braxton have an affair on their spouses at home so we can save on hotel rooms.

Everyone had high hopes for me and Chase and they're still sort of in the dark about why we didn't work out.

Well, at least they *were*.

"Holy shit. Didn't I tell you?" Chase says in a hushed voice.

"What?"

"Your guy just walked in," he says without ever looking up at the door, like he's undercover or something.

I just whirl my freakin' head all the way around in the booth to see Luke— Cliff— talk to a waitress and take a seat at a small table on the opposite side of the diner. He doesn't even look in our direction when he sits down. When it feels like I might die if I get caught gawking at him I turn around.

"Who *is* this guy?" April feels justified to ask now.

"Do you want to tell them or should I?" Chase says.

"I don't suppose I'd have the option of keeping this a private matter?"

"Miss Forrester here was once in the Halcyon program,"

Chase announces. I jerk my neck back in offense.

"*Miss Forrester*?" I repeat.

"Wait, I thought their success rate was 99.999—"

"We're the one-thousandth of that percent."

"Holy shit."

"This guy's not... unstable is he?"

"Well, he did opt-out," I reply, even though they don't know the lingo. But it doesn't matter. They get the gist anyway.

"What an asshole," Braxton says.

"You better get rid of him before I do," Chase threatens. The booth tenses at Chase's little chivalrous/jealous hybrid outburst. I let him off the hook with a sigh. He's coming face to face with his competition after all, and he knows it.

But do I know it?

I force April out of her aisle seat in the booth and make my way to the other side of the diner. Luke is just minding his own business with coffee and a huge pastry, perusing his phone while wearing these black-rimmed glasses that add another dimension of hotness to him and oh my God I can't believe he's fucking here in my current reality how the *fuck* is any of this real??

"Hi," I say.

He looks up and smiles, bless my soul.

"Hi," he says as if I'm an unexpected delight. He gestures for me to sit down. I briefly entertain the idea that I might be dead or in a coma. Or some other state that's more real than a dream. "Any idea what's good here?" he asks.

"What are you doing here?" I question him.

"Just in the neighborhood."

"Your neighborhood is three hours away in Dallas?" I reply unconvinced.

"Sometimes."

"So now you're following me?"

"Can I help it that we're going to the same show?" he smiles, stirring sugar packets into his coffee.

I sigh, strengthening my non-existent resolve. "I told you. Well, actually I didn't..." I begin, already sounding like a noob as I remember that awkward confrontation from last night.

"It's good to see you and all, but I don't know what this is about. This grand gesture thing you're doing. You and me," I gesture back and forth between us, "that's never happening. You opted out, remember?"

"Of course, I remember."

"Good. Because we're not doing this, alright?"

"I just wanna talk. If you're not busy."

Talk?

Six years of talking? Right now?

How??

"Don't you have a life to get back to?" I responsibly change the subject. I only half want to know the answer.

"Not really," he says. Whew. I don't know why, but I don't want him to have a life.

"I could probably have you arrested or something."

"You could."

"Did you look it up before you came all the way out here?"

"I didn't have to. I'm a cop."

A cop?!??

I take a moment to sit back in gleeful astonishment. And also enjoy his trademark slow smirk.

"Get the fuck out of here," I smile.

"Highway patrol. Going on four years."

I smile big against my will, thinking of him wearing a uniform, pilot sunglasses and wielding government authority.

"I'm utterly blown away by that information."

"Never pegged me for a law and order guy, huh?" he smiles.

"Never pegged you as a 'pick a profession of any kind' guy."

He chuckles, taking another sip of his coffee as he nods.

"Aren't you loaded or something?"

"In a manner of speaking."

"So you're a cop for fun?"

"Let's just say I had an epiphany," he cryptically replies. Oh my God I love him.

"Explains you expertly tailing us. And the donut," I add. He takes a big bite.

"Want one?"

"No thanks."

"I take it they're your mortal enemy now," he chews, wiping his fingers on a napkin.

"They always were."

He finishes chewing, rubbing residual crumbs between his thick fingers and I try not to watch his every move.

"You look good, *prasice*. I meant to tell you."

He inadvertently starts my pussy up, strong and dependable after years of neglect. Like Han Solo and the Millennium Falcon. That nickname.

"Little pig," I reply.

"What's that?"

"That's what *prasice* means. In Croatian. It means '*little pig*'? Really?"

He just smiles, looking at me as though I'm a constellation.

Only now do I realize this is a trap. I look down at the table until I can think straight and come up with a plan of escape.

"It's just a term of endearment," he says.

"So is 'little tiger.' You could've called me that. Or 'darling' or…"

"'*Prasice*' suits you. No matter what size you are."

"Why's that?"

"I don't know, you're just… cute. And sweet."

Uggghhh.

He was never like this. Sentimental. Not when I knew him.

"And I like to eat shit? Roll around in the mud?"

"Just because I speak Croatian doesn't mean I studied the etymology. It's a term of endearment."

"You're honestly trying to tell me you didn't know you were calling me 'little pig'?"

"I'm saying it's not literal."

"Convenient."

"You really think I was insulting you behind your back that entire time?" He squints, as though the idea just dawned on him. As though I'm the cynical one.

"You certainly couldn't call me a pig to my face, now could you?"

"Lyric—"

"You admitted you never loved me."

I have to wait for him to finish a thoughtful sip before I get a rebuttal.

"That doesn't mean it wasn't real. It just means that I didn't know what love was."

"And now you do?"

He sighs with a smile and sits back in his chair.

My eyes return to the table and I dig my fingernails into my arm and focus on not smiling back.

I don't want to complete the circuit but I can't help the feeling of wholeness that I know he also feels.

He's happy to be doing anything together again. Even fight. We did plenty of that. My nails are still in my arm, by the way.

"So, the guitar player. I take it he's the boyfriend?" he says.

"He's my writing partner."

"And your boyfriend."

I don't fault him for seeing us on stage and thinking that we're fucking each other's brains out afterwards. The chemistry took us both back and for a good year or so, he would've been right.

"Is this your way of asking if we're sleeping together?"

"I've no right to that information, we both know that."

"Is that your way of saying you already know?"

"I'm saying what I mean already, Lyric. Bria," he corrects himself. Oh my fucking God.

"I have no intention of trusting you. Ever. About anything."

"Fair enough," he says.

"We dated. For a while."

"But not anymore?"

Goddamn, he's so calm. Like a god. What's his deal?

"You jealous?" I ask with a raised eyebrow.

"No," he grinned.

"Why not?"

He moves a finger across his bottom lip as if contemplating if he should say what he's thinking.

He breaks out into a super sexy, super confident smile as he finally eyes me, I guess deciding to stay quiet.

My blood grows hot, both with anger and desire. Because he's smug and he knows he has me. My anger is dissipating against my will.

Damn.

Okay, so maybe Halcyon was *not* smoke and mirrors. My sense of time is all fucked up and I have an unusually strong urge to get on top of this table.

Cliff is my Match. And the fact that I don't want him to be is irrelevant.

"I'm not telling you anything about my life."

"Why not?"

"You wanted to talk and we're talking. You don't get to know me out here."

"Honestly sitting here talking to you. Seeing you. Feels unreal. Like I'm getting away with something."

I don't answer because I will say something equally raw and honest that will put me in a place where I don't have control.

"Your boyfriend is giving us the evil eye," he grins.

Jeez. There's a puddle in my underwear and Luke is wearing hipster glasses and referring to himself as Cliff. Like he was just an actor playing that part all those years ago.

"He's not my boyfriend. But I better get back. You'll be at the show tonight, right?"

"If you want."

"Sure," I shrug, hopefully conveying indifference.

"I'd like to see you before that. If I could."

YES.

"Not a chance."

"I'm staying at the Roundtree. Right across from the venue."

FUCK. YES.

"You arrogant bastard."

"I just wanna talk, *prasice*."

"Don't call me that."

"Preferably with my hands down your pants, but... I'll settle for whatever you give me."

Shivers seize my body and I don't dare look up until they subside. But they won't. *Oh my God oh my God oh my God oh*

80

my God...

"I take back that last statement," he says.

How did he know I wanted his hand down my pants???

I can't break.

He seems to have changed but... my heart.

I just can't.

I let him stew in uncertainty and guilt a bit longer before I answer.

"I'll be there. But only because we do need to talk. And then you're gonna drive back to wherever the hell you came from. Because I'm waist-deep in my own life right now. And you're the last person I would ever add to it."

"I understand."

"We have a studio session today, and then practice after that. I'll come by right before that since it's in that area. Around 1."

"I'll be waiting."

"Huh," I laugh. "I ought to stand you up. That'd make us even then, huh *Cliff*?"

He lowers his gaze. "Hardly."

Ah. I've found his cryptonite. Turns out it's guilt. It has the opposite effect on me, because I suddenly have the strength to be the first to walk away.

I get up from the table without another response and return to our booth. I must have one hell of a look on my face because no one says anything to me. It's a good thing too, because I wouldn't have been able to hear them over the sound of my pumping heart, which feels like it's working so hard I breathe like I'm drowning in blood.

He drove all the way here just to talk. Really.

What an arrogant jerk. Following me all around town like some psychopath, who got his favorite childhood toy sold in a garage sale.

He used me up for six months and then said "no thanks."

Did he really think that after a 12 sentence exchange I was willing to *fuck* and forget it all, like this was all water under the bridge?

If he thinks that I'm just gonna knock on the door of his hotel room, peel off my clothes piece by piece so he can devour my tight buxom body with his eyes while I watch...

Shit. I want him.

"Bria, how much is the rate for this studio?"

"What?"

"How much time did you buy?"

"Time did I buy for what?"

"Jesus," Chase rolls his eyes and gets up from the table in a huff.

Everyone's quiet. A bit dramatic, I think, as the rest of us follow suit.

Braxton leaves the tip. For a second I feel guilty, but then I remember that Chase and I aren't together anymore and that I've always tried my best not to lead him on. Except for maybe when we're on stage.

But he gets it. It's part of our thing. He's my partner, I lean on him. I'm totally *not* using him. We're performers. It's part of our *thing*.

He's going to have to pay up if he wants to get anything out of me, I think, as we head back to the hotel. I just gotta think of something he can give me that I want. Ideally, something that *isn't*, in fact, the same thing that *he* wants. What the fuck do I want?

I draw myself a bath once I get back to the room.

A naughty one. For old time's sake.

Like the one that got him to touch me for the first time and never stop. There's no handheld showerhead in this mid-priced dump, so I inch my pelvis right up to the running faucet. Jeez, I hope there's no hidden cameras in this place.

I probably shouldn't be so turned on about a flashback so juvenile and desperate as the first time I witnessed Luke's naked body aroused by mine in the shower.

We were both a couple of noobs, looking for someone to complete us. Or at least, I was.

He was just forced to go by his parents, in some hail marry attempt to grow him via getting fucked until the Peter Pan syndrome left his system. It didn't work.

I was a virgin, hoping I could pay money to find someone who I could trust would love me for me and no other reason. Also didn't work.

It's borderline abusive what we did to each other.

And yet... I shamelessly resurrect every toe-curling moment we had until I'm gripping the edge of the tub and choking back frantic, resonant moans in the echo-ey bathroom.

And worse, I dared to add to them the moments that had not happened.

Yet.

Halcyon: Six Years Ago

Incredibly fancy chicken and dumplings for lunch. A broth made with white wine— and tomato, oddly enough. Pillowy dumplings to die for.

I hung back at the dining hall while Luke went ahead to his solo counseling session, shamelessly refilling my second bowl, which was only half empty so it was technically my third. I didn't see Jem until she went up to me in line and elbowed me.

"Hey, no cutsies," someone behind us said.

"Mind your business, T'Challa," she said to the white guy behind us. I couldn't tell if that name choice made me want to hang out with him, or if it didn't.

"How ya holdin' up?" Jem asked me.

"I'm in line for seconds," I cheerily said, as though that answered it.

"No sex yet, I take it?"

"Uh, definitely not."

"What's his deal?"

"His deal is that I disgust him," I sighed.

"I doubt *that's* true."

"I don't. He gave me this whole spiel about how he was confident there was a mix-up, and it should be cleared up soon."

Jem had a look of stoic shock.

"...You've *gotta* be fucking kidding me."

"I wish I was."

Jem gave me an alarmed touch to the shoulder that put me on edge.

Oh no, was I putting up with abusive patterns of behavior again?

"This, you should definitely bring up to your therapist. Whatever you want to be cleared up, he'll bring up in your Match's personal session. It's not just, you know, like confession. He'll slap him around good if he needs to."

"Really?"

"Yeah. I mean, I can't verify that for sure, but once I started bringing up real, pointed issues in my personal sessions, Darren always came back like a new man, singing a totally different tune."

"Really?" I said again, feeling dangerously hopeful.

"Yeah. And the confidentiality is real, as far as I can tell. He's heard some ugly stuff. Our counselor Dr. Mayfield's like a steel trap."

"You guys look so well-adjusted and... well-suited. I just don't see how you guys could have issues."

"Well, I can't tell you the whole of it because it's not mine to tell, but let's just say some heavy shit came out that Darren's never said outloud. Early. And this program brought out the nastiness before the week was up. The program doesn't fix you. It just gives you the confidence and tools to get to the other side of it."

"I hear you, but I don't know what fixes the trauma of finding out you have a fat match."

"Another piece of advice? When you go in there, make sure the person you're worried about is you, and not him."

I took Jem's advice and vented to Dr. Payton the next day.

Not at first. At first, I just sat there. He simply stayed silent until I was ready to talk. I perused the intimidating bookcase behind him that scaled the entire 10-foot wall. Every single book seemed to be related to psychology. There were a few standouts. Shakespeare. Dante's Inferno. George Orwell.

"There are these shortbread cookies that I like to buy. They're sweet, but they're buttery. One of the best flavors in the world. I told myself when I get married, I want a cake with icing that tastes just like those cookies. If I have to develop it myself, I will. I've thought a lot about it. I think salted butter instead of unsalted would probably make all the difference."

Dr. Payton just listens to me from the other side of the desk.

"Although, I think salt does something chemically to the process of frosting... and maybe that's why they don't use it.

85

Like it doesn't get fluffy or something."

"How are you holding up?"

At that, I just break down.

The pity party is in full swing now.

Why me, why why why.

Ugh. I'm so tired of asking that. More than having the occasion to, even. Dr. Payton offers me a Kleenex.

"I just keep reliving that look on his face, during processing," I sniffed, my eyes averted to one side of the room in shame. "I had arrived first, and I could see the lobby doors open. He sort of... met eyes with me while he was a ways off down that long hallway and then... he looked away. Like I was a stranger." A tear fell as I spoke.

"I mean I *was* but... like he was just passing by, you know? He was looking for the *real* girl. And then he looked at me again and I could tell it was dawning on him. I wasn't just some random girl on the bench. And he looked away *again* like... he just didn't want it to be true."

There was a clock in his office that ticked off every quarter of a second, a constant gizmo like a tiny washing machine.

"Are you sure you're not exaggerating this insecurity you have in your mind, Lyric?"

I fumbled the balled up tissue in my hand. "You heard him the other day. We didn't speak to each other the entire first day, and finally he comes in apologizing, not for the way he's acting but for the program."

"How so?"

"He was just saying the program got it wrong and apologizing that Halcyon was putting me through this and that he hoped everything was gonna be fixed soon."

"What did you think about that?" he said in a million-dollar

86

therapist way.

"I thought he was in denial and it made me feel like shit."

"You haven't brought any of this up to him?"

"Of course not, I mean... he's a stranger that doesn't seem to like me very much."

"Do *you* think the program got it wrong?"

I furrowed my brow and shrugged. "Well... I *doubt* it. And like, I know I'm big or whatever, but he's not exactly a prize himself. I mean he's kind of funny looking, wouldn't you agree?"

Dr. Payton put a hand under his chin as if hiding his amusement.

"And he's kind of a jerk. Arrogant. And yeah, I expected there to be an adjustment period, but if he won't even go along with the program, I don't know how we're ever going to get past it."

"Why did you expect there to be an adjustment period?"

"Oh. Well..." I gestured up and down my whole body with my hands. "I don't know, I'm kinda just used to doing that. I didn't think you guys would find some plus-size fetish guy to pair me up with, and I kind of wouldn't want that, so. At least in here I know he's not just tolerating me. So there's that."

"Tolerating you?"

I took a deep breath and tried to keep it succinct. "I had a boyfriend once. You could hardly call him that. You could say I come from a prominent family. And my other sister, she's gorgeous. I won't go into a bunch of stories, but let's just say I have reason to be leery of men on the outside."

Dr. Payton stayed quiet a moment before launching into his recommendation.

"I think the both of you are a bit too focused on physical appearances. Your matching is primarily based on strong biological and psychological factors that are proven successful markers across countless studies of romantic partners. My advice would be to put your confidence in that, rather than your past experiences."

"So basically, you're saying 'trust the program'?"

"Indeed."

I silently looked down at my folded hands, turning them inside out, exposing my palms.

"He's masturbating."

Dr. Payton gave my confession a bit of silent gravity before answering, "How do you mean?"

"He thinks I don't know. He thinks I can't hear. Or I'm asleep. There aren't any doors for fuck's sake."

"How does that make you feel?"

"Boy, you really are a therapist, aren't you?"

Dr. Payton pointed to the degrees on his wall.

"I don't know. At first it surprised me, obviously. It was a little repulsive."

"Only a little?"

"Yeah, I mean... I can't be a hypocrite about it. Just because I'm more discrete than him."

"Have you masturbated since being here?"

I felt safe enough to tell the truth. "Every day."

"Lyric, these first few weeks are critical. Most matches are already having sex within the first week of the program."

"So I've noticed."

"I realize you're not there yet, but we can't forget the goal. Eventually you'll have to get beyond the roommate phase and actually communicate."

"About what?"

"What you just told me seems like a good start."

"Like, 'hey, can you not jack-off five feet away from me like a registered sex offender?'"

"Did it occur to you that maybe he *wants* you to overhear these... sessions?"

I couldn't control the heat to my nipples, under my arms at the words. I tried to scoot back into my chair until I disappeared, but no luck.

"....No."

"You should let him know they agitate you."

"They don't agitate me it's just... he's being such a snob about this, but so sloppy about *that*, that it's just... unattractive."

"We'll bring this up at our next joint counseling session."

"Do we have to?"

"This is what I'm here for, Lyric. Every couple has their own unique set of adjustments to make. This isn't just a bizarre sex resort. We're here to work. At times, it will be uncomfortable."

"It's just that... I thought we had confidentiality."

"We do, Lyric. But this isn't confession. He's had no problems voicing his issues. The same confidence is available for you."

I sighed.

"In the meantime I recommend that you force the issue. As soon as possible. Catch him in the act. You'll feel more confident about being direct in that moment."

"Permission to leave a bit early then?"

Dr. Payton gave me a smirk.

"This isn't the military, Lyric. Feel free to leave at anytime."

9

Cliff

An hour or two after we left the diner, there's a knock on my hotel room door. My heart floods.

I slowly walk to the door and linger there for just a moment. It's not every day that I open a door and Lyric is just standing there. And I don't know how many more times I'll have.

She gives me the cordial grin of a stranger when the door opens and she makes her way in, as though I'm in her way.

"You came."

"Told you I would."

My eyes follow her as I close the door.

"Sorry if I got a little... comfortable back there, by the way."

"What do you mean?" she asks over her shoulder.

"At the diner. I didn't mean to be so... forward. Being around you again just—"

"I get it," she curtly cut me off.

"You do?"

"I do," she let out a breath she must've been holding.

"So, um... Cliff the highway patrolman, huh?" she says my

90

name like it's as foreign on her tongue as it is to my ears.

"That's me."

"That's you. Where you from?"

"Uh, Chicago, more or less."

"Windy City," she comments.

"Yeah."

To anyone else this would be small talk. But the small stuff is the only stuff we don't know about each other.

"What brings you to Texas?" she asks.

"You, of course."

"Of course," she smiles. "How long are you here for?" she asks.

"I... actually live here."

"You live here. In Dallas?"

"Houston."

A stunned cache of questions builds behind her eyes.

"That's where *I* live..." she replied, a bit stunned.

"Really?" I deadpan. I don't pretend to be shocked.

"For how long?"

"About a year now."

More stunned silence.

"The answer is yes."

"Yes, what?"

"I came out here to find you."

A second burden lifts off me as I confess to her.

"I was sorta hoping it would happen organically. Looking for a sign, I guess. That you would take me back. A sign to tell me to go after you no matter what."

"And then I joined a band."

"And then you joined a band."

Bria shakes her head and laughs.

"But I knew about you before the band."

"You did?"

I nod. "You weren't exactly a needle in a haystack."

"No," she laughs, looking at the family picture displayed on my phone laying on the side table. She picks it up. "Is this your parents?"

"Yes."

"Still living?"

"Yes."

"You look like your dad," she says before launching into more questions. "How long have you known?"

"Known what?"

"Who I was."

"...Few years."

"Must be nice. Finding you was next to impossible," she remarks.

"You tried to find me?"

"Of course. In a futile kind of way. When I had the urge to torture myself. I didn't get very far, as you can imagine. Pathetically pointless."

I lower my head. "I, uh... wow. That's... wow."

"What?"

"I just... never considered that you would... do that."

"Well. Closure on my end was pretty much non-existent, so."

"Right." I swallow as I launch right in. "Lyric, I want you to know th—"

"Bria."

"What?"

"It's Bria. You called me Lyric."

"Sorry. I'm probably gonna do that a lot," I laugh, but I instantly want to take the words back. Presumptuous much?

Bria's look confirms my suspicion.

"You live here but you haven't been to any other shows before," she blurts. "Why?"

"How do you know?"

"Trust me, I know."

I run nervous fingers through my hair. "You're right. I was still hoping for that organic meeting, I guess. Bumping into you at the grocery store, or something I guess. I got cold feet. Once the possibility became real."

"So what changed?"

"Started hearing your name around town. Figured I better try now while it's still only a $10 cover."

Bria laughs. "Too cheap to pay the big bucks?"

"More like... I didn't want to make it seem like I was only coming around because you made it big or... when you started losing the weight, I already—"

"So... what took you so long?" she cuts me off impatiently.

"So long for what?"

She scoffs. "You said you knew about me. For years, apparently."

I open my mouth, but the mountain of excuses is too large to make its way out of my guilt-ridden throat. I know I owe her all the explanations, but it's shameful.

"Well... I didn't *know* know. I'd hoped," I say.

Bria continues a shallow pace around my room as if she could possibly be interested in the decor.

"I saw you while I was in the... in Chicago," I catch myself. "On TV. It was surreal, I thought I was hallucinating. Have a seat," I gesture towards a table and chair.

"No need. This won't take long," she refuses.

But her reply makes me think maybe *I* should sit down.

"I had a whole speech planned, you know?" she continues. "I've had several speeches planned, actually. For years. I had questions for years. They changed over time. It was basically all the same thing. 'What happened,' 'How could you,' 'Why why why...'" she gestures with her hands, refusing to make eye contact with me.

I don't know why she's putting up this facade of invulnerability. She must be hoping that six years apart will make it so that I won't see through it.

But the fact that she's using it at all stings enough. And knowing how her mind must've obsessed all these years. My heart skips as she moves a piece of hair behind her ear.

"But I'm genuinely past all that. There's no explanation you could give me that could satisfy me. And I'm done with dissatisfied. Forever."

My hope sinks. Because I can see she's telling the truth. She looks different, she talks differently. She doesn't even have the same name as the girl I knew, so I'm practically talking to a stranger.

"I understand," I muster, swallowing any pleas for mercy.

"Still. That doesn't make you useless," she retorts, a stoic look in her eyes. I shudder.

It's such a movie villain answer that at first I can't think of what she could be talking about.

Surely she doesn't mean sex.

Maybe she isn't so different.

"Bria... I'm not sure I follow."

"Sure you do," she leaned against the bathroom door frame, "you probably went through a period like I did, where you thought Halcyon was bullshit. But it isn't. Seeing you last night, being with you now. It's more than just memories. You *are* my

94

Match."

I lower my head, fiddling with a matchbook at the small table, suddenly shy. She does feel it.

"I want you too," she says. "There's no use denying that, I do. And I want you to make love to me. Like you haven't seen me in six years and you won't ever see me again."

My heart accelerates at her first three words, and continues until she gets to the last.

"You're saying... you want... one last hurrah."

"Precisely."

"I can do that," I say.

"Good."

"But that doesn't mean that I will. Tempting as that offer is."

"Why not?"

"Because of all the ways I pictured this going, it was with or without you. Never with only a piece of you. And so... I'm not giving in."

Bria smiles and my heart jolts again.

"With or without me, huh?"

"That's right."

She's genuinely amused as she laughs.

"I think you will. Give in."

"Why's that?"

"For the same reason you think you can waltz right back into my life and whisk me away. You think I don't know how much you want me? I'm not a size 6, but I'm sure as shit not a 22 anymore."

I don't know what to make of that statement. Has the weight loss turned her into a bitch?

"I do want you. But that's not the only reason."

"But it's one of them."

95

"I suppose," I admit with a shrug. "But if I can't have all of you, I'm not much interested."

"Did you even hear what I said?"

"Loud and clear."

"I don't believe a word out of your mouth," she glares. "You're wasting your time trying to win me back."

"I'm not trying to win you back."

She rears back a bit as though I've slapped her.

Shit. Why did I say it like that?

"Then you get nothing."

"Then I get nothing," I shrug.

As prepared as I was for this outcome, coming this close to her only to lose her causes grief to bloom all over my body.

Bria quietly heads to the door and it feels like my heart's in a vice as I'm already trying to memorize the sight of her walking away.

But she stops just as the door opens.

She lets out a little laugh as she turns and slams it shut in front of her, turning to face me.

I survive another heart attack as her actions give me another glimmer of hope.

She's bluffing. Of course, she's bluffing.

"You really got some nerve. Do you have any idea how much you owe me?"

"A lot. But I'm not giving in."

Bria uncrosses her arms. "Alright, *Cliff*. Think of it this way. We're playing South by Southwest this weekend. This is the show that's going to launch us. I've made sure of it. If you're not leaving without me, then you've gotta convince me to turn my back on my whole life, my entire band, on everything that I've worked for. And I'm telling you right now, without that magic dick of yours, you don't stand a chance."

I can't help grinning. She hasn't forgotten a thing.

"It's hardly magic."

"I think I would know better than you."

Could she have been experiencing the same colorless sex without me all these years? Even with Chase, the band hottie boyfriend she eye-fucks on stage every night?

It's a risk. A big risk.

I've never been more vulnerable. The thought of coming so close just to lose her again, presumably forever, is a total mindfuck.

But I have a mindfuck coming to me.

She trusted me, and I left her there alone. I have to be willing to let her choose the same path. Or I'll never rest.

I stand up. "Come here," I say.

She looks a bit frightened as she answers. "No."

"I don't wanna do anything, I just want to smell you."

She furrows her brow. "Smell me?"

"Yes."

"...Not unless we have a deal."

I don't hesitate. "We have a deal."

"Good. I'll come back here after my show."

"And you stay the whole night."

"Fine." She heads for the door and my stammering stops her.

"Do I need um... I mean... are you using... anything?"

Bria tilts her head and smiles at my shyness.

The women were given a Halcyon-patented cocktail of birth control, and tested for STIs before being admitted.

It was a bit like heaven, really. Not the worry-free aspect, but the trust. So much trust.

"That's considerate of you but... I just had my period, I'll be

97

fine."

"I can still suit up, if you want."

"Why? Don't tell me you doubled up on skanks since you've been out," she raises an eyebrow.

"You really do know me," I mutter.

"Oh no. Are you serious?" she laugh-moans, presumably to keep from crying.

I smile. She's taking this part a lot better than I imagined.

"Yeah, after I left uh... let's just say there was a lot of burning."

"Oh, for fuck's sake. So what are we talking about, Herpes? Hep C?" she sighs.

Jesus. Maybe she's taking this a little too well.

"Uh, none of the above."

"Chase had Herpes," she confides. The *fuck.*

"Is that so?"

"When we were together. I mean, he still has it obviously, just... we're not together. Anymore."

I don't draw attention to the fact that she's telling me about her life even though she said she wouldn't.

"Occupational hazard, I guess," I dismiss tactfully.

"Yeah. He's been in bands non-stop since he was about 16."

I take a deep and hopefully non-judgemental breath. "So, does that mean you..."

"No. No, we were careful. Really careful. Which is why I was sorta looking forward to... not having to be, but looks like I can't catch a break."

"I'm clean, I swear," I vow, going overboard. Obviously, my dick is not going to let me back out of this. "I got paperwork to prove it, I just... you never know. It's up to you."

Bria just rubs her forehead wearily.

"Nevermind just... I'll decide later."

"I'm sorry. I never meant to spring all that on you, but since you brought it up—"

"So what, you just left the program and started fucking girls?"

Ah. Okay, so she was taking it well for the moment. Gotta watch out for that delayed reaction.

I fumble around, trying to come clean as tactfully as possible.

"I don't like to think about it now, but, um... basically I knew I lost you. Well... 'lost' isn't quite strong enough. I... threw you away and... it was hard. Living with myself. Day to day. Really dark. I just did whatever I could to take my mind off of it. It wasn't... it happened, and I won't make excuses."

Her eyes turn sympathetic and...I don't know. Uncertain.

"What about after that?" she asks.

"After what?"

"This 'dark period.' Any relationships?"

"There's been a few. You?"

"Nice try."

I smirk. "Couldn't hold a candle to our worst day, though. Know what I mean?"

She still won't meet my eyes for longer than a second or two. She nods and heads for the door as I follow closely behind. Suddenly she turns around once she gets to the door.

"Just um, pick something up. Just in case I make the prudent choice. But I probably won't. If I'm staying the whole night, things are gonna get irresponsible."

My mouth goes dry as my brain tries to manage the open floodgates of fantasy about the near future.

"You think we're really going to open this door and then... shut it right back again?" I caution her.

"We have to. What are you doing?"

Abruptly I stop closing the distance between us.

"You said I could smell you."

"Oh," she giggles before awkwardly standing still as I approach her.

I stand so close that we're barely touching. I don't force her to look at me. I just steady myself with my hands on her shoulders and inhale her scent, starting with her hair.

Bria laughs a little as she takes a whiff of her own of me. Emotions mercilessly erupt out of my eyes and ears, nose and mouth. She absent-mindedly tugs at my t-shirt. A mistake.

I engulf her in an embrace and I'm like Superman in the sun. My wandering nose makes its way down her neck where her skin is unbearably soft.

Bria tilts her head some to accommodate me and then suddenly backs away, probably feeling my uncontrollable boner. A soundless gasp escapes her and our eyes meet.

Instinctively, I start reading her body like braille. I know if she eyes my lips it means she wants to keep going. Like hypnosis, I see her eyes move.

I lean in, unconsciously, uncontrollably. Bria stops me with her hand, forceful enough that I freeze.

"One kiss…" I bargain, like a junkie. With every intention of taking more. Much more.

"After the show," she urges.

But the show is 40 years away in Halcyon time.

Before I can object she serves me a meek explanation.

"I sing better when I'm suffering."

And with that, Bria shuts the door and leaves.

10

Luke

its.

It was, unfortunately, all I could think about after a week of no pornography at Halcyon. Or video games. The days were impossibly long.

What did humans do before any of this? I wondered to myself. Even fucking could only take up so much time in a person's day.

Thankfully, the campus offered some reprieve. A gym, pools. A rec room on each floor. There were more social things available, but I sure as shit wasn't in the mood for that.

I tried to get the attention of some of the other women I saw at the gym or the pool.

I tried to hold conversations with them, but it was no use. It was worse than high-school level rejection, trying to pry anything out of women who were already paired with someone.

It was beyond unavailability. It was like they had blinders on. Uber focused. I'm pretty sure the way one woman scampered off, she was ready to report me or something. Good.

Maybe it'll get me kicked out of this place.

I started experiencing what unfortunately was an all too

common occurrence throughout my life with Lyric.

It seemed like since grade school, I was always drawing some poor lonely soul that I could care less about.

And after becoming completely exasperated by said soul, who couldn't seem to catch a hint, I would have to do the mean thing and tell them to go away.

Lyric was the embodiment of this phenomenon, the culmination of my entire life's romantic story.

The less I showed interest in Lyric, the more she seemed to like me.

She asked if I wanted to take a walk with her. Asked if I had any game suggestions for the deck of cards she brought. She struck up conversations that ended after about five lines. Made up reasons to ask about lights on or off, the use of towels, the noise level of her headphones.

I heard the shuffling from her nylon uniform once the front door opened and closed. She was back from her counseling session. I braced myself for another forced interaction.

"You're awfully quiet, I thought you were gone."

"Nope."

"I saw the infamous Dey and Samantha in the hallway finally. Jem was right, they're totally hot."

"Cool."

"Sure you don't want to borrow a book or..."

Having reached my breaking point on the matter, I found myself particularly unable to control my shortness.

"Listen, Lyric, can you just... not talk? To me?"

"Uh... sure."

Quietly, Lyric retreated to her room, where she faithfully remained and kept her promise.

It didn't take long for me to regret my assumption.

She was simply being a nice person, I realized. She was always a bit more outgoing than me when we got to the dining hall, talking to Jem and Darren or whoever was there.

Only a few times did someone ask why I was so quiet, and she cordially covered for me.

If it wasn't for her demeanor, people would suspect that our time at Halcyon was going as horrible as it actually was. And the questions would be worse.

By the time my first solo counseling session rolled around, I still hadn't gotten over myself well enough to apologize to her.

"So, Luke."

"Dr. Payton," I said, unconsciously bouncing my knees.

"How have you been adjusting?"

"Um, well enough, I guess. I mean, I'm bored out of my mind."

"Bored?"

"Yeah, I mean there's nothing to do around here."

"Nothing to do?"

"Yeah, is there an echo in here?" I scoffed. "Nothing to do in here."

"Like what?"

"Like no TV, no xbox, no internet. No phone."

"Well, that's because you do have some*one* to do, in a manner of speaking."

I adopted a blank expression of grasping for understanding.

"You mean... Lyric?"

"Your Match, Lyric, yes."

"Well, to be perfectly honest, Dr., I am in no way physically attracted to Lyric. And I'm pretty sure the feeling is mutual."

"What makes you say that?"

"I don't know. She's not sending any of the usual female signals of interest."

"...And what are these "usual female signals"?

"I don't know. Eye contact, flirting. She doesn't even make an effort at conversation anymore. She just goes to her room and reads or listens to music or whatever she does."

"'Her' room?"

"Yeah, I gave her the big bed."

"...You 'gave her the big bed.'"

"Jesus, there really *is* an echo in here."

"Has it occurred to you that Lyric might be hurt by your actions?"

"Of course. I mean, I told her not to talk to me."

Dr. Payton refrained from repeating my apparently awe-inspiring statement, which I appreciated. If this is him being unbiased, he's failing miserably.

"You see, there's this phenomenon, in my life, where girls that I'm not interested in, show interest in me, and it just pisses me off," I explained. "And I thought that's what Lyric was doing, but now I think she was just trying to be nice."

"What about the girls that you *are* interested in?"

I scoff bitterly and shake my head. "Never give me the time of day. Only one ever did. Stacey, my ex-fiancée. I thought my luck was finally changing. Maybe I just needed to get to college, grow up or whatever. But she just railroaded me."

"How long have you been dealing with this phenomenon?"

"Since I've been alive, it seems like."

"Is it possible that you are exuding a certain desperation and anxiety approaching the women you want, which is causing them to reject you? And the lack of self-consciousness and artifice you have with the women you *don't* approach is attracting them even more?"

My eyes narrowed, as though information was being downloaded to my brain.

"Something tells me you're not asking me that because you *don't* know the answer."

"So Lyric was the recipient of this resentment?"

"Yeah," I said. "I don't know why it makes me feel like shit to think I might have disappointed her. It's not like it's my fault. She seems like a real sweetheart. She deserves better than what this program is doing to her, I'll tell you that."

"You seem to be convinced that the blame lies entirely on the program."

"Absolutely. I mean, they clearly got my test results all skewed. And then I had to wait this obscene amount of time to get picked and now it's no wonder. If I ever get out of this place alive I'll be pursuing legal action."

Dr. Payton maintained his wise, curious-looking poker face.

"Do you not find Lyric attractive?"

"No, I mean... she's beautiful and all. I'm just not a chubby chaser. At all."

"Beautiful how?"

"I mean, she's easy on the eyes. Beautiful face. Pouty lips. Like a model. Really sweet."

"It's her size that you object to," Dr. Payton deduced.

"I know plenty of guys that are into that, believe me. But it's just not my thing. Honestly, it seems a bit unhealthy for her to even be here, the size that she is. I'm starting to think this place is a little unscrupulous."

Dr. Payton's expression started to slip, but he caught himself.

"I understand from your earlier evaluation that you had 20+ hour a week habit of porn consumption," he suddenly said.

I shrugged at the non-sequitur. "At the time of orientation, yes that was true. I stopped completely for a while, but then it picked back up in the new year. Now it's more like ten or so hours— well it was before I got here. Now it's officially nil."

"How are you holding up?"

"Honestly, not well, Doc. I'm cranky as fuck. I think I might be going through withdrawals."

"Completely normal," said Dr. Payton.

"It's hard to jack off in peace when you're joined at the hip to a roommate in a house with no door."

"That is the point, of course, Luke."

I sighed, despondent. "Well. Since we're being honest, I have a bad feeling it's gonna be a long six months."

"How do you feel about that?"

"How do I feel about my feeling?" I snickered sarcastically. "I don't know. I'm still sort of hoping for a miracle, I guess."

"Your brain is in the process of rewiring itself to adjust to a natural threshold of stimuli. It may take a few more weeks, but I suspect you'll have your miracle."

What, he thought I would miraculously wake up one day attracted to Lyric?

"...That's not quite the miracle I had in mind," I replied with wide eyes.

"You were hoping to suddenly wake up next to Christie Brinkley?" Dr. Payton asked.

"Who's that?"

"I would tell you to ask Magellan, but you can't," Dr. Payton teased.

"Listen, Doc, I understand your reasoning. You think because I've been jacking off to unrealistic depictions of women since I was twelve, that now I have the expectations of a Burmese sultan, but that's not me. I'm not that guy."

"Not what guy?"

"I'm not a moron, okay? I know how to be realistic. Lyric is not just 'out of my comfort zone,' I'd have better luck with my sister. I'm telling you, it's not there."

"If you could wake up tomorrow feeling attracted to Lyric, would you consider that a win?" Dr. Payton asked.

I thought about that for a second. Impossible as it sounded, something about it appealed to me.

"...I don't know. I mean... if by some miracle that happens, it would still mean that my real Match is somewhere out there still, looking for me. I don't know that I could be satisfied with that."

"I'll make a deal with you, Luke, Dr. Payton bargained as he removed his glasses to clean them. "If you promise to keep an open mind, by the six-week mark if there's been no change in progress, and with Lyric's permission, I will personally recommend your compatibility re-evaluation."

"That's all I ask."

"In the meantime, it wouldn't hurt to get to know Lyric. With this little insight into your past history with women, it might be nice to make friends with a woman when there's no sexual tension present. You could pick her brain. Ask her what attracts her to you, what you're doing right."

I don't know why I didn't divulge to Dr. Payton the fantasy I'd had about Lyric the other night while quietly whacking off.

It was a little embarrassing, but I was starting to trust this guy. He seemed legit.

"I guess you're right. I hadn't thought of that. How long would it take to hear back?"

"...Hear back?"

"About the compatibility re-evaluation."

Dr. Payton kept his expression neutral, but for some reason, I could sense he was exasperated.

"Expect another six weeks."

Six weeks...

I rubbed my forehead worriedly. "So I could spend three of my six months in here with the wrong person?"

Dr. Payton put his tongue in his cheek.

"In the scheme of your entire life, does it really seem that long?"

"Touché, Dr. Payton," I said as I stood, feeling better. "I appreciate this. Really, I do."

The doctor managed a smile.

"Peace of mind is a powerful motivator. I'm more than happy to help."

* * *

I started to wake up in the mornings to Lyric's amplified humming in the shower.

My foggy mind awakened itself straining to hear and anticipating the next angelic sound.

Sometimes I woke up to the deafening sounds of her blow dryer. On those days she emerged from the bathroom with her hair completely straight and looking like the celebrity she almost certainly was.

Other days her hair was pulled back in a high tight ponytail, the tail being a perfect poof like a human topiary.

On the days I'd awaken hearing her return from swimming, she was usually wearing her hair in a kinetic, airy looking afro made of tight curls.

Usually I retreat to the couch or to my room, but one day I instead crowded the doorway of her room until she looked up and removed an ear of her headphones.

"Hey," I said.

"Hey."

"You still got that deck of cards?"

The two of us sat at the kitchen nook playing Go Fish.

"So um... Lyric, huh?" I began without looking up from my hand.

"What?"

"You chose the name Lyric. You a musician or what?"

"You could say that. I just love music I guess," she shrugged. I gave her a disapproving look.

"I could say that? Are you a musician or aren't you?"

She relinquished a nervous smile. "I dabble. Piano. Guitar. Mandolin. Got any eights?"

I handed her what I had. "So you *are* a musician," I pushed.

"My entire family are musicians in some capacity, so it's hard to think of myself that way. Not when you've grown up around real ones," she clarified.

"Any two's?"

"Go fish."

I pulled a card from the deck. "So you really are famous."

"What?"

"Jem said you looked familiar the other day. Like you were famous."

She fumbled a bit. "Oh. Well... you could say I'm sorta famous by proxy, I guess. But mostly on the industry side. I don't know. I don't wanna say too much. Got any threes?"

"Go fish. I'm not mega into music, so. I'm sure I wouldn't know you."

"You'd be surprised," she said with intrigue. I raised an eyebrow.

"What, are you like, Michael Jackson's cousin or something?"

"I've been to his house."

"You're shitting me."

"I was pretty little, so I don't remember."

"He didn't like... touch you. Did he?"

"...I don't think so."

It was quiet for a moment until we both snickered at the same time.

"It's your turn," she laughed.

"Are you sure?"

"Yup."

"Uh... sevens," I blurted.

She handed over her sevens.

"What about you? Luke. You a Star Wars fan?"

"Is it that obvious?"

"Nah. Lucky guess. Any fives?"

I handed over my fives.

"We got a barn burner on our hands," she smiled.

"Looks like it," I grinned. "You like Star Wars?"

"Sure."

"Really?"

"The way you feel about music is probably how I feel about Star Wars," she summated.

"Fair enough."

"You related to George Lucas by any chance?"

"I wish," I scoffed.

"I know you can't tell me specifics but... just how rich are you? On a scale of one to ten."

"I've no idea," I admitted.

I had an idea, of course, it's the standard answer we give to outsiders. It's evasive without being an outright lie.

"*Damn*," she remarked.

She seemed rich enough to know what "I don't know" means.

"Did you go to college?" she asked.

"I did."

"What'd you study?"

"Finance."

"Hm. Really?" she cocked her head as though surprised.

"I hated it."

"Ah," she says, as if that explained something. "What'd you do after college?"

"Nothing, honestly. I had a job. I lost it. Before I came here."

"A job doing what?" she asked.

"Nothing worth mentioning."

"We've got nothing but time here, Luke."

I sighed extra loud. "There's at least ten other things we could do that are more interesting than talking about my life."

There was an awkward silence while the thought of sex flashed before my brain, and hers too if her silence was any indication.

My pulse shot up. Lyric stayed looking down at the coffee table as if she'd swept the thought away as quickly as she could.

"...I'm sure that's not true," she said, laying her winning hand out on the coffee table. "I win."

"Good for you," I said non-ironically.

"Wanna go again?"

"Nah," I answered.

She grabbed the cards and leftover deck to needlessly shuffle them before putting them back in their pack.

She gave me a flirty look, but I think that's just her face.

"So, you were saying?"

She wanted to keep the conversation going.

I gave in, chuckling. "I basically filed paperwork that ensured people who lost their jobs couldn't file for unemployment."

"Wow, that sounds... terrible."

"Not really. There are pretty shitty employees out there, it turns out."

"I see."

An impossibly silent moment passed between us. The imposing silence of a distractionless room.

But I was at least starting to see the benefit of talking. We'd shaved at least 20 minutes off the day with just one round of Go Fish. I threw the ball back to her.

"What do you do?"

"I'm in school. For music business. Naturally. Only had a semester left when they called."

"Oh. Sounds like we're both kind of... still getting our feet wet. How old are you?"

"I'll be 22 soon. You?"

"25," I said. I nodded towards her. "You seem kind of young to be in a program like this."

"Oh. Well... when you come from a family like mine, there's not that much 'go out and see the world' left. There are a few things I haven't done yet." she confided.

She shrunk a bit once the words left her mouth, adorably.

"This program, it kinda gives you an excuse to do something responsible and dumb at the same time."

"Yeah. I think that's their gimmick," I said.

"Their gimmick?"

"Yeah. How they get you."

She stopped and gave me a squinting look.

"So... what did Dr. Payton say about... did you tell him your doubts about me?" she asked.

I shifted in my seat. "Um, well, we're supposed to keep that confidential, but yeah, I told him about it."

When I didn't go further, she nudged her head forward a bit, an obvious need in the air for me to expound further.

"I don't suppose you could tell me his suggestion," she said.

"Well, he agreed to re-evaluate me if there's been no change in six weeks."

"No change?" she tilted her head.

I swallowed.

"Well... you know. If I'm... if I don't have a change of heart."

"I see," she finally said, after the meaning of my words finally clicked.

My stomach churned as my mouth started running out of preservation.

"No offense to you, Lyric it's just... you seem super cool—"

"*Don't*... do that," she cut me off. She put the cards back in their pack and didn't move from the table. I didn't either.

"It wouldn't be right away," I reassured her, "and not without your permission. And then after that..." my voice trailed off.

"After that what?"

Shit. Just get it over with.

I finally looked up at her. "It takes... another six weeks for the re-evaluation to be completed."

She pushed her chair back from the table and, panic breathing, stood up.

"Three months.   I'm stuck in here with you for three months??"

I sat where I was, watching her pace absent-mindedly around the living room.

"...Lyric—"

"Of course you'll have my permission to fuck off after *three months* of this! You know, you're not exactly God's gift to women, Luke," she lodged at me.

"Okay. You're right. I deserve that."

"And just what am I supposed to do? Once you get 're-evaluated'?"

"If they got my Match wrong, then it stands to reason that yours is still out there too."

"Oh my God, dude. You're *delusional*," she shook her head with a bitter laugh.

"What?" I asked curiously.

"You think this is McDonald's or something? They just got your order wrong? You really think they would risk possibly mishandling our information? They could get sued. You think they would risk losing the public's trust like that?"

I rolled my eyes. "Trust me, a big giant company like this has got to have some fucked up shit goin' on. Guarantee they've got $9.00 an hour community college rejects watching the monitors in here and jackin' off to what's on them."

"You'd know all about that, wouldn't you," she muttered.

"...'Scuse me?" I furrowed my brow.

My heart sped up. Did she know about the porn addiction? Who would've told her?

Would Dr. Payton rat me out?

She went on as though I hadn't spoken. "And so, after six weeks, when you find out what literally *everyone* around you already knows, then what? Then we're 'sposed to just... what, be a couple?"

I kept my surprised expression. "If you're really my Match, then you'll have my full undivided attention."

"Oh, lucky me!" she declared sarcastically.

"Yeah. Lucky you," I replied, with a sarcastic bite of my own.

She gave me a long look before she shook her head in disbelief with a laugh.

"Fine, asshole. Spin your wheels if you want. Don't even *think* about touching me for the next six weeks."

"Don't worry, I won't," I said.

"And keep your jack off sessions relegated to the shower like a normal person," she added on the way to her room.

"Ditto," I said at her back.

If she heard me at all, she pretended not to notice.

11

Luke

Things got a bit tense after our confrontation, as you can imagine.

She went to lunch the next day without saying a word. When she got back, I was just getting dressed.

"Did you go to lunch already?"

"Eat a dick."

"...Very mature."

We'd already had our counseling session right before the blowup, so Dr. Payton wasn't around to give her some rational advice.

I had no idea what she was telling the other "inmates." I was pretty much a pariah when I went into the dining hall alone. But I was relieved to not have to put up a united front in view of strangers that don't give a shit.

As requested, I kept my jack-off sessions relegated to the shower, which became a highlight of my morning.

I usually woke to the sounds of her shower anyway, but I found myself perking my ears, waiting to hear similar signs of self-pleasuring. I had a knack for it for some reason, knowing when other people were masturbating. An odd talent.

Finally, that weekend I was rewarded with one of her quiet moans, clipped and muffled like she'd put a hand over her mouth.

Must've been too good to keep quiet, I thought, my morning wood that much harder. Already I was reliving the angelic sound.

I had a folder on my laptop at home devoted to my favorite videos with the best moaning. I miss my moaning collection.

I was jealous but wouldn't be for long, as I was now wide awake and due for a shower of my own.

After a long week of the silent treatment, we would be forced to interact all weekend— or at least if we wanted to eat.

This was our first weekend where we were out of doggy bags and would have to cook together. I heard the package arrive just as I was shaving.

For some reason, I came out of the bathroom right away, in just my towel. I came around the corner just in time to see Lyric enthusiastically begin shuffling through ingredients, arranging the vegetables and perusing the recipes.

"This is supposed to feed us for an entire weekend?" I spoke up. Lyric turned around and looked startled to see me. She gave me a contentious little once over and then answered.

"I think we get another box tomorrow."

"Is this a work camp?"

"What's your deal?" she glared, exasperated.

"Nothing. It just sort of seems like we're paying a buncha money to fend for ourselves, which is what we were already doing before we got here."

"Somehow I doubt you're doing much of that," she replied.

Well. At least she was talking to me.

I put on a pair of sweatpants and joined her in the kitchen.

"What about you, money bags?" I teased.

"What about me what?"

"When's the last time you had to cook for yourself?"

"My family cooks together. A lot. Your mom or dad never cook?"

I go through my memory banks. "My mom used to cook a bunch. Really elaborate shit that took all day. Now she pretty much relies on the help."

Lyric stopped in her tracks.

"...Are you telling me that you still live at home? And you have servants that cook for you every day?"

"Not every day. I sometimes eat fast food."

"Oh... my God," she said, as if I offended her.

"What?"

"So what, you just... live at home and bleed your parents dry? Is that it?"

"Look, don't judge me, princess. Isn't that what you do?" I said, playfully offended.

"As soon as I graduate, I'm going out on my own," she asserted. "I sort of can't fuckin' wait to be out on my own. What's *your* plan exactly? What the hell are you even getting out of this program? I know you're not about to tell me it was your idea to apply."

"You're right, I'm not gonna say that."

Lyric just shook her head and laughed. "Lemme guess: your parents are trying to set your grown-ass up with a wife because you're incapable of taking care of yourself?"

"...Actually it was just my mom's idea."

"Jesus Christ," Lyric scoffed and shook her head again. I huffed a little laugh watching her. She cracked a smile.

"What?"

"Care to be re-evaluated?" I raised an eyebrow.

She sighed. "It's tempting." She grabbed the clear plastic bag of tomatoes and handed them to me.

"Think you can manage to cut a tomato?"

I grabbed the bag and handled them like they were alien produce as I fished one out and onto the counter.

"In the event you get re-assigned, let me send you off with a new skill. It's called 'usefulness.' Trust me, you're gonna need it. Your Match can thank me later."

I groaned a groan of laziness.

"Sorry, is this boring you?"

"A little."

"You got something else to do?"

"No, I guess I don't."

"Good," she said.

And that's when it happened. Lyric absent-mindedly began singing.

"While you were away I started lovin' you/ Oh looooovin' you…"

I froze mid-cut and looked over at Lyric who didn't seem fazed by the sweet sound that her mouth just produced.

She didn't even seem to know it happened. She busied herself with an avocado until she noticed I was staring. She stopped with a doe-eyed look that further arrested me.

"What?"

"You were singing."

"Oh. Yeah. Sorry, I do that."

"No, it was nice."

"…Thanks," she replied in a small voice.

Lyric didn't resume her song and a small part of me was forlorn. Meanwhile, I couldn't stop shaking and it took me even longer to cut up one tomato. Because for a split second Lyric

119

looked exactly like my ex-girlfriend Stacey.

More specifically, she looked like Erika Leigh, this actress I'd been obsessed with since I was about 14.

Part of the reason I'd fallen in love with Stacey was that she had the same build and mannerisms and shade of chestnut brown hair.

But I didn't understand how Lyric, being the antithesis of Erika Leigh in practically all ways, could somehow have her face in her face.

Was it some kind of facial symmetry they shared? Some sort of... essence?

I was starting to wonder if I should entertain the idea that the program was real. And that whatever biological markers drew me to Erika Leigh in the first place had nothing to do with the woman herself. Or maybe... the woman herself enhanced what drew me to her...

My mind continued this chicken or egg biological syllogism as my heart dipped and fluttered unconsciously.

No wonder Lyric's face caught my eye almost immediately. I'd had to do a double-take.

Holy shit... was she really my match?

I had to admit it was interesting. A compelling piece of evidence, but I couldn't just leave the issue to rest. Not if, in six weeks, I could know for sure.

About an hour later we were eating fettuccine with roasted tomatoes and this buttery, avocado-based sauce.

"Holy fuck, this is good," I commented as we ate.

"Finally, something we agree on," she said with a full mouth.

"The food's pretty stellar here, I gotta admit."

"Pasta's basically my crack. There's a little left, do you want it?"

"No, take it," I grinned.

"What?" she asked.

"Nothing," I answered. I was going to say something about the way she totally owned her appetite, but there's no way she would take that as a compliment.

"So what are you listening to in those headphones of yours?"

"Oh. Um, sometimes music. Podcasts. Audiobooks."

"Podcasts about what?"

"Music business stuff mostly. 2 Dope Queens."

"Dope Queens?"

"Never mind."

"Anything you think I would be into?"

"Um... based on what I've seen so far, I'm gonna go with 'no.'"

"Oh. What about the audio books?"

She chewed and knitted her brow. "What's with the interrogation?"

I shrugged in surrender. "I'm not interrogating you, I'm just bored. And jealous. I didn't think to bring downloaded shit here."

"What would you have brought?"

"I don't know. Some pirated movies. TV shows."

"You're only allowed 1GB of data."

"Ugh. So many rules."

"They're only bothersome to people who don't like their Match."

I scoffed. "Lyric, I like you fine, it's just—"

"So, you admit that you're really my Match."

I hesitated, not knowing if it was a trap.

"Well, for now, yes. There's a good chance you really are."

"You don't say."

"I'm not ruling it out, I just—"

"Want to know for sure," she parroted me.

"Right."

"Right."

"Okay, so, what about the audiobooks?"

She gave me a little mischievous glance, a smile at the corner of her lips. "Definitely not your thing."

I couldn't control my smile as I gave her a suspicious eye.

"Don't tell me you're into like, 50 Shades and all that."

"Okay, I won't."

"Oh my God, Lyric," I chuckled.

"I don't want to hear your opinion."

"No wonder you seem like such a prude."

"What??" she jerked her head back.

"What is with women and these books? I honestly don't get it."

She gives me a steady glare like she's about to lay into me. But it suddenly softens, like she's decided against it. "No, I don't suppose you would," she says, stabbing her pasta with a fork.

"What's that supposed to mean?"

"It means if you knew something about women, you probably wouldn't be here."

I scoffed, nursing a wound to my pride.

"You think I'm here because I can't get a woman?"

"I honestly haven't thought that much about it, but it seems like the only logical conclusion."

"Literally anyone can get a woman. You'd have to be a moron to *not* be able to. It's just not every woman is worth getting."

"I see," her eyes widened sarcastically.

Okay, two can play at this game.

"So... you've been listening to porn books for two weeks?" I ask.

"Basically."

I laughed.

"Have you ever even had sex?"

"No."

"Oh my God," I rolled my eyes, trying not to smile. It was kind of adorable.

"I take it you have?"

"Uh... yeah."

"Okay," she shrugged.

"No wonder you're so into those things. They're nothing like reality."

"Well, it's not really your problem, now is it?" she answered defensively.

I grinned.

"No, I guess not," I replied.

* * *

So, I might've stopped in to Lyric's room on purpose right after my shower a few days later.

I patted my hair dry with a towel, shirtless with my pajama bottoms hanging on my hips. Her hair was straightened this morning and sitting on top of her head in a thick, messy bun. Kind of a weird choice after you spend an hour in the bathroom straightening it, but whatever.

Lyric tried to look nonchalant while I stood there half naked and glistening, but she's got a terrible poker face.

It's a simple pleasure that costs nothing and amused me. The days are long around here.

"Okay, I give in." I said.

"Give in to what?" she asked as I laid beside her in bed.

"Give me an ear," I replied, nodding towards her iPad.

"I'll do you one better," she said, whipping out a tiny egg shaped speaker and hooking it up to it.

I chuckled. "You sure do come prepared."

"I had this crazy idea that my Match would love music just as much as I did."

"Alright, I get it."

"Get what?"

"Neither of us got what we wanted," I said.

"I never said that," Lyric sighed.

"You don't have to."

"I don't know what I want," she replied. "That's why I'm here."

"You need Halcyon to tell you what you want?"

"I'm relying on Halcyon to give me a better chance in here than I would have out there."

"...I don't see you having trouble finding a guy."

"No?"

"You're outgoing, fun, talented, pretty," I rattled off. She rolled her eyes, but not before smiling.

"...With a gorgeous sister," she dared to add, looking down.

"Ah, now I see. You were being upstaged."

"More like... used," she said, her eyes wandering. Either she was lost in thought or checking me out.

"Sorry."

"Wasn't your fault."

"So, what are we listening to?"

"...What kind of heat level are you comfortable with?" she asked with a squint.

"Give me the dirtiest thing you got."

"...I don't think you know what you're asking," she countered with a raised eyebrow.

I laughed. "Alright, I'll leave it up to you then."

"You laugh like you're from the 1930's," she suddenly remarked.

That only made me laugh again. "What does that even mean?"

Lyric chose a book called "All the Queen's Men," a historical romance about a princess from an African tribe who is betrothed to a future king and gets taken to a fictional European land.

It was a weird thing to be doing in the middle of the afternoon for more than one reason.

Typically, audiobooks just made me tired and I always got distracted and had to rewind a hundred times before I finally just gave up. I certainly never listened to an audiobook while laying next to someone in bed.

And maybe it was because I hadn't used a single media device in 15 days, but the lush description of this world practically wrapped itself around me.

The story was about six princesses from a fictional African tribe, prized for their smooth skin as dark as a night sky. Their father was a chief, and they were said to each be the product of an ancient goddess since they had no mother.

The European prince chose one girl to be his wife in exchange for access to a river. The prince waited six years to come back for the girl who was now a woman. They were to be married in the European country but it took a month to get there by boat. Turns out he'd been obsessed with her the whole time, but pretended to be diplomatic so he could get more out of the chief.

The prince was impatient to make love to her in secret on the way home, but the princess had never seen a boat and was violently ill...

Lyric pushed pause and got up out of bed.

"What are you doing?" I said.

"It's lunch time."

"No fucking way it's lunch time already."

She gave me her biggest laugh to date.

"You can't turn it off now, I insisted, "he finally got to see her muff."

"I see you're enjoying the story," she pointed to my semi-erection.

"We have an hour before they're done serving lunch."

"Trust me, you want to get lunch over with before you go any further," she grinned.

I was tempted to stay behind and have the most satisfying jerk off session of my life, but my stomach won out.

I decided to amuse Lyric in pretty much the only way I know how, which was to make an ass of myself. So, when we made it through the line I scarfed down my food in record time, which she found hilarious.

It had the added bonus of making her feel comfortable enough to eat like a normal human.

We got back to the barracks and I instantly went back in her room and jumped into the king-sized bed.

"Fire it up," I said.

"You can get under the covers in case you need to, you know, hide things."

"I'm not gonna jack off in front of you."

"I know, I just meant—"

"Unless you want me to," I offered. The hesitation was adorable.

"That's very generous, but I was talking about erections. If you jack off in front of me, I'm just gonna jill off in front of you."

I narrowed my eyes in silence. "'Jill off?'"

"Yeah, you know. Jack and Jill," she clarified with a wave of her hand.

"I get the reference, I just don't understand... like where did you hear that?"

"It's a thing."

"It's not a thing."

"It doesn't matter, I'm just saying be forewarned. Are you gonna behave yourself or not?"

"...I think so." I stifle my grin. Hearing Lyric talk candidly about virginal sexcapades satisfied me in a deep place.

She gave me a raised eyebrow as I got underneath the covers and waited for the naughtiest bedtime story ever.

The time between lunch and dinner went by like a breeze as we finished the story about the European prince's obsession with his dark-skinned bride, who haunted his dreams as he slept.

12

Bria

I can barely concentrate after leaving Cliff's hotel room.

Everything in me wanted to jump his bones and not leave his room until time for soundcheck. If that would've even been enough.

I shake my head, hoping to clear these cobwebs but it's impossible. All my brain can do is re-live the conversation while my insides try and fail not to unsettle all this buried emotion.

He was out there. Fucking other women. While I was "in here," in my imprisoned mind, in that body, picking up the pieces.

And it feels like someone's running my soul through a sewing machine. All his unsatisfactory answers like seawater to my thirsty heart.

I shouldn't have let him smell me and I shouldn't have smelled him back. Instantly the scent came back to me and warped six years of time into a half-second.

I thought if I didn't return his embrace, if I just kept my arms at my sides and looked straight ahead, into his hard chest that I once kissed until my lips were raw... I still feel the tip of his nose behind my ear.

I'm within walking distance to the studio where we had a recording session, still in a trance by the time I arrive. Somewhere between ecstasy and agony. The ecstasy of knowing that suddenly, on a random afternoon, Luke and I were in the same room again. And that in a few hours I'm going to be the recipient of the best sex I both do and don't deserve. The agony of it not happening right this minute. Or the next. Or the next.

I don't know much about this Cliff dude, but Luke?!?!!??

Luke could stay erect after a climax and make us both come at least three times in one session. He's one of those guys that likes to look deep into your eyes at all times, even kissing. It's like having sex with an owl and I'm fucking here for it.

I'm sure we looked ridiculous and emo our first time doing it, but for me, it was like being made love to by a fallen angel. The thought of it makes me shiver, and then it makes me mad all over again.

He fucking left me. And spent the last six years with God only knows who—

"Bria?"

"What?"

"I said we might need to cut 'Do or Die' from the set tonight."

"I heard that part."

"Are you sure?"

I take a minute to answer. "Yes."

"Everything alright?"

"Yeah, just ready to get in the booth."

We cut one song, and it's... fine. Just fine.

I was prepared to use all the shit from this afternoon and lay it out on the microphone but it all just falls flat. It's constipated, it's disjointed from the group, and I can feel it. It's a thousand bucks down the drain and even the engineer knows it. But no one says anything.

And unfortunately, all I can see in my mind is a countdown to after the show.

"So um... where were you earlier?" Chase asks.

"Just... taking a breather."

"Because we took a stroll downtown and some of the other acts were out and about. A few brands. Shook some hands, but our manager was nowhere to be found."

That was a dig at me, of course. "Tomorrow, I'm all yours, I promise."

"You know, if all goes according to plan, there's a lot more touring where this came from," he lectures.

"You don't know think I know that?" I reply. "This band is my life. I don't have a back-up plan, I'm all in."

"Uh... okay, but that's not what I'm talking about."

"What *are* you talking about?"

"...Listen, Bri. We need to talk for a minute," Chase says.

By "we" he means the entire band and me.

They've all been a unit longer without me, so I allow it. For now.

"I know what you're going to say, and it's fine."

"What am I going to say?"

"You're going to say that I've been acting weird ever since Lu... Cliff showed up last night, and I know. I know, you're right, and it's fine."

"I was going to say that there are five other people here that love you and have been your family for five years—"

"Do you? Love me?"

"Of course."

"Because it feels like you're trying to remind me of how much pressure is riding on all of this like I don't know. Like I'd be

130

willing to just... leave you all out in the lurch. I know the pressure I'm under. I got this."

"We're all under the same amount of pressure, Bri."

"Which is it, Chase? You can do this without me, or can't you? Because I can't seem to win an argument around here."

"I fucking hate this guy already," he mutters under his breath.

"Really? Because you've been so subtle up to now."

"We're *this close*, Bria—"

"YOU WOULDN'T EVEN HAVE *CONCEIVED* OF THIS IF IT WASN'T FOR ME. BACK OFF!"

Everyone else quiets as another tempest moves through the two strongest personalities of the group.

Chase and I can have the kind of fights that almost ensure would be followed up with the greatest sex you could imagine.

It should have. And it never did. Even with me practically heaving myself into an ancient trance underneath him, I just couldn't force myself inside the passion that Chase was clearly feeling.

Chase simply walks out of the room. Since the arguments can no longer be construed as an outlet of my secret infatuation, he has to take them at face value. I see the realization dawning that I'm genuinely just annoyed with him.

I'm mad at myself, but I don't move. The band awkwardly shifts and the engineer pretends not to be here— a move that seems practiced— which only makes me feel worse.

"I'm so tired of you all acting like you're at the mercy of my moods."

"Sure. We're free to do and say whatever we want," Jacob speaks up sarcastically.

What in the actual fuck.

"Who has something to say to me? Besides you?"

Chelsea speaks up.

"We're away from our families for this tour. We all have full-time jobs—"

"This band *is* my full-time job."

"For now. You have a famous family to fall back on."

"My 'famous family' is nothing to fall back on."

"You're right, it's worse. You have something to prove."

"My reasons for being here are just as valid. That's not fair."

"We're just worried. That's all."

"Of what? My personal life has nothing to do with the commitment I have to this band."

Everyone's quiet, but not out of contrition.

Do they really not believe me?

"We're doing South by Southwest. On our own steam. Everything is riding on this. Why the hell would I try so hard to get us all here?"

"And after you've succeeded? What then?"

"Then we ride the fucking wave! We deserve it."

"Your mother is Minnie Forrester. We could've used the break four years ago."

Four *years* ago, are they mental?

"Now we're tight. We've got a good set, the right songs. What the hell did I know about leading a band? You think I wanted to fall on my ass in front of my family? They all think I'm crazy, anyway. But they won't anymore."

Chase conveniently re-emerges, but it's not like he would've defended me if he'd stayed.

"So that's all that matters? Not looking like an ass in front of your family?"

"Of course not."

"What was wrong with us four years ago? We were doing fine

for eight years."

"And then Lori left," I say.

"And then Lori left."

"Right," I reply. Are we not on the same page here?

"What are you saying, Bri?"

"Okay, you know what? You guys can shit on me when I'm not here."

"Bria..."

"We're trying to have an honest conversation," Braxton chimes in.

"When SXSW is 24 hours away? Really?"

"When should we have it, Bria?"

Everyone's crazy if they think I'm gonna do this right now.

"I don't know. After. I'm going to the hotel."

"You mean to *his* hotel?" Chase digs.

Oh my gosh, I'm sooo ready to get laid.

"Depends on who has the better gym." I grab my shit and head for the door.

"What about rehearsal?" April meekly asks.

"I don't fucking need rehearsal," I shout behind me. "Call me when it's time to leave."

Halcyon— Six Years Ago

For the next week, Luke and I would continue to be cordial roommates.

I was an early riser, while Luke preferred to sleep. It was basically like living with a stoner.

We ate meals together in relative silence. We sometimes played cards in silence.

By now, whatever politeness we'd been hanging on to had faded and we were simply living our nerdy, doorless lives. We talked to ourselves, sang to ourselves. We discovered we had similar tastes in movies.

"You've never seen Goodfellas?"

"It's been on my list forever, but no."

"You have to see it, if you liked The Departed, you'd like this movie."

"Tell it to me right now."

"What?"

"Narrate the entire movie to me, and don't leave anything out," he said. I laughed and laughed.

We were so goddamn bored. And Luke has this great way of being unexpectedly funny. You wouldn't even expect him to understand what a joke is. And then... *bam.*

The next day, we were both awake early in time for breakfast. Luke insisted on a shower, but I just got dressed and tried to make my hair presentable.

Luke emerged from the bathroom, a towel tied around his middle with his hair still dripping, just as I was zipping into my suit.

I looked up to see him already watching me, as I unabashedly watched him.

I didn't have the confidence yet to question the moment or let it linger. I gave him a double-take of shy confusion. He had mercy on me with small talk.

"What's up with these jumpsuits, anyway?" he said.

"Right? I feel like a janitor," I smoothly replied.

"Maybe it has some kind of psychological effect. Takes away individuality," he theorized, disappearing behind the wall that separated our rooms. "Keeps men from eyeing other chicks too close while they're in here."

I furrowed my brow and rolled my eyes where he couldn't see.

"...Pretty sure they're just trying to keep laundry from becoming a nightmare."

"Maybe they're trying to hasten some level of intimacy because you have to get completely naked just to take a dump," he said. I gave him a charmingly nerdy laugh.

We were back in the dining hall that was much more full than it had been the last two weeks. It seemed the newest residents were coming out of the honeymoon phase.

"Lotta new people this week," Luke said. He was too oblivious to see me roll my eyes.

I spotted Jem in line and she waved me over to cut halfway through. Thankfully, no one minded.

"What's on the menu?" I asked.

"Osso bucco."

"Holy shit."

"Around month four, you won't feel that way, trust me."

"One more month right?"

"Essentially. Darren wants to get married right away once we get out of here."

"Awww..." I said, digging my fingernails into my own fist. "Any idea on what he does?"

"Something about pharmaceuticals."

"Not the street kind, I hope."

"Me too," she said. Her face brightened. "Hey, you guys should come hang out with us tomorrow."

"Saturday?"

"Yeah, around the firepit. Some of us 'elders.' Anyone who's not busy fucking each other comes out on the patio around 6, when it starts to get dark."

"Well, we *definitely* qualify for that shindig," I said, sounding a little bitter.

"This is abuse, Lyric," Jem asserted, concerned.

"I don't know, between me and you, sometimes I catch him looking at me. I think I'm wearing him down."

Jem wasn't so easily impressed. "Ugh! If he wasn't your match I'd tell you to just dump his ass."

"He's still convinced that they're gonna re-evaluate him after six weeks."

"Which is when?"

"We're about halfway there."

"I can't believe your therapist would even suggest that."

"Dr. Payton knows what he's doing. Honestly, he'd just be unbearable otherwise," I rationalize. "He can get a little self-defeatist, I think."

Jem shakes her head in disbelief. "Well, I admire you, Lyric. I couldn't do it."

I shrugged, not wanting her pity. "I'm sure I can drag him to a hangout tomorrow. We'll be there."

"What else do you have to do, right?" Jem winked.

* * *

"Do you think you could pretend to be a normal human tonight?" I asked Luke after lunch.

"Why? What's up?"

I laughed. "I can't just get a 'yes'?"

"No."

"Jem invited us to a bonfire type deal. And she's basically the only person that knows you're refusing to fuck me. So, I think if you can just smile occasionally and look brooding, everyone will just think you're shy or something."

"I am shy."

"Really," I asked unconvinced.

"Yes."

"Okay then... try to just be a movie version of yourself, please. If that makes sense."

"It does."

It was a pleasant 68 degrees when we went out to the campus' large outdoor area that had a pavilion, a few grills, and a large recessed fire pit surrounded by benches.

"There they are," Jem announced, getting up to greet me with a hug. She even extended Luke a warm side hug that earned her a grin I was jealous of.

I sat at the end of one bench, right underneath the load-bearing iron feet. It felt sturdy and sure underneath me and my shoulders relaxed.

I'd broken a chair at an outdoor restaurant once, while I was out with my sister and my mom. Around ten years ago, thank God. Before smart phones got too smart. I was only 12.

I wasn't big enough to break a chair but I believed I was, especially after that. The paps following us could barely snap a family-feeding picture for laughing.

"*These fucking chairs. I just broke one myself yesterday*," the waitress went on and on as she helped me into another one. She got a $500 tip that day. Every once in awhile I think about it and wish we'd given her more.

Luke looked at me surprised when I sat down. The spot I picked didn't have an empty space for him to sit next to me.

"Really?" he teased.

"The last thing I need is to be the fat chick that broke a bench outside," I attempted some self-deprecating humor. Not my usual go-to, but I wanted to test the crowd.

"What?" Luke gave me an offended tone, surprisingly. There was a resounding chorus behind him as well, as though I was making fun of someone else there.

"My fears are warranted, people, let's just leave it at that."

"Honestly, Lyric, you're not that big. I've seen chicks that look like they could die any minute, walking around like queens."

"I carry it well, I'll admit that," I backpedaled, as if forced to now pay myself a compliment. The group giggled.

"What do you think, Luke, does she carry it well?" one of the guys directed at him.

I turned from hot to cold, a plastic smile glued to my face nervously.

I was ready to interrupt him with another zinger rather than see the hesitation all over his face. One look at Darren and I knew that Jem had been talking to him about us.

"She *absolutely* carries it well," he muttered without hesitation, sitting across from me on the other side of the fire. A few of the girls "aww"ed and the guys chuckled knowingly as if they knew what that meant. As if they assumed he was one of those guys. That like... girls like me.

I gave him a private look, a mix of shock, fluster and coquettishness. He returned my gaze with a grin and then looked away.

"What?" he laughed when he looked up and I was still looking at him.

"Oh my gosh, *nothing*," I looked away, girlishly smiling.

Everyone laughed at the two of us. They should have, it was cute. We seemed like we were in a puppy love phase.

"Dey, get up so Luke can sit next to Lyric," Jem suddenly ordered.

"Where's Sam going to sit?" he giggled.

Jem continued to re-organize the seating chart until she was satisfied. Luke came and sat next to me, one arm resting behind me on the back of the bench.

It was just one arm. It was barely touching me. But nothing had ever felt so good in my life.

I looked over at him and he was already looking down at me. I felt like the paramedics had shocked me one too many times.

And yet it was familiar. Comfortable enough to go in for a kiss, but in no way confident that it's what he would even want.

Top that with the reddest, juiciest cherry of electricity, arousal a warm blanket over my insides. If he looked at my lips right now, I would probably just explode.

I suddenly looked away from him, giggling, unaware of the audience we apparently had.

"You two are adorable. You must be pretty new."

"Yeah. Three weeks."

"Three weeks?!"

"What the hell are you guys doing down here with us fogies?"

"Yeah, you guys should still be fucking each other's brains out."

"Leave them alone, you guys," Jem came to our rescue. "They're doing it right, if you ask me. Get all the junk out at the beginning and enjoy the rest of your time here," she added, cryptically. Which sort of didn't help. A sheepish look appeared in her eye.

Thankfully, everyone's attention was suddenly drawn to the foreign language being spoken in the corner.

Dey was talking to his match Samantha, who hadn't known English. Luke turned in their direction with special interest.

"Ti si iz hrvatstva?" he suddenly blurted in an unrecognizable pattern of syllables. Audible gasps could be heard and Saman-

tha's face lit up at once.

"What?!" Dey exclaimed

"Oh my God!" I cried.

The two continued to talk as if no one else was there. I could only deduce that he was explaining the context for knowing Croatian. Samantha was in absolute raptures and it made everyone laugh, especially her match, Dey, who'd picked up the language quite well in their time at Halcyon.

I didn't understand a word but it was graceful and authoritative and dark. And he spoke it with an ease that was almost unnerving. Like a spy.

Who *is* this fuckin' guy?

Finally, they were done and Luke looked over to find me with my mouth wide open and my brow in an accusatory knit.

"What? My grandmother never learned English."

I responded by hitting him hard in the chest. The group laughed.

"Ow."

"You said there wasn't anything interesting about you," I accused him. The group laughed again.

We returned to the room when I asked if he was ready to go and he admitted he was.

I nodded and smiled. He'd more than done his duty. I wasn't going to ask more of him. Everyone assumed we were going back to the room to have sex. Because why wouldn't we?

I had an unusual pit of sadness in my gut on the way back to the room. The more he showed me, the less I could be as neutral as I was before we sat around the fire pit.

The dark, brooding language falling off Luke's lips had etched itself in my mind, and I wanted to hear more. And I wanted him to want to share it with me. But he didn't.

"Think I'm gonna get in the shower," he said.

Hmmm.... now what could possibly have him "taking a shower" twice in one day?

Besides sheer sexual depravity, of course.

"Not so fast, you. Come here," I demanded. He complied with a slight grin as I put my hands on my hips, a square look in my eye.

"What are the odds that you would be speaking Croatian tonight?"

"Small world."

"When were you gonna tell me that you knew a foreign language?"

"I don't know," he shrugged.

"Gonna seduce your 'real' Match with that, huh?"

His grinning lips parted like he wanted to say something, but instead he just rolled his eyes and walked off.

"Am I done here, Constable?" he said. Lol, what the fuck.

"You were awfully nice to me down there," I added.

"You deserve it."

"Did you mean it?" I raised my voice as he disappeared from view. He made me wait a second or two for his answer.

"Every word," he answered back.

13

Luke

I *got to see Lyric's impossibly large cleavage yesterday.* So that was nice.

Whatever it was wrapped in was black lace and nice. Just sitting there all cradled, like two perfect puppies.

Oddly firm, to be so big. Like they might be fake, but that would be weird of her to have fake tits. I guess they're just perfect.

And then she just... zipped up and hid them away, like a duffle bag or something.

They might've been the most perfect tits that exist.

They were big enough to write my full name across them. Like, with a pen or... with anything, really.

Anyway, what can I say, they were nice. Everything about them was nice. Trust me, I know tits. You'll just have to take my word for it.

The next day we barely talked, I'm not sure why. I thought we had a pretty good night at the bonfire, but I wasn't gonna bring anything up if she wasn't. Maybe I was overreacting. But after three weeks I knew a quiet Lyric was an unhappy Lyric.

We got to the dining hall where she instantly left me and went off to find some people who weren't treating her like shit, as I was. I stayed behind in line and tried not to imagine the black lace bra she was wearing underneath that jumpsuit. Did she pack that for me?

She and Jem sat down, with Darren and I still in line. I watched her sit across from Jem, barely touching her food as if absorbed with what Jem was saying.

Jem caught me staring and leaned over to Lyric who turned to look in my direction.

Lyric waved, cordially, like one of those popular girls who are also nice. I didn't want to wave back like a doofus so I just stood there. They both laughed at me. I tried to keep it up, but eventually I had to grin.

Lyric laughs at me a lot. She thinks I'm pretty funny. She's got no reason to lie so I trust it.

She eats different when it's just us. I found that a little odd. I had to conclude she felt anxiety eating in public. I didn't know the first thing about how to broach the subject, so I brought it up to Dr. Payton in our weekly one on one session.

"It's strange, because she seems so confident, otherwise. When we're alone. And then we get in the dining hall and she's like a gollum."

"Can you blame her for being self-conscious when her insecurities are constantly being reinforced by others, such as yourself?"

"Careful Doc, your bias is showing."

"Then let me be clear: I'm team Lyric."

"Ohoho," I slowly nodded with a laugh.

"But I find it interesting that she feels more anxiety in public than when the two of you are alone."

"Must mean she knows I'm not all bad," I found the silver lining.

"Or perhaps she is projecting the perceived anxiety that you feel onto her? Being seen with her?"

I scoffed as though that were ridiculous. "Of course I don't mind being *seen* with her."

"You just mind being romantically linked with her."

I quietly chewed a thumbnail, prepared to change the subject. But really it was the same subject.

"I think I understand why Stacey left me."

"Your previous girlfriend," Dr. Payton filled in.

I nodded. "I was so afraid of rejection, and yet simultaneously afraid to hurt her, which resulted in the wasting of both our time."

"Are you still in love with Stacey?"

"Absolutely not."

"Why do you think Stacey's on your mind right now?"

"Stacey's always on my mind. But just as a reminder. Of what I did wrong, what I did right. What not to do again."

"You fear you are doing the same thing again?" Dr. Payton deduced.

"I fear that it's my only setting."

"Even with the program's assurance of emotional and biological compatibility?"

"My faith in that assurance was shaken the moment I got here."

"Be that as it may, this could prove to be an opportunity to do things differently than you've ever done them. Move on from that particular lesson in your life?" he counseled.

"Lyric's already teaching me a lot."

"How so?"

"That whole thing about Stacey. I mean, here I am with a woman who's the complete opposite of Stacey in just about every way, but I'm still doing the same thing," I reasoned aloud. "I mean, I'm not desperate to hold on to Lyric or anything, like I was Stacey, but it feels like I'm in limbo just the same."

"You're in limbo with Lyric?"

"Yeah. I mean, she's not my Match, but she could be."

"...She could be?"

I sighed, exasperated. The echo was back.

"Yes, I'm not a moron. I know this place isn't McDonald's. The likelihood that they would just get my 'order wrong' is... slim. I mean, if you guys mismatched one person the impact would be like, catastrophic."

Dr. Payton seemed to be stifling a victorious grin. Smug bastard. A credit to his professionalism, he stayed engaged.

"But until you know for sure, you're in limbo," he summated.

"No. It's all a series of limbos. After this one would come another one, if by some miracle I turn out to be right."

Dr. Payton knitted his brow in a way that meant he wanted me to expound.

"I mean, I like Lyric. She's like a super cool roommate. I had a roommate in college like that. Someone who was way cooler than I would ever otherwise be around. To me, he was just...a decent roommate. I didn't know it until we got around other people and I saw how magnetic he was.

"Sometimes I think I could learn to love her. Sometimes I think I might prefer it. Rather than meet some unrealistic ideal that incapacitates me. Or some other plain, pasty face girl for me to get used to," I said. "Lyric's not like anyone I've ever met or known in my life. She's got this beautiful voice. She's confident. Not in this overblown way, just... the way things've gone these last couple a' weeks I'd expect her to be ranting and raving and throwing fits, or being rude. But she's always warm. Everybody that talks to her loves her.

"She's definitely some kind of somebody on the outside, I believe that. Not just because of how she carries herself, but she does that thing that makes you feel special that she wants to even be around you.

"I don't want to start something with her that I won't finish, but do I really want some other poor bastard to get her?

"I mean, she's mine. If the program got it right, I mean… my biology picked her, or whatever the fuck. And then I think, should I even be letting a program dictate me this much? I mean isn't this how love begins for most people anyway?"

Dr. Payton listened faithfully with a neutral expression, one hand covering his mouth.

"All valuable things to think about," he relinquished his cross—legged sitting position.

"You know, Doc, some days it seems like you're helping me, and other days you just seem like a glorified priest."

Present Day

A knock on my door jolts me awake.

I'd fallen asleep in front of the television, a pizza box half empty and still open on the bed. I look around for my phone but the alarm clock catches my eye: 1:03 am.

My heart jolts me awake the rest of the way as my foggy mind reminds me what's happening.

Bria's at the door. She's come over directly after her set.

I felt sick when I went out to buy condoms. Maybe it was nerves. Took half a pill proactively. In case the sex got me too stressed and triggered night terrors. So far, so good.

I open the door and there she is, wearing a leather jacket with a graphic print tee underneath and jeans. Her hair's in a similar messy bun like it was in Houston, her makeup still dramatic and heavy from the show. She looks like the rockstar she is.

She stands there, wordless until I stand aside for her to step in. She walks slowly to the quaint table and chair set overlooking the pool and the parking lot before taking a seat.

"How was the show?" I inquire.

"Amazing. Especially when I noticed you weren't there."

I think she's serious. I smile. "I was going to come. But I thought the better of it."

"You did the right thing," she says without looking up at me. I sit across from her on the adjacent bed.

"I won't miss it tomorrow."

"You're really gonna drive to Austin?"

I just shrug, staring. Our eyes meet substantially for the first time, her eyes deep and dark. Bria huffs a laugh and grins, which is contagious.

"What is it?"

"Your... fashion sense hasn't changed at all, I see."

I look down at myself, shirtless with a pair of black sweatpants hanging low on my hips.

"Doing some working out yourself, huh?" she says.

"How'd you know?"

"I'm a bit of a gym rat, you could say. Yours are the shoulders of a man that works out."

"Force of habit, I guess," I reply, refusing to elaborate.

I was about to mention physical therapy but I easily stopped myself. I'm not even close to being ready to go into that.

Inwardly I cringe. So much to tell her, but where to start?

"Helps with the job," I say instead. "Helps me focus."

"I see," Bria nods absently before launching into her proposition. "Listen, it's already pretty late. We leave for Austin tomorrow. I can't stay the whole night."

Instantly I'm defensive. "We had a deal."

"I know, but... it is what it is," she says with cold realism.

She's trying to play me. Pretty sure I've used this technique before.

"Bria... if this is your way of screwing me over—"

"My way of *what*? Screwing *you* over?"

She *is* trying to play me. And she's using my mistakes to do it.

"Just get naked, Cliff."

"No, Bria."

She sits there giving me another cold stare before standing up.

"Fine. I will," she says.

Her leather jacket comes off first.

Maybe it's my 'fight or flight' kicking in, because I don't move. I can't. Even though my heart is beating heavy and my whole body is tensing, preparing to see Lyric naked again for the first time in six years, but also for the first time ever. So I guess my body picks 'fight.'

This isn't the agreement, this isn't the agreement, my mind protests as Bria's eyes catch mine in a tractor beam. She doesn't look down at herself at all as she removes her oversized t-shirt. Then her shoes.

Then she peels off her jeans, each piece slow and deliberate as she reveals her newly sculpted body to me in a dark olive green bra and panties.

The moment my eyes leave hers to peruse her body, she knows she's won. And the moment my eyes refused to meet hers again, she knew, that I knew, that I'd lost.

"I'm gonna take a shower, I think. Came straight from the stage, you know?" she says as she saunters over to the only other door in the room, feels around on the wall for the light and looks over her shoulder to see if I'm still watching, I presume.

I am.

She sends me a not so subtle sign of invitation before shutting the door behind her.

The shower was one of our favorite spots. I was never an early riser until I started waking up with a start at the sound of Lyric showering.

Once in the morning, always. We had nothing else to do but fuck each other.

I'm still frozen in place on the edge of the bed. My heart's in my mouth, my dick raging.

The running shower water puts my mind in such a frenzy that I give in to the urge to cry.

I cry because I'm overwhelmed. I cry because I'm here with her and the moment couldn't be any more wrong.

Her body. It's different now, beyond what my wildest dreams once were.

The shape of her is the same. Only smaller. She's still that heady mix of daintiness and heft. Still not worried about our hip bones ever meeting.

If I were still Luke, I'd be jumping up and down right now. Not because she's healthy but because Luke's happy.

Luke used to hound her about her weight, once to the point that they fought and she cried.

She looks like she works out every day, and I wonder is that Luke's doing.

Probably planning to slim down even more. If I ever make it

past this night, I'll do my best to put a stop to that.

Suddenly I hear a faint noise echoing from the other side of the door and my whole body goes hot, cold and then hot again.

No way is she fucking touching herself right now.

Step foot in that bathroom, and you lose, an inner voice cautions me.

She used to do the same thing in the program. Back when I was still refusing to touch her.

First time she did that it made me feel both horny and guilty. She didn't seem like the type to be doing it on purpose. Not at the time.

At the time, I figured she was probably at her wit's end with me and only did it when she thought I was sleeping. She was politely trying to get herself off.

Now, battling my will, body, and muscle-memory on the edge of the bed as I listen to Bria bring herself fully to orgasm in the shower, I'm realizing that she'd probably been doing it on purpose that whole time.

"Probably"? She was.

Dr. Payton said men are simple creatures, she'd giggled once, over dinner. I wouldn't be surprised if the bastard had told her to do it.

The sound of the water suddenly ceases.

The shower is over and I survived. I won. The victory is hollow.

I swallow involuntarily as the bathroom door swings open and steam comes barreling out. Bria emerges with a white towel covering her private bits, droplets still decorating her smooth brown shoulders. She takes a big breath, looking straight at me.

"I needed that," she smiles, talking about the shower and not the orgasm, I can tell. She carries her clothes bunched up in her hand to an empty chair.

"Got a little ahead of myself in there, hope you don't mind," she adds. Now she's referring to the orgasm. "I expected you to walk in at any minute and join me and then... I started thinking maybe you just left."

"I thought about it," I croak.

"What? Joining me or leaving?"

"Clearly the first one."

"Clearly," Bria looks down, probably at my pitched tent. "Tell me you bought the condoms."

"I did."

"Good."

"Where are you staying, tomorrow?" I ask.

"In Austin? Why?"

"It's just that you probably booked yours earlier than mine. Only thing I could find was a little outside the city."

"Cliff..." she sighs like I'm a puppy that won't go away.

"What?"

"You can't be serious."

"About what?"

"Go back to your life. Let me go back to mine," she offers.

That's impossible and she knows it, but I let her have it for now.

"Fine," I reply, "but we agreed to one night."

"We did," Bria sighs. "But I don't know that I can give it to you tomorrow night either. I mean, it's South by Southwest."

"Then drive back to Houston with me. Afterwards."

"...I don't know about that, Cliff," she lets me down easy.

"We have a lot of ground to cover, Bria. It's been a long six years. For me."

"For me too."

"There's a lot of things I need to say."

"No, you don't."

"Bria, please—"

"You could've left me a note, Luke."

Her use of my Halcyon name startles me.

"What?"

"When you opt-out? Because you know, you probably won't see this person ever again, so maybe you'd like to leave them with some parting words? Did you think they wouldn't tell me that they offered you that?"

It's officially starting. The punishment I both dread and long for.

"Did you immediately go out and find some other chick to fuck? *Cliff*?" she corrects herself.

My silence is damning and I can feel it.

Answering her would not appease either of us.

Suddenly she starts rummaging through my things. Plastic bags, the drawers of the nightstand.

"Where are the vests, Cliff."

If you fuck her you lose, the voice says again.

My shoulders slump a bit at that. Defeat surrounds me on every side. She's made it more than clear that it's now or never. And if by some miracle I manage to refuse, the small pile of grace I built is lost.

She's moved on, but she hasn't. She's not satisfied until she can have the chance to crush me the way I crushed her.

"I thought I could handle this," I sigh, "I thought after all this time I wasn't selfish anymore."

"Cliff, whatever bullshit you're saying, I'm not trying to hear it. I'm taking this dick. Tonight."

Oh God oh God oh God oh God...

I've been naive. This is the best I'm going to get. A glorious death.

My hope goes down in flames as she eventually finds the condoms in the desk drawer.

She drops her towel, her beautiful brown globes a fraction of their formal selves. Her nipples are smaller. Like they've been re-sculpted.

She seems proud of them. She should be, they're sexy.

She gets down on her knees in front of me, pulls out my manhood that's so erect it's practically pinned to my stomach.

She grunts before she gives it a slow, appreciative lick, from balls to tip, before taking it into her mouth with a moan.

I can only make strained noises like an animal in a trap. Her mouth drifts further and further down my shaft, and with it my sanity.

She's gotten better at this, I distantly realize, the sound of a condom wrapper ripping. A thick coating of guilt blankets me.

She was a virgin when she joined the program. Not that it matters. It doesn't matter. But to the old me, to Luke, it did. Back when I believed that women existed to make me happy.

Back when I was worried about what my parents would say when I brought Lyric home to them. Overweight. Clearly new money.

I would always ease my anxiety with one consolation: at least she hadn't been with anyone else.

Not that she loved me, even though I was a shit stain. Not that she was a decent human being. And she had every right to put me in my place but hadn't wanted to. Even though she seemed to have everything, but just wanted a soul mate, so she could "see life through him," as she'd said. And then she'd cried. Because I still hadn't touched her yet.

No. It wasn't any of that stuff that mattered. It was that she hadn't been with anyone else.

But even on that one consolation I supposedly valued, I'd opted out anyway. And then lost the little I had.

And I mean really, really lost it, it seemed. Because she's really, really good at giving head now.

And I should know. Because I've been with many, many more people now as well. More than I ever thought I would.

Because Halcyon enabled me to unlock Lyric. And when I unlocked her, I unlocked this secret I'd been missing my entire life. And then I drowned myself so deep in pussy using that secret, that I managed to unlock another one. A less pleasant one.

"Cliff? What the hell?"

I can't respond. I'm paralyzed, both with guilt and embarrassment, my erection and my dignity both dwindling.

My eyes blurred with tears. Bria is on her feet in an instant, naked and confrontational, eyeing me.

"What the hell's wrong with you?" she squints, eviscerating me.

I pull up my sweatpants, remove the empty condom and put my cock back beneath the waistband.

"This was a mistake, I think," I say. I walk over to Bria's clothes bunched up on the chair, gather them up and gruffly hand them to her before going into the bathroom and closing the door, sitting on the floor on the other side, my face red and raw.

14

Bria

I dress quietly in shock, looking around the empty hotel room.

I don't know which part he meant by it being a mistake. Us having sex, him coming to see me, or all of it.

But I'm being rejected again. By him.

What is it about him? What is it about me?

I'm losing my mind. My mind is fucking unraveling right now.

I should just walk out. This guy is crazy. Clearly. It's the only explanation.

But how could those six months have been fake?

I walk up to the bathroom door and knock.

"Luke?" I ask in a small voice. I could've tried the door, I know it's not locked.

But I don't really want to look at him. In fact, it's good there's a door between us.

"I've still got a few more pounds to go, I know. If that's what this is about."

Nothing.

"Can you at least just tell me what this is about? Because this...

I have these dreams about you every once in a while. Used to be all the time, but now it almost never happens. Well, until you started coming around, that is. And in almost all the dreams you're not saying anything, and your back is to me and you're walking away... away away away."

Still nothing.

Something takes over my body. I see my arm raise up and start loudly banging on the bathroom door. And I know that it's all coming up and out. At 2 am in a hotel room.

Part of me is relieved.

"Can you just tell me why you keep rejecting me? If you want me so much? You *LIAR*!!" I scream as I pound away at the door even more.

I can't even feel the pain as my mouth unleashes a string of cursing and I just want to destroy something and see it break. Irreparably.

My eye lands on the TV, which easily rips from the wall and cracks as it tumbles to the floor.

Well, that was lackluster, and now I might be going to jail tonight.

I put on my leather jacket, prepared to make a quick getaway if need be, and then get close enough to the door so I know he can hear me.

"Don't you ever fuckin' come near me again," I pant in a calm voice, the tears falling faster than I can wipe them. "I swear to God, I'm gonna have Chase kick your fuckin' ass like he wants to do anyway. And then I'm gonna have you killed, Cliff, I swear to fucking Christ. If you think I can't, show up to this *fucking* show tomorrow. I will tell my fucking father, who's been *dying* to have you killed, since two thousand and fuckin' *fourteen*, he just needed a name. And now I have one. Cliff..."

My voice trails off as I look around for identification. I see a discarded pair of pants and dig through pockets until I find a small brown leather wallet. I open it, confronted with the sight of an Illinois license. I wipe my nose and face with my sleeve.

"Novak. Cliff Novak the highway patrolman from Chicago..." I sob.

I hear a slight chuckle on the other side of the door. Either that or a sob. I don't stop to figure it out.

"It's not a threat, Cliff. I don't give a shit that you're a cop, you think I give a *fuck*? You think my dad would have you killed if he was worried about getting caught? You know how many fuckin' goblins come over to our house regularly? That would love to kill a cop and get paid?? Show up tomorrow, Cliff! Novak! Oh my God, I fucking hate you! I fucking hate you, Cliff," I wheeze. "If I ever see your face again, I swear you're fucking dead. I swear on my life!"

Halcyon— Six Years Ago

"Hey, you fell asleep," Luke informed me.

"What's that?"

"During the book. You missed like, two chapters."

Luke had taken his shower that morning and came straight to my room as he'd done every morning for the past week.

"Oh. Well, I've read it, so... don't worry about me. Where'd you leave off?"

"When they get back to Asgard or wherever the fuck."

"Azram."

"Right, and the king's right hand guy goes down on her in front of the prince."

"Oh... that's like my favorite part."

I typically fall asleep before him and wake up alone in bed. I can only assume he's left to get relief as soon as my eyes close. He gets extra squirmy during the sex parts.

And everytime he hears something that blows his mind, his reaction is so cartoonish I'm wondering if he's secretly a comedic genius.

I'm a little sad that he kept the book going without me, because that means I missed a loooot of real time reactions last night.

I got Luke hooked on historical romances. This was his first reverse harem.

Yeah, he definitely got off to that.

"You say that's not even the hottest book you have?"

"Well... it's probably about a seven. Out of ten."

"Holy shit. You've been holding out on me, Lyric," he said.

"What do you mean?" I laughed.

"You had a porn stash this whole time, and you didn't tell me."

"This is not pornography," I shook my head. "Pornography is pornography."

"What's the difference?" he scoffed.

"Maybe you can't tell the difference as a man, but I've watched porn and read romance novels. As a woman. They're not the same."

"That's not an answer, by the way," he said as he got cozy underneath my blanket.

"It's like the difference between doing cocaine and... jumping out of a plane."

"Okay. Which one's the cocaine?" he asked. I laughed.

"If you don't know, then there's nothing else I can say."

We tore ourselves away from the final chapters to go have lunch. Today it was sushi. I was plenty satisfied, but I also could stab someone in the neck for an Oreo. Just one Oreo.

"You think we could be friends after this, at least?" I suddenly asked.

He chewed thoughtfully. "You want to be friends?"

"Sure."

He looked at me skeptically.

"I already feel like you know me better than a lot of people," I clarified. "And vice versa, wouldn't you say?"

He reached for a piece of pickled ginger off my plate and dropped it in his mouth. "I would," he smacked.

"But I just remembered everyone who doesn't decide to stay together has to fuck off after this is over."

"I can't imagine how they think people won't be able to track each other down."

"Such an anarchist," I rolled my eyes, "I think they can sue you or arrest you or something."

"Honestly, anyone who can afford this place isn't worried about all that."

"And so far, they have 100% success, so there's been no need to test your theory out."

"Another fact that's probably horseshit," he said after gulping down the cucumber-infused green tea.

"What, the 100% success?"

"It's scientifically impossible," he dismissed.

"So, you think they're just lying about that?"

He laughed. I got defensive.

"Look, just because I believe what people tell me doesn't mean I'm naive."

He laughed again. I was so happy to be able to amuse him.

"That's exactly what it means," he chuckled.

When the laughter met his eyes it was pretty great. But not if it was at my expense.

"I just mean... forget it."

"There's nothing wrong with being naive, by the way," he tried to recover.

"There's nothing particularly great about being cynical."

He gave me a little nudge under the table with his knee.

"You're right. I'm sorry," he said, contrite. Instantly he was forgiven.

We went to see Dr. Payton, and it was the second week he hasn't been able to get much out of us. Mainly because we were just itching to get back to the room and finish "reading." And maybe he was just embarrassed or something, but I chose to believe he wanted there to be something private about this bizarre life of ours.

"So? Everything good?" Dr. Payton began.

"Great."

"Any breakthroughs?"

"...Sort of," I volunteered.

"Is that so?"

"Lyric brought a bunch of audiobooks on her tablet and we've been reading them together," he finished.

"I see. So you've found a common interest."

"That's right," Luke said. He kept a straight face while mine was dubious. I had a sudden urge to clear my throat.

"Well, that's good. Any arguments? Petty squabbles? This is usually about the time to expect those."

"None for me."

"Me either."

"Blink twice, Lyric, if your life is being threatened," he joked. I laughed and looked over at Luke, who barely gave me a smirk.

"Well, I have to say this is very interesting," Dr. Payton

remarked. "I can't tell if this platonic state you two have settled on has stifled your progress or hastened it. We'll have to keep monitoring it. I still have room for individual sessions this week. Just keep me posted."

We got back to the room and I stripped down to my standard fluffy girl uniform— an oversized sweatshirt and pajama bottoms.

Shyly I joined him under the covers without a word.

I decided that I was done reading and ready to start experiencing.

Only, I hadn't told Luke that.

If he noticed at all, he didn't say anything. Which indicated to me that he was willing to do non-descript, irresponsibly sexual acts with me that he might be ashamed of later.

Sharp arousal bloomed across the middle of my body as a game of sexual chess began.

I saw myself cuddling up to him and running my fingers down his bare, chiseled chest.

But as soon as I felt the weight of him next to me in bed, I pressed play on the speaker sitting on the night stand and turned away from him in bed.

Wordlessly, he moved behind me and I felt his arms slink across my middle. The warmth of his body on my back. And... his hardness.

Uncontrollably, I seized in his arms.

"You okay?" he asked. I nodded quickly.

"You've never spooned before?"

"Not with a boy."

"Not with a boy?" he snickered, teasing me a little.

"Shut up."

"You never had a penis rubbed up against you?"

161

"Shhh, you're missing the story."

"You're really soft. And warm."

"And chubby. Be quiet," I said.

"I'm chubby too now," he whispered.

"I noticed," I whispered back, my eyes closed.

It took an hour for me to finally relax. Or get horny enough to forget my nerves, one of the two.

"*Chapter 7...*" the speaker droned in a commanding voice.

"I love your smell," he suddenly remarked.

"You *love* it?"

He put his nose in my neck and took a big whiff, as if daring me to doubt him. I giggled, helplessly charmed.

"I don't think your new and improved Match would approve of this," I said, smugly.

"There's nothing wrong with cuddling," he defended. The bass in his voice was practically vibrating my soul.

"Hearing you say that word is super weird, just so you know."

"Cuddling" he said with a deadpan tone. He was acting a little out of the ordinary, but I guess I started it. Sort of. I reached for my tablet and went back about five minutes.

"I'm not really listening anymore," he said in a voice that was new to me, one that was lighter. My pulse rose but I wasn't too sure what that meant for me.

"Shh... concentrate, baby," I said.

Fuck, I didn't mean to call him baby. I ignored it and hoped he would do the same.

He must've heard me, because we laid there for nearly another hour, his boner adjusted against my back.

In my life I'd only ever made it to third base, but this was definitely the most prolonged contact I'd ever had with anyone, and my body was on this permanent fluttering frequency like I was coming down with something.

"Lyric."

"Huh."

"How wet are you right now?" he asked.

Maybe it was my hazy state, but I didn't find the question all that strange. "I don't know."

"On a scale of 1 to 10."

I craned my neck behind me to look at him with his beady stare and a vague smirk smugly on his face.

"So crass," I smiled.

"I can smell it."

"Can not."

"Can so," he insisted.

"You're totally bluffing."

"Lyric, we've been confined to a box for a month, and you've been listening to lady porn for most of it. I can smell your arousal."

"What, like a cat?"

"Like a normal human," he answered.

There was silence after that. "How come I can't smell it?" I asked.

He let go of me just to bust out into the biggest unexpected laugh I'd ever heard. I didn't see what was so funny about it, but it made me smile.

I was genuinely curious. I left my rhetorical question there to linger in the air and resumed laying there with my back to him. We were quiet for a little while. He was laying on his back behind me, his arms no longer around me. He was thinking. But I didn't know what about.

"Lyric....Lyric.....Lyric.....Lyric..."

"What," I replied.

"If I put my hand down your pants would you stop me?"

Strangely enough I saw this coming. It seemed pretty in-evitable, really. Even if it was simple curiosity. I'd gotten enough lingering looks from him by now.

But I felt like his question was a trap. A copout. Like he could blame me for whatever happened next. There was certainly nothing romantic about it.

"Lyric..."

"I heard you."

"Is that a yes?" he wondered.

"No."

"No, as in.... no, you wouldn't?"

"Yes. As in, no. I wouldn't."

A long moment went by. I wouldn't call it a hesitation. Or weighing his options. It was something else. All I knew was that his energy changed to something sober and deliberate as his weight shifted behind me on the bed.

I kept my eyes closed, but I felt him over me slightly.

Down his hand sank inside my pajama bottoms, between my legs.

Straight to old third base, for only the second time in my life. My knees opened slightly, to accommodate him.

"Holy cow," he remarked.

"You really are from the 1930's," I giggled.

"*To je prekrasno.*"

"Luke, don't you get all foreign and sexy on me now," I whined in frustration.

"*Želim to okusiti.*"

"Luke..."

He removed his hand, put it straight into his mouth and returned it between my legs. His fingers trailed the lips, my clit, my walls, all the way in and back out.

The words of the audiobook morphed into some ancient, syllabic nonsense. His face wasn't more than an inch from mine. My pulse was racing and I was so self-conscious I wanted to die. Meanwhile his head went back as though he were in ecstasy.

"Fuck," he whispered, sending uncontrollable sparks of arousal to my brain and back.

I rolled to my back with my knees up. Instantly he was in front of me on his own knees, tugging at my everything— my panties, my pajama bottoms, all at once.

I wanted to enjoy this all, but I couldn't feel anything. All I could do was watch him, lean and muscled, suddenly animalistic as his erection punched through the fabric of his sweatpants like an alien.

He pried my thighs apart and I gasped.

"What are you doing?" I breathed. He answered by disappearing between my legs, the sensation of what had to be his tongue on my labia.

"What are you doing?" I asked again, the only sentence I had available.

It was meant to convey that I had no expectations. And that I didn't want to be responsible for whatever happened next. Was I gonna fart in his face? Start peeing uncontrollably? I didn't know what to do. Suddenly it seemed like all these sex books had failed me.

He reared back up for a moment, in an intense staring match with my lady business. He locked an arm around one of my legs and dove back in.

I couldn't believe what I was seeing. The sight of him pleasuring me sent arresting shocks all over me. His tongue circling my clit answered those shocks with a bitter syrupy sensation, one that made both my pleasure and my desire rise unbearably.

"Oh God... oh my God..." I moaned. He answered with a few of his own.

I lost control. The rolling of his hot tongue, the pointing licks, the kisses. The pleasure was too intense. My dramatic moans drowned out the audiobook still playing in the background.

My hand went into his gorgeous dark hair, which I'd never touched before then, I realized.

"Oh fuck, baby, I'm gonna come..." I growled. Then the climax hit and it was like the star spangled banner behind my eyes.

I screamed, not caring about peeing or anything else until the orgasm let me go. Finally it did and my head hit the pillow.

I was still in the throes of ecstasy when I heard, "Let me see those tits."

My high still lingered but my dignity was long gone.

I mustered a bit of strength to sit up and remove my sweatshirt. I rested on my elbows to take a peak at him smearing my juices all over his cock and manhandling it furiously. My mouth involuntarily dropped at the sight.

"Yeah, open that pretty mouth, baby," he said. Almost all the bass in his voice had vanished, and now it was thin and frantic and it made me wish I hadn't come already.

I looked up at him and he was looking directly at me.

"That's right, look at me," he panted, "look at me I'm gonna come..."

And then he fuckin' did. Loud and long and all over me. My mouth dropped open even further.

"Fuck, baby," I moaned, as cum cooled all over my belly. He steadied himself with a hand on one of my knees still open and bent, panting. Finally, he let out a pretty long sigh and let himself collapse dramatically on the other end of the bed, his head beading sweat and hanging slightly off the edge. I couldn't help laughing.

"Feel better?" I said. He didn't answer. I laughed again.

I could see that his eyes were open. His cock was limp and his sweatpants were around his knees. He seemed beyond content.

So was I. And yet afraid of how much I wanted more.

I laid back on the bed a complete mess and let out a contented sigh of my own. Oral sex is great, was my last conscious thought.

"*Fuck*!" Luke's voice woke me out of my slumber.

I opened my eyes but everything was pitch black.

"What time is it?"

I checked my tablet. "7:30," I replied.

"Get up," he said, tossing me a jumpsuit, "or we're gonna miss dinner."

Luckily for us, the dining hall doesn't close completely at 8pm. They just stop serving at 8pm. At 7:48 we were in there.

I felt a little gross. I woke up covered in dry fluids, put a jumpsuit on in a dash and rushed downstairs.

We didn't have time to discuss what happened, and the longer time went on without conversation, the worse I made it in my mind.

I looked over at his stupid face, scarfing down food. He was clueless. He'd gotten off and the whole thing was forgotten about.

No way was I going to be the first to bring up what happened. No way was I going to follow behind him like some puppy just because he gave me my first bonafide sexual experience.

Chilean sea bass, microgreens, mashed chickpeas. It was delicious as hell, but I wasn't in the mood for sea bass.

"What's wrong with you?" he said.

"Nothing."

167

"Eat."

"I'm not really that hungry," I muttered. He gave me a "yeah right" look.

"Ugh, God," I scoffed, instantly repelled by him. Abruptly I got up from my seat.

I pretended not to see some of our peeps in the corner on the way out and back to the room.

I discarded my dirty jumpsuit in the laundry chute, grabbed my speaker from the room and played my "desert island" playlist in the bathroom while I ran a bath.

There's not enough Nick Drake on this list. I allotted myself only 100 songs and had to choose between Pink Moon and Things Behind the Sun. For some reason I thought it was a good idea to forego both of them and choose Black Eyed Dog.

I should've just picked Things Behind the Sun and got on with it. Even though it gives me nightmares if I fall asleep listening to it.

I only put on two songs each by my must-haves, and five by Jeff Buckley and I'm not sorry. I'm glad I trusted my instincts, because I was feeling the kind of ineffable emotion that only Jeff Buckley could reach and articulate.

Lilac Wine was on, and I was about to have myself a good cry during the good part, when I heard the front door latch.

I lamented the timing as I heard footsteps along various parts of the room and waited, in case he came around the corner.

It's nearly impossible to hear someone enter the bathroom. Let's just say I know from personal experience. I waited a bit more for Luke to appear in the bathroom, but he didn't.

The song changed to Pachad, an obscure number by Yael Naim.

Let's be honest here, half of these are songs I wanted to fuck to. This one not so much. Well, maybe not before the first 54 seconds.

I closed my eyes. I was so jealous of her clean, earnest, unpretentious vocal, those and others like her. The kind that makes you not care that you can't understand a word. I hum the affecting melody.

The next song is Janelle Monae, my vocal twin— in tone only, not in style. Or influences, probably. Say You'll Go, another song I could fuck to. Jeez, I made a fuck playlist, didn't I?

The battery on my speaker died halfway through the song. I could vaguely hear it playing on the tablet from my room.

"*Loove is not a faaaaaaaantasy....*" I sung along. I opened my eyes, gathered an armful of fading bubbles and cover my chest.

"*It's more for you...*fuck!!" I scream.

The corner of my eye caught Luke, standing against the wall, arms crossed like the tallest ninja in the world.

"Mother*fuck*..." I panted. I was so startled that I was pissed.

My poor heart. I felt bad for it, as it worked overtime.

"I brought you back a doggy bag."

"How long have you been standing there?"

"I don't know," he said.

"One song? Two songs??"

"Your musical taste is... intimidating," he remarked, unzipping out of his jumpsuit. He had on a pair of boxers underneath, which I didn't know he owned. I always assumed he was freeballing it under those sweatpants of his.

His kissable shoulders rippled mysteriously as he shed both jumpsuit and boxers and left them in a heap as he walked toward the shower. Naturally I gawked at his ass, having seen it now twice today.

"I can give you some privacy," I offered, watching the untouched canvas of his broad back as he walked in front of me.

"No need."

"I'm almost done."

"No you're not," he scoffed as he turned on the shower.

The shower was see-through, a somewhat obvious design choice. And I was glad of it, because I was unapologetically enjoying the show.

It was my first time seeing Luke's naked form in its full glory, his cock dangling at half mast and boasting a size that relieved me. He wasn't small. He wasn't huge. He was perfect.

Everything about him was perfect. Physically, at least.

I licked my dry and trembling lips. I heard Luke's rumbling laugh on the other side of the glass.

"See something you like?" he asked.

"I could ask you the same question, you know," I said, reaching for the hot water knob on the faucet.

"You're taking all my hot water," he cried. He quickly turned his water off. "Shit," he cursed.

"Serves you right," I said.

"What'd I do?"

"Nothing," I said. "Except maybe be yourself. That's the problem."

He gave me his weird, honking 1930's laugh.

"Keep laughing," I mildly threatened, my bath water renewed by the steamy heat from the faucet.

Luke began to lather the washcloth in his hand and leaned against the shower wall. We faced each other's naked bodies.

"As you were," he said, lathering up his arms and chest.

"As I was?"

"You were about to get off, were you not?"

My pulse quickened again. "Uhh... I don't know," I admit with a furrowed brow.

170

"Please, you had the place to yourself and no one takes baths to get clean."

"Says you. On both of those statements."

"You can keep acting as if I'm not here," he suggested.

"Well, first of all *that's* impossible. Secondly, I don't want to."

"You sort of owe me," he said. "You know, for blowing your mind this afternoon?"

I smiled. So he *was* willing to acknowledge what happened. "Technically, that was a privilege," I said. He cracked a big smile.

This is clearly his favorite subject. He definitely looked happier.

"Should I start?" he asked, the washcloth lingering around his bobbing manhood before continuing it's journey down his legs and back up.

My brain was trying to catch up. Shouldn't we talk about the first thing that happened, before we add to the tally? Was he going to tell me what's going on in that brain of his?

The answer to that question was probably "nothing" if his dick was any indication. I started to feel used. Which oddly felt kind of hot. I was shit at bargaining.

"I'm not sure what you want," I confessed.

"I want you to put on a show for me."

I broke into a nervous smiling, biting my lip to keep it from trembling.

So, this is happening.

My mind was completely blank. I didn't know the first thing about putting on a show.

But I knew how to get myself off in a bathtub.

I turned on the tepid faucet water and reached for the hand-held. I wanted a lot more control for what was suddenly turning into a sex romp that Luke was willing to participate in.

I leaned back, left my legs bent at the knees and opened them wide, glancing over at Luke who was now fully erect, still lathered and giving his cock slow and special attention.

It should be no surprise to me that Luke could stroke himself like he had the gold in the jerk-off Olympics. But it was clear from the way he handled his member that he knew how to give himself pleasure. And he seemed to know how to do the same with my body. Watching him go from slow to fast to no strokes at all, to rubbing the tip, his nuts, his thighs, I imagined him being just as attentive to me, all the while looking straight at my body as though I were a feast, the way he was now.

I looked away, already breathless and frantic, afraid to come too quickly under Luke's rapt focus. I aimed the showerhead at some nothing spot on my vagina, rubbing the inside of my thigh with one hand, while my mind was neurotically trying to find my inner vixen.

"Rub that soap on your tits," Luke suggested.

I grabbed the soap with a smirk on my face, lathered and started to rub, the shower stall filling with Luke's quiet breathless whispers of encouragement.

15

Luke

Maybe it was because I hadn't seen a porno in over a month.

Or because more and more I had found myself noticing the way Lyric's giant tits rested in her jumpsuit, and in the untied robe she sometimes ran past my room in when she thought I was still sleeping.

And that, despite her size, her body did everything right. Her height made her statuesque. Her waist cinched like she was a drawing. Her legs narrowed as they lengthened like two perfect carrot sticks. Her ass was too much for one man and borderline obscene.

And watching Lyric touch herself in the bath practically had me so dizzy with arousal I was seeing stars.

If I was home right now after a month of no porn, this was exactly the bizarro rabbit hole shit I would randomly click on first.

I put off stroking myself and let the feel of the washcloth work me into a frenzy while my eyes feasted on the sight of Lyric's charcoal nipples slathered with white soap, white soap that should be my jizz, I thought with conviction.

Lyric put a soapy hand between her legs before reaching for the handheld again and teasing the area in a circle.

"I wanna watch you come," I confessed.

"You first," she said.

"No way."

"Let's make it a tie," she grinned. She put a free hand behind her head and let her gaze rest on my naked form, a lazy grip around my shaft. I gave it a quick once over from base to tip, in danger of spilling over the edge with just one stroke.

I watched as she looked mesmerized, no longer teasing, but zeroing in on her clit while I fondled myself between both hands, my hips simulating sex, finally returning to the faithful maneuver of hand to cock, faster and faster until she couldn't watch anymore.

She belted a month long pent-up groan as her orgasm came up and out, holding the handheld steady over her clit.

Her sex clenched again and again along with her teeth as she groaned and moaned through the sensation.

I was fully detached from reality, stroking myself frantically and watching the first of only a handful of female orgasms I'd ever witnessed. It was fascinating and exhilarating and a little repulsive. Alien and alienating. And the image I was officially addicted to as I felt myself teetering over the edge.

"Oh shit, are you about to come again??" I muttered in disbelief, the last intelligible thing I would ever utter before my load hit the shower stall glass.

My head snapped back against my will and so did my eyes, as my orgasm went soundlessly on and on.

"Fuck!" Lyric cried as she came tumbling after, having watched the entire spectacle, I'm sure. Breathlessly she closed her eyes and leaned back in the tub, looking like a cold and boneless mess.

Once my vision returned fully, I started the shower water back up and the stall was enveloped in steam in under a minute. By the time I was done rinsing off, Lyric was gone and the bath was empty.

I heard singing coming from outside as I wrapped a towel around my waist and found Lyric in front of the dresser in her room, her white satin robe with the palm tree print loosely tied over her lacey black bra and underwear. A different one than the one I got jizz all over this afternoon.

I smirked. How many of those did she have?

I looked at the reflection of her dark body in her expensive robe, her plump breasts sitting in her custom lingerie.

I was close enough that she heard me and stopped singing, but she didn't look up. Finally she faced the reflection in the mirror and seemed startled to see me there behind her.

We both looked at the sight of ourselves in the mirror. I never thought of my skin as pale until then as I drew close to her, and watched my arms appear around her waist in the mirror's reflection, my head on her shoulder.

"Did I make you happy back there?" I grinned into her ear.

I looked down at her, but Lyric was still just staring and staring into the mirror, like it was a portrait. I looked at her through the reflection and chuckled.

"Did you hear me?" I asked.

"You asked am I happy?"

"You were singing."

"When?"

"Just now," I laughed.

"Oh."

"You sing when you're happy."

"Do I?"

"You're very sexy, Lyric," I whispered.

"Thanks for noticing."

She watched my fingers undo the loose knot of her robe. One went inside her underwear, to the dark triangle between her legs.

"You don't have to do that," her voice cracked.

"Do what?"

"What you're doing right now."

"I know that, Lyric, I want to," I assured her in a low voice.

"I know, I just meant... whatever you decide to... I'm not expecting—"

"Stop, Lyric. Just stop."

I moved my hands to her neck and peeled the satin robe from her shoulders.

The drapey fabric fell from her body into a pile. She examined the sight of my hands roaming her hips. I got to her middle and her eyes averted away to look at nothing.

"Watch me," I said, meeting her scared eyes in the mirror.

She returned my gaze, then watched me touch her body as if bored.

"Stop worrying about me, *prasice*. I'm an asshole." Lyric blew breath out of her cheeks, her eyes watered.

I felt like I'd woken up from a month long dream. Lyric was one of the most gorgeous women that ever walked the planet. And she actually cared about what I did. And what I did affected her. Either adversely or otherwise.

When I touched her she came alive, like I was fuckin' Gepetto. And that's just plain stupid, like having the sun shine a little brighter just because you're awake.

It's stupid, but it is what it is.

Is Lyric really biologically inclined to love me? Did the program get it right?

I put my lips on her shoulder and kissed. She closed her eyes, her breath erratic. I slowly caressed her, gently kissing up to her neck, conscious of what I owed her after a month of misunderstanding what I was doing here, making her feel unwanted in the process. Her eyes were just as alluring closed as they were open.

My tongue jutted out and gently flicked her skin. Her brow knitted and she stiffened a little, as if mistrusting the moment. Slowly she yielded, craning her neck to one side.

This newfound power of mine sent a rush to my cock with each new reaction. I moaned a curse and her eyes clenched.

"Are you ready for round three?" I asked.

"Aren't you tired?"

"It takes a lot to tire me out."

"By round three you mean... sex?" she confirmed in a shakey breath.

"That's exactly what I mean. Don't tell me you're not ready," I slightly raised an eyebrow.

"No, I am, it's just... you're getting re-evaluated in two weeks."

"I'm not doing that shit anymore."

"What, why?" she wondered with concern.

"Because it doesn't matter."

"What do you mean it doesn't matter?"

"Don't start repeating everything I say, Lyric, you heard me."

"It does matter. You might not believe in the program, but I still do."

"Look at me," I said with a stern expression, still facing us in the mirror. "I want you, Lyric. Do you believe in that?"

"I'm not letting you touch me until you promise me that you'll get re-evaluated," she returned my stern gaze. "Because unlike you, I know what it's going to say."

Her face was so fucking stunning that I could've barfed. Suddenly, like I'd had too many shots.

"Fine," I agreed.

"Good."

"Now go lay down over there. Don't take anything else off."

She smiled a gorgeous smile with her eyes and bit her lip again as she complied. I let my towel fall to the floor, crawled onto the bed and loomed over her, my own hair falling into view of her prettily excited face.

"I'm going to make love to you now," I said softly. "Would you like that?"

Lyric only nodded.

"Is that what you want?" I asked in her ear, barely audible.

All of my atoms vibrated as she breathlessly answered, "Yes."

* * *

For the first time ever, I woke up first.

I turned over in the big bed, confronted by the sight of a sleeping Lyric next to me, her pouty lips and sharp cheekbones turning her sleeping visage dramatic even with her eyes closed. I traced her lips with my finger as they slowly spread into a smile.

Her eyes popped open with a million words in them. Or rather, the same words a few hundred thousand times.

There was a knowing in them. Of sex, of me, of herself. The change was profound. Naked, but still mysterious.

The knowing spread to her lips and she smiled. I could only

drink it in and stare. After awhile she laughed and looked down shyly for a moment. When she looked back up, she saw that I hadn't moved and laughed again.

She reached over and kissed my motionless lips earnestly. I grabbed her face when she was about to pull away, requesting more.

Lyric's sexual power was in her kiss.

I didn't know that. Not until I was literally on top of her, which was the first time I ever kissed her mouth.

It was something primal and innocent, almost maternal, like a repressed memory of being breastfed.

I was stunned and I wanted to cry. I never wanted it to end. And then her tongue shyly intervened and turned every bit of it to dark, bottomless craving.

She did the same thing to me this morning. I was back on top of her in an instant.

We didn't show up for breakfast that day. Or lunch.

I didn't want to eat. I wanted to watch Lyric take my dick into her body and get more pleasure from it than anyone has a right to. And that was going to be my new food.

We made it to dinner. She made a beeline to an open booth, which are usually all taken up.

Not that we would ever really use one before. They're usually occupied by two excessively lovey-dovey inmates, so I knew what she was after. More than even the sex.

We spent a month sitting across from each other in the same sexless arrangement, saving face in front of everyone. Now that we'd been intimate she wanted more than to sit across from me. She wanted a booth.

It was only fair. I brought us both a tray and caught Jem scampering out of my spot on my way to the booth.

"What'd she want?" I muttered as I sat down.

"Don't be grumpy."

"I wasn't. Just curious."

"Well, she knows about our... struggles."

"Pretty sure everyone does," my eyes widened.

"You think?"

"Lyric, there are no TV's here. Trust me, word spread."

"Well anyway, I told her I would fill in the details later."

I smile, a bite of food on its way to my mouth. "What kind of details?"

She just responded by fondling me under the table as she grinned.

The next day was my session with Dr. Payton. I sat silent in his office for nearly ten minutes, the sound of the clock becoming white noise the longer I sat wordless in the chair.

Dr. Payton didn't force us to talk in solo sessions and we had to initiate. I munched on a thumbnail as I prepared to put my thoughts to words.

"So, Lyric and I had sex the other night."

"Oh," Dr. Payton said in a rare moment of surprise. "How was that?"

"It was um... it caught me off guard."

"How so?"

I looked down at his socks as I usually do, to help me concentrate.

"I just expected the sex with my Match to be this fiery, all-consuming thing. And in a way it is. But the way it's happened. It's more like a match. Or a candle. Than this... inferno."

"So you now believe Lyric to be your Match."

"I do."

Dr. Payton sat back in his chair.

"Who initiated?" he asked.

"I did."

"Why?"

I stared at the empty space between us where there should be a desk, but instead it's Dr. Payton's crossed legs, his pants ridden up enough that I can see a bit of his ankle. It's more vulnerable than I perceive him being.

"I don't know. I wanted to, I guess."

"Why did you want to?"

Normally, I would tease Dr. Payton about his tedious questioning but today I was keen to know, myself.

"It sort of started off small and then it just... escalated."

"How did it start off small?"

My mind went to the memory and my entire body jolted. My concentration divided. It felt compulsive, against my will.

"I put my hand down her pants."

"I see."

"I asked her if I could."

"Of course."

"And then... one thing led to another," I gestured as I leaned forward.

"As they do."

"I mean... the way I see it, it was inevitable."

"How so?"

"I don't know. Me and my issues, she and hers." My thumbnail returned to my mouth. "Eventually, we were going to... look to each other, I guess."

"And will you still be requesting your re-evaluation?"

"I promised Lyric that I would."

"You did?"

"She wouldn't sleep with me until I promised."

Dr. Payton looked concerned. "Any idea why?"

"She wants me to have the re-assurance. And also, she's pretty confident in the results."

"What about you?"

"I genuinely don't care anymore."

"Why's that?"

"Because last night made me realize that I don't even want to be subject to what some program picked for me," I retorted. "Lyric's a great person. Quality. She's got this creative soul. And she's turned on by me for some reason, so... I took control of the situation. And I don't care if that decision was right or wrong. And I don't care what the evaluation says."

"Fair enough," nodded Dr. Payton.

"This doesn't mean I'm in love with her."

"No?"

"No," I quickly shook my head. "And I don't think she's in love with me. I think that... I'm her first. So the feelings she has for me are by default. I guess the same goes for me. I can feel myself feeling... possessive, in a way."

"Keep in mind, you're only one month into the program," the doctor reminded me.

"I have. But I want to be honest."

"That's good."

"I know enough about Lyric to say that I know she's great. And that she deserves love."

"Do you think that you deserve love?" Dr. Payton asked.

"I honestly don't know. And to be honest, I'm not sure I care. Not about not deserving love, but about being loved."

"You don't care about being loved?"

I frowned a bit as I shrugged, searching my mind. "No. I think... I'm figuring out what fuels me. And it has something

182

to do with women, I don't know, being grateful to me or something."

"...Uh-huh."

"There's some kind of pattern here, don't you think? Wounded birds and what not?" I offered.

"You think Lyric is a wounded bird?"

"In a way. She's insecure about her weight. Doesn't like compliments. She's a great singer. Like... gifted. She doesn't think she's that good."

"But you seem to have trouble when these... 'wounded birds' move on and 'leave the nest,' as it were. Isn't that right?"

"But that's what's different this time about Lyric," I said, sitting forward in my chair again. "Because I don't have this crippling attachment to her."

"But you do have some attachment?"

I cleared my throat and rambled on. "Of course, I mean... we've spent a lot of hours together. She's getting to know parts of me that I would never choose to show anyone. And she's a doll to me. I don't know what you call it. 'Friendship' is too broad, especially now that we've had sex... well actually, maybe that's the exact right word. Maybe it's just friendship that's gotten more shitty, not the word itself. But it feels like if she needed me to kill someone, I would do it without wondering what they did to deserve it. They clearly had it coming."

"You trust her, and that's valuable to you," concluded Dr. Payton.

"Yes."

"And you find that more fulfilling than being loved."

"There's more... I don't know," I gestured with my hands as I shifted in my seat, "I don't feel stifled by my own fear. There's a freedom to just appreciate her. And appreciate her appreciating me. A part of me still wants the sweeping, all-consuming love story. In fact, I don't know that I could abandon it completely."

"No one is suggesting that you have to. The program is not here to force to people to feel things they don't. Or to fulfill an ideal. It's to present you with a monogamous option that will ensure the highest outcome of success based on scientific research. This is why all candidates have the option to opt-out once the program is completed."

"Which is a little coersive, don't you think?" I argued.

"In what way?"

"What if you like the person, and you may choose that person down the road, let's say?"

"Research suggests that it's better for the rejected candidate to sever ties with the Match that has decided to move on."

"That's not fair. People grow and change."

Dr. Payton recited Halcyon's talking points. "Candidates that choose Halcyon are typically wearied by the modern system of finding a mate by the time they apply. So far we've had success 100% of the time, so this is a moot point."

"How do you verify those numbers?"

"By a voluntary survey system sent to every graduating couple. Which also boasts 100% participation."

"Is that so," I said with a slight groan.

"It is."

"How do you know those people aren't just miserable with the person they settled with? Too afraid to find someone better out there because of the brainwashing that this program is constantly bombarding you with?"

Dr. Payton thought for a moment and then gave a slight nod. "I suppose we don't."

"Well, I respect that you're willing to admit that."

He let out a sigh of enthusiasm. "Well, I think this has been a productive session, don't you?"

"I do."

"Anything else you want to discuss?"

"Nope."

He shooed me away as he placed his reading glasses back on his face.

"Off you go then."

16

Bria

Another dream.

This time in front of Cliff, yelling until I'm hoarse. He's still mute, but he has anguish in his face. I notice it but I don't stop yelling. *He really does care*, I think.

The dream changes inexplicably and I'm sitting with Dr. Payton, doing my Halcyon exit interview.

This time, when he rattles off the terms and conditions of opting out I'm resolved to say "yes."

My heart floods with fear. I'm afraid I'll never be able to match what I had with him. I stuff it all down with the proof I have of the past.

He never loved you. He only wants the new and improved you. He saw you on TV and wants to cash in. But he couldn't pull it off with a straight face. Or a hard dick.

I told our therapist Dr. Payton I was opting out. He took me to a separate exit where I could see Luke behind double-sided glass. He was waiting for me on a bench at check-out. It was so detailed that I woke myself up studying him, pitying his clueless face.

I made a mistake, I thought. The flood of fear overtakes me.

I wake up with a gasp.

I sit up on the edge of the bed crying, not knowing who my tears are for.

Because I know what the dream means. Or at least, I think I do.

Oh God, was that him? What he *felt*? That instant suffocating grief?

I like being in a melancholy space before a show, but this is too much. This is an emergency.

I reach for my phone. 4 am. Meaning it's 2 am in LA.

Mom's either still up, or willing to answer.

"Mom," I sniff.

"Bria, honey, what's wrong?"

I spill the entire contents of the last three days over the phone, up to and including what happened in his hotel room. My mom's one of those types of moms. A shock, I know.

"Well baby, it sounds like he's trying to win you back and you won't let him."

"That's exactly what's happening," I admit.

"So... I don't understand here. You surprised or... what?"

"I can't trust him, Mama."

"I understand. Sounds like *he* understands. Sounds like he's trying to give you a wide berth but he's also letting you know that he's here and he's not goin' anywhere. No matter what you decide. Also sounds like he's got standards. You tryin' to use him for some good and you got him fucked up. I'mma be honest Bri, I'm likin' this dude."

"He's a cop now, too."

"You love civil servants!"

"I know."

"And you say he's been in Houston this whole time?"

"For about a year."

"Bria, this is a no-brainer. Marry that man."

"What?!? That's what you got out of that?"

"Yes. You know how many times we had to hear about 'Luke this' and 'Luke that'? I wanna meet the man as soon as possible."

"Sounds to me like you'll do anything to get some grandchildren."

"Sounds to me like the program *works*, honey. On a delay in your case, but still."

"He left me. Alone at check-out. Then he just shows up six years later? Like... I'm in the middle of living my life."

"It's messy, I get it. But if he wanted you back, because he made a mistake, was there really any right way for him to do this?"

Fuck, she's right. She's right and it feels so good when Mom knows just what she's talking about.

Feels like a warm blanket, like when you come home from school and the kids made fun of you and Mom is there when you get home, instead of on tour. And you make cookies in the kitchen and eat the whole plate watching movies.

But Mom never seemed to understand that I still had school the next day, and the day after that, and the day after that. And a plate of cookies was the source of the problem, not the solution. So I'm wary to trust her.

"It's not fair. I'm the same person I was then. He knows that. Why did *my* love story have to be the one to get fucked up? I just... I really, really did not need that, you know?"

"Oh, Bria. I'm so sorry that happened. If he never says it, let me say it," she lets her voice drip with so much sympathy that I curl into a ball and put the phone on speaker next to me, just as I did when I was at my heaviest and I called my sister because I couldn't get out of bed.

I get to thinking about Skye, but Mom cuts through my thoughts.

"But you know what? I think you *did* need it. Because you're not the same person. You would not be where you are now without what happened. You'd be some... housewife to an immature man, who resented you every day. And you'd be big and hopeless, and afraid to wake up and see that one day he's gone, thinkin' all this time he was just doin' you a favor by being with you.

"Now I know I'm not you, but I feel like I am. I feel like I went through it, watching you go through it. And it hurt like hell. For me. I can only imagine what it was for you.

"But you gotta admit Bri, this? This is *muuuch* much better than what it would've been. If everything went according to plan."

Damn. She's really, really right and I know it.

I'm all fucked up. Because I'm realizing maybe my love story isn't a failure. It doesn't have to be over.

What if it's still happening? What if it's still being written?

"I gotta go Mom, you're fuckin' up my mind right now."

I get up, pacing the room.

I want to talk to him so bad I feel like I'm going to jump out of my skin. But what would I say? I just want to yell more, and for him to listen, like in the dream. I told myself I was done asking why, but I'm not. I told him I was too, and he complied a little too easily. It's the one thing he refuses to give me.

Ugh, *no*. No, he's a liar. He's a liar and I'm a chump.

I hate being attached to him. I just feel tainted. My world's

189

tainted, Texas is tainted because he's been living in it. This tour is tainted. The way I feel right now, I just want to lay in bed and stop. And dammit, I want a plate of cookies.

"So shattered/broken in pieces..."

No. I refuse to write.

I can't stomach the thought of turning this into art any longer. I'm just broken, and there's nothing beautiful about it.

"There I go/Trying to outrun that lovesick/thinkin' it will never catch me."

"Wow," I say aloud, getting up from my bed, exasperated. I have to be up in four hours, but sleep just isn't happening.

I rummage through my bag for my notebook with the silver hologram cover and begin to write.

Around 5 am I drift asleep, only to have my alarm go off an hour later.

I'm learning a valuable lesson today. One, never ever plan a gig this far in advance. Because your old boyfriend just might randomly show up and drain all your enthusiasm and motivation.

Two, there's a chance the band is right to be worried.

I love my life, and love being on stage. But as long as I'm Minnie Forrester's daughter all this will ever be for me is a hobby. The moment it stops being fun, I'm out. The rest of them, however, would just have to stop.

They really are subject to my whims. It's not fair to me, but it isn't to them either.

And whether *that* was fair or not was irrelevant. It's just the way it is. Band life.

I need to keep it going. For all of us. And I can do that if I don't have to do everything.

Which means after this tour, I need to fire myself. From either managing or singing. But I think that choice is pretty obvious.

For three hours, I sleep terribly in the back of the van on the way to Austin, and it'll have to do. Two shows today. Two tomorrow. Promo for MeTv, local radio stations, and Fader Magazine. Heaven help me.

I'm going to be forced to mention my weight loss and my mother 58 times today each, but I'm going to make it through. I have to. Chances are we'll be playing for strangers for the next two days, but if I find one die-hard in the audience I am clinging to that die-hard for dear life.

Also, maybe I should just get over myself and hire a hair and makeup person. I've proven I can be normal long enough— and the shit hasn't even worked, exactly no one was fooled. I need to save time. And my arms.

Thankfully, we get there by 10 am and by noon, we're done with everything but one show and one interview, because managing. It's going to be very very hard to replace me.

In the press area there are little tents everywhere with each media outlet having its own setup.

MeTv outranks and outclasses everyone there, with a full spread of food, couches, and a booth for taking selfies. The headliners won't be around until tomorrow, so today is mostly big fish in small ponds like us. The interviewer and crew seem enthusiastic to sit down with us, however.

"Now Bria, we caught up with your sister Skye on the set of her new movie, Souless, and this is what she had to say about the last time you spoke."

Skye's the one who introduced me to Chase, the one who convinced me to move to Houston. I owe my current life to her.

I feel like pins and needles are stabbing me everywhere as

191

I'm blindsided with a clip of Skye looking overly made up and slightly disheveled from a day of shooting.

"Uh, we talk. We talk all the time. We both live in Houston, I've been in Vancouver shooting, I know she's touring right now and doing really well so, we're both busy. You know how Forrester's do. Gotta keep busy, gotta be in the spotlight."

Whaaaaat the fuck does that mean, is all I can think as the interviewer fades to background noise, continuing to segue into his next question.

I don't really hear it, but I get the gist. They know not to come out and ask, but everyone wants to know if the rumors are true, if Skye and me are beefing. And it's my job to put out the fire.

Short answer: we are. But not on my end. Let's just say, once I stopped being the "fat Forrester," there was a disturbance in the Force.

But unlike Skye, I've got no problems grinning and bearing it on behalf of the family. Since I've been doing it pretty much my entire life.

As I said, I didn't hear the question, but I've got my pre-made, non-answer answer ready.

"We just saw each other during the holidays. We do a holiday movie marathon every year, I mean it's honestly... I think we're just now starting to have an actual normal relationship, where we're two separate people with different lives and careers and ambitions so... we're family. Whatever people like to report, it's all love, I wish her well and... I'll see her at Dad's birthday. If not before."

Lesson number four: time to hire a publicist.

The interview's over once they're done talking to me and it makes me cringe that they don't even have any questions for Chase.

He doesn't seem to mind as he turns to me on our way out of the press area. We head further down the road towards the small village set up of stages.

"You're a trooper," Chase says.

"It's for a good cause," I shrug.

"I didn't know they were gonna ask that."

"I did. It's fine. Any publicity is good publicity."

Chase nods a bit and I just look at him. I want to say more and I know he does too, but not about the same thing. I shake my head.

"What?" he says.

I take his arm by force and we walk ahead of the rest of the band.

"I wish you would've just fucked her," I mutter in a low voice.

Chase scoffed.

"I fucked you."

"I know. You ruined her life, you know that?"

He chuckled a little. "I'm sorry you have her for a sister."

"Why? You didn't do it."

As soon as we get to our assigned stage we unload gear and find out that we won't get to do soundcheck.

"Band Name Lyric, you guys are up in five," a stage manager says.

"I'm exhausted," I confess.

"You comin' with us to eat barbecue?" Braxton asks.

"That's paleo, isn't it?" I joke.

Just then I feel my back pocket vibrate.

It's a text from my mom.

I open it and it's just a really long link.

I click and it opens a browser window: 'Search results for Cliff Novak Chicago, Ill.'

At first I don't understand what I'm staring at. Some five year old story about a guy getting hit by a bus. They're all the same story. Then another set about Novak Electric.

I don't understand why my mother would send me this.

"Bria we're up."

Wait, Novak Electric. Holy fuck, is that... like *all* that's him?

Suddenly I see his face in one article. A conspiracy blogger. 'When Struggling Chicago Newspaper Refuses to Bury a Story, Novak Electric Buys It.'

These are not about different Cliff Novaks, they're all about the same one.

"Bria, you okay?"

I haven't moved. I've been frozen in the same spot for I don't know how long, scrolling and clicking.

The information is bombarding me, and yet I feel like it's not telling me anything. What was I thinking, clicking on this right *now*??

I feel a strange set of hands pushing me from backstage. Probably the stage manager. I peel my eyes away from my phone and try to find my mark as I go out to the smallish stage and confront the crowd with my mind in a fog. I'm on autopilot as my shaky hand reaches for a mic stand in front of me.

"Hi, we're A Band Name Lyric," I say conversationally.

Wait, I'm not supposed to do that, I was just going to launch into the first song like we did in Houston. Dammit.

All I can think about is getting the chance to pour over everything I just read, but I force my mind to the present. One of these shows needs to hit or this was all for nothing.

I hear Braxton behind me counting off the first song just as I lock eyes with a familiar face. One die-hard. Not of the band, but of me.

There's Cliff, his eyes smiling. My mind, body, and soul begin to recharge against my will.

I love you, he mouths.

17

Cliff

I woke up this morning with every intention of driving home, convinced that I'd screwed the pooch and that I'd been fooling myself that any of this could come out any differently.

I've held on to Felix's words all these years, "make yourself into the kind of guy that deserves her."

But Felix isn't some fairy godmother, he was just trying to get me off a ledge. And it worked. I hoped it would work a different way and it didn't. Bria wants to have me killed, and moving to Texas isn't going to reverse that. Believe me, I understand. I almost did the job myself once.

But when it came time to either take the 35 or the 45, I nearly crashed the car. I followed every sign for Austin until I was here.

Bria looks a little dazed when she gets on stage, and I wonder if that's my doing. She seems nervous. Exhausted. And that's definitely my doing.

We lock eyes. She looks at me almost with awe and I wonder if I've suddenly become part of the act. She holds on to my gaze like a lifeline as she sings and a lightning bolt shoots through me.

She seems to get her second wind, but I can't yet tell if that's a good sign. She could just as easily be working up the energy to punch me out after the show.

She's brilliant, as usual. I see glimpses of the old Bria, of Lyric. In her mannerisms, her facial expressions. It makes me smile.

I wait with bated breath every second, hoping to catch another golden moment of eye contact. I never take my eyes away and I'm rewarded, more than a few times.

Their set quickly ends to well-received applause, and the next band is hurried on stage behind them.

I wait by the sidelines for the band to finish breaking down, official-looking crew-members whooshing by on each side of me, giving me a once over as they carry black and metal cases of various sizes and shapes at their sides.

But no one says anything. Now I'm concerned that maybe security's a little *too* lax around here.

"'Scuse me, are you supposed to be back here?"

"He's okay," I hear Bria's voice. Our eyes meet for a long moment before something else takes her attention.

A little while later I get the same question, this time from an older guy with a goatee.

"Bria says I'm okay," I say.

"Who?"

"Bria Forrester," I repeat, pointing at the lone brown girl standing fifteen feet away. Bria senses a conversation concerning her and turns in my direction. The older gentleman stays put. Finally, she walks over.

"Is there a problem?"

"He's not wearing a lanyard."

"*I'm* not wearing a lanyard."

"He needs a lanyard if he's gonna be back here."

Bria grabs my hand and pulls me over to where the rest of her band is packing up gear.

"Here. Grab a case," she says. "I don't have a lot of pull out here so..." she puts her arm on both of my shoulders like she's knighting me, "You're now the tour manager if anyone asks."

"Where do you have a lot of pull?"

"Pretty much everywhere else."

"Is that right?" I grin.

"Yep."

"I don't believe we've met," I hear a voice behind me. I turn around to see the guitarist staring me down, "I'm Chase."

Chase is supposed to be beating me up today. But from the looks of it, she hasn't mentioned last night to him or anyone else.

"Cliff," I say, extending my hand. He takes it.

"So I guess you're responsible for that set?"

"What do you mean?"

"I mean... I haven't seen Bria perform like that in months. Only thing different is you."

"I don't know if I can take credit for that."

"Sure you can."

"Does that mean... you approve?" I ask.

"I don't think it matters."

"It does."

He seems to appreciate the comment. We both get the sense that Bria reasonably and tactfully caught one of us up on the other.

"I see you've gotten acquainted," Bria comes over. "Chase, they're saying we gotta move the van."

"Excuse me," he says. Bria watches him walk away like she's

dreading being alone with me. Finally, she looks at me and takes a breath.

"Hey."

"Hi."

"I meant what I said last night. About showing your face today."

"I know," I reply.

"You think I'm full of shit?"

"No."

"You just... not afraid to die, huh?" she smiles. I grin a little and shrug in response.

"Grab a guitar case. Walk with me."

We walk to the back of the venue where there's a small loading dock and a few spaces to park. Chase is already expertly backing up their van with their trailer attached and we start loading.

One by one the other members come by carrying gear and Bria rushes through an introduction for each one.

"You coming with us to Franklin's?" the blonde one named April asks me.

Bria's eyeing me in the corner. I can feel that she wants me to stay. But I can't.

"Actually, I have to get back on the road right after this."

"Oh no," April whines while Bria goes to grab more gear with a disappointed air. "Well, hopefully, this isn't the last we'll see of you," April says.

"Me too," I reply.

"I'll walk with you to your car," Bria offers.

"It's kind of far away."

"Good, it'll give us time to talk. April, save me a seat?"

"Don't you two run off together," April smirks, "Chase can't sing lead."

"He can, he just *won't*," Bria retorts. "I won't be long."

Bria locks up the trailer hitched to their van, puts her arm in mine, and leans on me as we start to walk.

She gives me an intense look, one I recognize but I don't know what's brought it on. Or what she wants to tell me with it.

She must see my fear because her face softens suddenly and she just smiles, leading the way.

We fight the flow of crowd traffic, live musicians, and performers on every corner. It's a bit too loud to talk but I don't think either of us mind. I feel so content that if I drifted off to sleep at this moment I might never wake up.

After a while, Bria un-links her arm and puts her hand in my hand. We look at each other and lose concentration on the simple task of walking, bumping into people left and right.

"A Band Name Lyric!" some random guy with beer in a plastic cup points to her, "you're Lyric!"

Bria gives me a knowing grin. I give her one back as the crowd dies down the further we get from the action.

"Sorry I flipped out on you last night," she says.

I huff a little laugh. "Not the first time you've gone nuclear on me."

She gives me a reminiscing chuckle. "No, I guess not. Sorry, I'm so... volatile."

"You had every right to be angry, then and now."

Bria just shakes her head. "No, I didn't. I overreacted. I haven't been thinking about you at all in this."

"Thinking about me?"

"How scary this must be for you to do what you're doing."

"What am I doing?" I ask.

"You don't know?"

"Just want to hear it in your words."

Bria moves a piece of her hair from her eyes. "I guess you're... trying to win me back or... pick up where we left off."

I purse my lips nervously. "What do you think about that?"

"I think... I don't have a choice."

"Of course you do," I argue. I don't really understand what she means by the answer, but I don't agree. I'm not here to force anything.

She eyes me for a long while and I can't help but return her penetrating stare. No matter how deep it goes there's no fear or apprehension. Only love.

She takes my hand again, brings the back of it to her lips, and kisses.

"No, I don't think I do," she sighs as we trek uphill towards the garage.

We take the elevator to the top and my black Suburban is parked in the first spot, the concrete structure overlooking downtown.

"You picked one hell of a gas guzzler to follow me around Texas with."

"Costs about as much as it did to rent a car. I like having a lot of legroom."

"What happened to your Maserati dreams?" she asks. I laugh, remembering the weird shit I aspired to in the program. I didn't mention it, but I'm sure she gathered that my family could afford it.

"Felix gave me this."

"Is that the guy you came with the other night?"

"Yeah. He's my best friend."

"Will I get to meet him?"

"Of course."

"When you opted out... did they let you see me?" she suddenly asks.

"What do you mean?"

"Like through a double-sided mirror or something. Did you see me waiting for you?"

I find her question odd. "No."

"Huh," she says. "I had a dream last night."

"Ah," I nod and smile knowingly. No one has a subconscious like Lyric's. "What was it?"

"I was back at Halcyon. In the exit interview, but as my present self. Like it was a do-ever. I told Dr. Payton I wanted to opt-out, because...you were a liar and I hated you and... They took me to this side door and I saw you. Waiting. And it was like, the worst. Like I knew I made a mistake. Instantly."

It means everything that she understands before I even say anything. My sweet, sensitive Lyric.

I lower my head, emotional. Humbled.

"What is it?"

"I'm such a bastard."

"Is that what happened?"

I simply nod. She grabs my face with both her hands but I just can't look at her.

"I talked to my mom last night. After I woke up in the middle of the night from that dream. You know what she said?"

"What?" I whisper.

"She said if we left Halcyon together that day, it would've been a disaster. I would've been an insecure mess, waiting for you to leave me. You would've eventually resented me. Taken me for granted and left me anyway, and you know what? She's right. We're much better people now, both of us. So when you think about it, you actually did the right thing."

Her words floor me. They flood me with so much relief.

Somehow my head finds her shoulder and she quietly holds on to my sobbing frame.

If Lyric can forgive me, then so can I.

She slowly wraps her arms around my shoulders and lets me hold her. Really hold her. For the first time in six years. And there's nothing more I want to say or do besides this. I close my eyes, willing my emotions to subside.

She holds me back and I know she's waiting for the embrace to become more than just that, but first things first. I just want to hold her a while.

"Are you sure you can't stay?" she asks. Her question makes me so high I'm light-headed.

I shake my head. "I'm going on shift as soon as I get back. I used up all my PTO."

"You mean *I* used it up."

"You didn't. You were perfect," I say as I finally let go. I brush her cheek with the back of my hand. Her hand goes on top of mine and her eyes close like she's in ecstasy. I don't know what happened between last night and today, but I'm grateful for it.

"You're perfect. You know that? You always were," I say.

"I can't believe you're here. I can't believe you came," she says as a single tear falls.

I can't believe my ears. Is this really my life right now?

My thumb trails her bottom lip feeling surreal, feeling content enough to die. I fucking won somehow.

"You still owe me a kiss," I say.

"God, do not kiss me right now," she rolls her eyes. She hates starting what can't be finished. *Me*, on the other hand...

"You remember the first song you sang to me?" I ask.

She thinks for a moment then laughs.

"*Give me a kiss to build a dream on...*" she sings the first bar.

"So?"

She sighs. "Fine. You first."

"No. Both of us at the same time."

Our foreheads meet and the years melt away as this time I take her face in my hands.

Her warm soft lips turn my insides to lava. We hear a sudden thud of the door leading to the stairs not far off, lone footsteps, and then a wolf whistle, but we can barely even react until we get our fill.

I can't believe it's been six years since we kissed. And it's so hungry, so savory that it's making me blind with arousal.

By the time I pull away, no more than an inch away from her mouth, Bria's eyes are full of stars and I know mine are too. We eye each other's lips.

"I was afraid of that."

"You should've given me one night."

"It wouldn't have been enough," she said. Her brow knits subtly. "By the way, what happened... in your hotel room last night?"

My gaze shifts to my feet. "You mean—"

"Yeah. That's never happened before. *Ever.*"

My heart sickens thinking back to that moment. Hearing about those dreams, thinking of how she blamed herself.

"Bria, you're beautiful. The fact you think that could've possibly been about *that* is... insane."

"...So what happened?"

I sighed. "All I could think about was how much better you are at giving head now. And how it's my fault. That you're better at giving head."

She looks into my eyes for a long moment. Finally, she shakes her head and laughs.

"What's funny?" I crack a smile.

"What do you mean?" she gains her composure well enough to ask. "There's nothing *not* funny about it."

"Can I call you?" I ask.

She shakes her head, still chuckling, gesturing for my phone and I retrieve it from my back pocket.

She puts her phone number in it and calls herself. Her phone plays a Lauryn Hill ringtone and suddenly stops.

"Let me know when you make it back," she says.

"When will you be back?" I ask.

She sighs as if exhausted just thinking about it. "Tomorrow or the next day. It depends on if we want to drive through the night. Three of us have regular jobs to get back to."

"I'd like to see you again. When you get back."

"Cliff..." she grins like a shy high schooler.

"What?"

She rolls her eyes and waves a hand, as if I've offended her. "Nothing. As soon as I get back, I'm coming over. How's that?" she coos. Oh my God.

"I love you," I reply uncontrollably. I don't know what the etiquette is and I don't care. I can only distantly register that she doesn't say it back.

It doesn't matter. Maybe she isn't ready. But I'm ready. I'm ready to say it over and over.

"I don't want to say goodbye," she says.

"Me either," I confess.

"We've never had to do it before."

"No, I guess technically we haven't."

"Sorry you came all this way for just a kiss," she says with hooded eyes.

"I'm not," I say as I go in for another peck that becomes two, then three. I grab her by her new and improved hips.

She used to be so shy when I put my hands on her. As much as I tried to undo the damage I caused by rejecting her that first month, she could never fully convince herself that loving her body didn't require some level of sacrifice for me.

Now, the apologies are gone from her eyes. She wants me, but more than that, she wants me to want her.

And she doesn't want to hear that I always want her no matter what size she is. She wants to reap the fruit of her labor. She reaches for my belt buckle.

"What are you doing?"

"If I'm going to get through another day of band-ing, I need more than a kiss."

"I need the whole night."

"You can have all the nights. And the days," she blurts, her eyes like two blazing black stars. For a moment I'm utterly speechless.

"You'd say anything to get in my pants right now," I reply.

"I mean it," she laughs.

Damn my pride. She just confessed she wants me back and everything in me wants to... celebrate. All over her. Right here and now. But I can't.

"When you get back. I promise."

"What if I die on the way home?"

"Don't die on the way home."

"What if *you* die on the way home?" she guilts me. Impressive.

"I won't."

"You can't promise that."

Her words jab me in the feels, and I realize that the last time we left each other, maybe we didn't say goodbye but she certainly never saw me again, even though I'd promised then too.

She's not just trying to guilt me to get what she's after. It's my fault that it hurts too much to hope.

"Wait here," I instruct her as I move towards the trunk. I open it and start stowing away the seats in the back two rows.

It's sketch, but the windows are as low a tint as they're legally allowed to be.

I can still make it back in plenty of time if I never have to leave the 6th floor of the parking garage.

"If the Suburban's rockin' don't come a-knockin'?"

"There shouldn't be that much rocking, but try to keep it down."

"Aren't you an officer of the law?" she smirks.

"Yes. Think about that. Really hard."

"Oh, I will," she says as she climbs in through the back and I lock the doors with the remote.

With the seats down, there's enough room for us to lay down comfortably, but we're not exactly here to camp out.

"You should wear more skirts," I suggest as she painstakingly removes her jeans.

"Maybe I will, now that you're around," she giggled.

"You still walk around in just your robe?" I ask. I barely get the question out before she's kissing me, her beautiful body again on display for me in just her t-shirt and bikini underwear. She grabs my belt buckle again.

"Not me, just you," I break away from her mouth.

"Bullshit."

She sits up on her elbows between the front two seats with her palms down at her sides and her legs up.

It only takes a second for my descent into madness to begin, me on all fours in front of her, with my hands on her knees holding them open.

I don't know what expression I'm making, but I can see from the corner of my eye she's watching me.

She's losing breath already, her hand shaky as it goes hastily between her thighs.

I'm already diving down headfirst by the time she pulls back the fabric of her underwear. She winces.

"Ohmigod, Luke. I mean— shit," she curses, either in defeat or pleasure, I'm not sure.

I really don't give a shit what she calls me. Both names send me into the stratosphere and for different reasons.

She puts her hand in my hair and forgets all about that 'try to keep it down' thing I told her. A distant car alarm sobers her but only a little.

I stop to pull her underwear all the way off and dive back in with both hands wrapped around her thighs, a fraction of their former selves.

All of me is vibrating like a tuning fork. The taste of her on my tongue again, the smell of her on my lips. It's just like the first time, when every lick elicited a surprised and grateful thrill from her throat.

Her hips undulate underneath me. I quicken my pace of long swirling strokes around her clit until she's begging me not to stop.

"Shit, I'm coming already," she laments as she lazily grits her teeth.

Slowly her eyes roll, her body arches and she comes in a way I don't recognize, quietly with her whole body tensing as she lets out a strained moan. Holy *fuck*.

The air of sex is causing delirium. I have to keep licking and sucking and kissing, slowly as she comes down, so that I can come down. Gotta stay on task, gotta get bored. Until she's boneless and unable to resist. If she retains an ounce of strength, I'm toast.

This, I owe her, but we won't be fucking for the first time in six years in a parking garage. I may have to pull over ten times with the smell of her lingering in the back of my car on the way home, and the panties I'm gonna make her leave behind, but I won't rush any part of this.

As I slowly cover the haven between her thighs with kisses, I can hear her sharp gasps everywhere my tongue touches. I realize the gasps are her quiet sobs.

I have an idea what the sobs are for. For lost time, gratitude, release, ecstasy, anger, pick an emotion. I resign myself to her service, her pleasure.

Soon a second orgasm washes over her as she shouts out my instructions, each demand sending throbbing courses of arousal through my veins. I've got blue balls so bad by the end that I might be running a fever.

I leave Bria a sopping mess in the back of my SUV, nodded off like an addict off the wagon. She probably hasn't had much sleep and I hope she doesn't drive tomorrow night.

I drive her down an alley that's the closest route to the restaurant.

"You sure the band's still here?"

"Positive," she says. She gives me another long look of a million words, what seems like the 100th today.

I won't complain. Or ask why. I send her a million-word look of my own. When she gets back to Houston, I may not ever use words again.

"Thanks for the ride," she caresses my mouth with her thumb and gives me a peck. "Let me know when you've made it."

"I've made it," I say.

Her smile is more radiant than I remember, which seems impossible. Or maybe caused by me. Which also seems impossible.

"Home, I meant."

"Oh, okay."

She shuts the door and walks along the side of the brick building in the opposite direction. I can see her turn back in the rearview, not sure if I'm watching her.

She gives me a small wave just in case and disappears into the crowd of festival-goers.

18

Chase

Five years Ago

Hollywood parties. I hated them.

Only had to ever go to one to know that I just wanted write the songs and play the guitar.

That worked for awhile, until the music video came out and teenage girls started showing up to our shitty shows. No one cared that we were trying to save indie music, as if we could do that.

The money tore us apart. Those industry vampires fed me a load of bullshit, told me I was good enough to go my own way. I trusted them to tell me if I was only mediocre. But why would they?

When I started to catch wind, they dulled my senses with drugs and women. They found a cash cow, fattened me up and fed off me for years until I finally wisened up and got the hell out of there.

So it gives me the shakes to be back here. Literally.

I can tell there's cocaine at this party. From the range of guests with nothing in common, huddled in bathrooms and sitting too close to each other on couches, to the deadening barrage of the DJ's playlist.

What's even crazier is that this isn't even Hollywood. It's fucking Houston.

But I guess, all scenes are essentially the same and can pop up anywhere. Strange how I seem to find them, no matter how far I move away.

But I'm not here for myself, I'm here for the band.

Lori left us, and it shook us to our core. How do you lose a lead singer without losing the heart of the band?

Surprisingly, we've managed to stay together. We all wanna keep going.

And so, I volunteered to use my remaining industry clout to hurl myself into the belly of the beast and bring back a diamond.

I can't go back to the innocence of being one of five LA dudes, skipping school, writing and playing music and being best friends. But I can get back to the heart of it.

C.H.L.O.E. had been at it four years when I joined. Playing clubs, pounding the pavement. They got close to a deal a few times, enough to catch people's attention, but everything fell through. Everyone sat back and waited for them to blow up. And no one lifted a finger to help them.

They needed a guitarist and I needed a band. I needed one bad. And they rescued me.

They were focused, disciplined. Cohesive. Better than half the famous bands out there. Weary, but at least not looking for that validation of an LA deal. And local, thank God.

Skye's a good fit. A high-ish profile looking for some street cred. I hate that I ever learned this lesson, but looks don't hurt, only help. Frosting for the cupcake. Stylistically it could be a disaster, or it could be kick-ass. I don't know what kind of person she is, but the word around town is she's professional, which is not a lightly thrown-around word.

"So, my sister's the one that convinced me to audition for you guys," Skye says, digging an olive straight out of her dirty martini and into her mouth.

"Oh yeah?"

"Yeah, she saw you guys at the Velvet Room a few years back."

"No shit."

"Yeah, she's like... a music buff. I mean, I guess we all are, but she wants to go behind the scenes. Be the next Diddy, or whatever."

"Diddy, huh?"

"Yeah. I told her she should come manage us. I mean... if I decide to be your lead singer, that is."

"Well, you would still have to audition."

"Of course."

"You're a hell of a vocalist, but it has to be a good fit, you know?"

"You know my sister writes a little bit."

Here we go. Nepotism powers on.

Even though I wouldn't mind entertaining a few ideas from a singer with Minnie Forrester's genes in them, I can already feel Skye trying to sink her talons into something that's not even really hers yet, and that's a bad sign.

"She's been writing poetry for years, but it's like the floodgates suddenly opened. I'm not wowed by a lot but *wow*, she's like, no joke."

"Sounds like you're very supportive of your sister."

"I am. She's my little dunkin' donut," she says in a diminuitive voice. "But she's all grown up now. Just went through kind of a bad break up actually."

I slowly nod my head after that little bit of context. I can't say I follow the gossip columns, but it's hard not to know that the tabloids have been having a field day with Bria Forrester's ballooning weight. Cruel, dark shit. Kinda surprised that there's a relationship story behind all that.

Which, of course, makes me feel like an asshole. Can't imagine the type of trust issues a big girl from a famous family must have.

"What's your sister's name again?" I ask.

You never act like you know anything that's going on outside of yourself in LA. Not with just anyone. Can't let any old stranger know you have a bit of humanity left.

"Bria. Forrester. She's in school for music business right now, but obviously that's just her being... extra. She doesn't even wanna work for Dad when she graduates, where she'd be guaranteed whatever job she wants."

"Well, Tar Baby's a rap label, isn't it?"

"Yeah, but Bria's into all kinds of music. Daddy would give her a whole department if she asked for it. But she's never been all that good with knowing when to take advantage of a good thing."

Ugh. This may not work out.

"Some people just don't have a knack a for it."

"Is it okay if I bring her with me to the audition?"

"Who, Bria? Sure, bring as many family members as you want."

"She's gonna flip out. Her fat little face just lit *up* when I told her you called. I'm telling you, she even remembered you from Soul Society, even before you started 5 Seasons of Summer."

God. Such a fucking stupid band name.

"Well, she sounds like a cool chick. I can't wait to meet her."

We can still do the audition. The band's excited for new blood and I already told them this was happening.

We'll probably have to keep looking, but for some reason I still feel good about it. Things are off to a good start, and that's always a good sign of things to come.

Present Day

It takes an hour for Bria to walk this Cliff fucker back to his car.

Finally, I spot her coming up the walk of the restaurant. From my place at the booth, I can see her approaching the entrance looking dazed and distracted and stifling a smile. She gets inside and the waitress directs her to where we're already seated. In that time, she's managed to completely wipe all traces of contentment from her face.

That makes me feel bad. If I wasn't here, she'd be telling the story of their alley finger-bang or whatever the fuck took so long.

I don't mean to be like this. It's bad enough that I'm in love with her. It's bad enough that she doesn't feel the same and probably never has.

But it means a lot that she's willing to spare me. She doesn't have to do that. One of us should be as happy as possible.

She takes the seat next to mine that was left purposely vacant without a word of discussion.

"Smells good," she says, picking through a random basket of meat. "Did you order me anything?"

"Just ordered a buncha shit to split," I say. Bria's sort of the treasurer of the group. She's got the degree, discipline and the least motive to cheat us. Braxton's an accountant in real life but he refuses to do the job.

"I wanna do 'Fast Car' tomorrow."

I smile. The song's perfect for her voice and her vibe, but she took it out because she didn't like the comparisons.

"We can take out Dreams."

"We don't have to."

"That's three covers. But as long as you don't mind. What's with the change of heart?"

"I just need something to look forward to, to get me through tomorrow."

When she talks like that she makes it clear she's not hungry for it. It's easy for her and she could just as easily do something else.

But I can't tell anymore if it's that, or if this Cliff guy is really discombobulating her that much.

"Oh my gosh," she moans as she takes a bite of the brisket. "Keep that away from me."

"So, did you and Cliff get things... sorted out?"

"When were they out of sorts?"

"Um... when you sang Big Girls Cry and then had a shouting match with him outside the club."

"Ohhh yeah, that," she nods her head. "Yeah, I guess you could say we got things sorted out."

"So what's the verdict?

"What do you mean?"

"Should I be worried about you or not?"

"You should absolutely not be worried about me."

"Why's that?"

She sits back in her chair with a confident look. "You know those commercials where they say, 'Brought to you by Novak Industries, a family company.'?"

"Yeah."

"Yeah, that's his people."

"Get the fuck," I chuckle in disbelief. She just slowly nods her head with an I'm- surprised-but-not eyeroll. I laugh again.

"Well, he could definitely afford Halcyon, couldn't he?"

"His parents. He kept saying his parents paid for it. He wouldn't go into it. Neither of us would. Or could."

"He's a trust fund kid. No wonder he has time to follow you around Texas."

"Actually, he's a cop."

"He's a what?"

"Highway patrol in Houston."

I just furrow my brow, not knowing where to start.

"I don't quite have the whole story yet. I had to get that first part from my mom. She looked him up on Magellan and sent me the link."

"Okay so... as impressive as that is, you haven't answered my question, really. Is he for real or—"

"He's for real," she says. That's when the smile returns, breaking through the cracks of her cool facade. She looks more than happy. She looks... tranquil.

Fuck. I still fuckin' hate this guy. I will always hate this guy. And if he was the guy after me instead of before me, this whole thing would be going a hell of a lot differently.

But I can't get anywhere near the Bria that only he seems to intimately know. And I can't hate what he brings out of her. Which is the thing I love seeing the most. Maybe more than the woman herself.

"So what happens now, you marry this guy and become a cadrillionaire?"

"Skye is going to shit herself to death," she smiles.

That makes me choke on my own spit, thinking of Skye painting on a fake smile for the course of an entire wedding.

What a hateful bitch. Couldn't stand to see Bria become something other than her overweight baby sister. It was as if the more Bria's outside matched her insides, the more Skye withered and died. They haven't been seen in the same room in over a year.

"So what does that mean for us?" I ask. She gives me a concerned deer in headlights look, obviously paranoid that I mean her and I. For fuck's sake, I'm not a teenage girl.

"The band," I let her off the hook. "He wants you barefoot and pregnant or what?"

"We haven't gotten that far yet," she says right before she sips her water through a straw.

I raise both my eyebrows. "I don't hear you objecting."

"Do you *wanna* be done?" she asks.

"No."

"But I get the sense that you don't think this will last forever."

"I can't speak for everyone else, but as long as you're doing music, I'm doing music."

"It's funny that you say that because CowTown Records offered us a deal," she says.

I raise an eyebrow. CowTown's a legit label. Run by two guys that were just small-time when I was coming up in the clubs in LA. They've stayed indie. It's a good fit. But I'm waiting to hear Bria tell me how her priorities have changed.

"Was it a deal or a meeting?" I ask.

"Is there a difference?"

"Yeah, a big one. 'Deal' means they want to sign us. 'Meeting' means they want to cut everyone and keep you."

"...You don't know that," she denies.

"When's the meeting?" I ask. Because I know it's a meeting.

She sips water through a straw as if stalling. "I didn't give them a definite answer."

"You probably won't be able to go to bat for all of us."

"Fuck that," she shakes her head.

"But you can make a case for me. April and Chelsea might be hired as background singers rather than members of the band. Pay scale's different."

"Gotta be honest, I don't know what I want anymore," she confesses.

"I was afraid you'd say that."

"No, I mean I still want to sing. With you guys. I want our shows to be packed. I want the shit that we make to sell. Touring's not my favorite."

"We're not exactly doing it in style."

"I'm not Lori. I'm not in danger of hating it. I don't even mind the image stuff, being out front. I fucking hate when they don't acknowledge you."

I just sit back and let her talk it out.

"I don't see this ending. I don't see myself doing this with anyone else. It's not like I need the money."

"So? What are our terms?"

"We keep paying the costs. Of everything. Small tours. I can bite the bullet, with another act of our choice on the roster. All we need is their distribution. It's literally all we need."

"I like it."

"Think we can get it?"

"Most of it. You never know."

"When should I tell everyone?"

I sigh. We'll see how this turns out. But for now, it's a win.

"Tell them now. They're exhausted."

19

Bria

I'm glad I decided to do Fast Car.

There wasn't a single die-hard in the crowd but they all knew that song.

We made a hell of an impression. Less than 24 hours and there's been one or two clips made according my Magellan alert. The band was in good spirits, especially after hearing about the meeting. I didn't tell them Chase's version of the news.

Also, I told them that I'm firing myself from one of my roles and left it to a vote. Everyone voted unanimously to have me stay on as lead singer, which sort of made the manager in me feel shitty.

Texas is a big fucking state. I've never been so excited to see my little car in Chase's parking lot once we get back to Houston around midnight the next night.

"You gonna be alright on the road?"

"Fine."

"Why do I feel like you're on your way to see this rent-a-boyfriend?"

"...He's working."

Chase cocks his head to one side and rolls his eyes.

"You're gonna have to get used to him," I say.

"So I was just a rebound that entire time?"

"...Not the *entire* time..."

"Jesus," he says, looking a bit like a beat dog.

"I didn't bring Halcyon up because it was embarrassing."

"It's just that I thought we told each other everything."

"Well. Now you know it all."

"I don't know the details."

"Oh, geez."

"So this program, it puts your life into a computer and out comes your perfect match?"

"Seems that way. Didn't always seem like that at the time."

"What was it about him? That captured you, I mean?"

"Chase..."

"What?"

"What is this?"

"You're special, Bri. I just wanna know why he's good enough."

"And not you?"

"Forget me."

I take a moment to think about how I was going to boil down the intense intimacy cultivated in that concentration of six months. And how insane it was to think time could erase what we built and how foolish it would be to try. Like bulldozing ancient Roman ruins for gentrification.

"He taught me how to love myself. By accident. Without him, there would've been no us. No band. None of it."

He's silent for a while, then he nods.

"Our dynamic. On stage," I begin, not sure how to word what I'm thinking. "That's.... all real. To me. You know that, right?"

"I know," he says, sounding clipped.

"We're still best friends."

"Best friends?"

"Yeah, did you not know that?"

"First I'm hearing about it."

"We're best friends," I reiterate.

He gives me a slow grin. "Send me a text when you make it back."

After a few minutes of being on the highway, I realize how much I lied about being fine on the road. I can't believe how exhausted I am. I should've slept on the way home but, I couldn't sleep for the anticipation of being home.

Cliff would be off in a few hours, and I was hoping to take a nap before he called. I hadn't even thought about the fact that I might sleep our first night together away. But between the decision to pick what music to play to keep myself awake, I'm already nodding off.

I'm roughly ten minutes from home. I think about powering through, but then I remember the conversation we had before he left. *"What if I die on the way home?"*

"Don't," had essentially been his response.

I let out a heaving sigh as I do something I've never before had to do: pull over to the side of a remote stretch of road at an ungodly hour, and sleep.

I don't want to sleep in another vehicle. Especially when I have to lock all my doors and will the car to look like it's not worth bothering. I desperately want to be home already and not look at a dashboard for at least two days.

I want my bed, soft warm and luxurious. But I won't die in pursuit of it.

I take the keys out of the ignition and keep them in my hand in case... I don't know, the Hulk punches through the glass and tries to turn the ignition while I'm sleeping. I keep my phone in the center console where it vibrates like crazy when someone calls.

The moment he's free, he'll call. I'll get a few winks in, drive home, no big deal.

A knock on my driver's side window interrupts my plan.

I startle awake, feeling dead, so I know haven't been asleep long.

The soundless, unmistakable strobe of blue and red glows around my whole car like a super intense party's been going on while I was out.

I'm still too out of it to grasp my surroundings. I'm wondering if something happened while I was asleep, not quite understanding that *I* am that something.

There's another knock and a bright light in my face, and I sit up, realizing I should've texted someone to let them know where I am before I—

"Roll down your window for me," a familiar voice says through the muffled glass.

I stop, a little confused.

I know that voice anywhere.

But what's Cliff doing here with the cops *OH MY GOD.*

I turn over just the battery on the car to roll my window down. I am then confronted with the sight of Luke... in a brown cop's uniform.

I have a thing for civil servants, the memory comes back to me as I reconcile the gun on his hip.

We were in bed when I said that, like we usually were.

No way is he a cop just because I said that.

"Hi there," he says.

"Oh my God."

"Everything okay?"

"Yeah, I made it home. Well... not quite, I was pretty exhausted. In fact, I think I might still be dreaming," I ramble, eyeing the name tag, the badge, the undershirt peeking out right below the top of his collar. Holy shit, he's even got pens in his shirt pocket.

"Home from where?" he asks.

And then it hits me: he did become a cop for me.

And now he's role-playing. My body sends a shock down there every time my mind entertains another scenario that should never happen in real life.

"Austin."

"What's in Austin?"

"SXSW. I'm a singer. In a band."

"Oh yeah? Anyone I've ever heard of?"

"Well, we're really good, so... I doubt it."

He slowly smirks. "Where's home?"

"Bellaire. About ten minutes from here."

"What's the address?" he asks. Hmmm... I don't watch a lot of crime TV but I'm pretty sure that's not a standard question.

"...Sorry, am I under arrest or something?"

"You refusing to answer my question?" he sternly asks. Holy hell.

"You still haven't identified yourself," I smirk.

"...Yeah, I did."

"No, you didn't," I giggle.

"...Did so."

"You didn't. I'm reporting you, Officer.... Novak," I laugh, eyeing his name tag.

"Hand over that license and registration. Giggle pants."

"Are you serious, right now?" I stare at him. I let down the visor where I keep the registration and hand it over.

"Any drugs in the car, rock star?" he teases, as I fish my license out of my purse.

"No."

"Is this address up to date?" he asks once I hand it over.

"Yes," I coo, ready to flirt my way out of this situation if need be. "That's where I'll be all night tonight."

"Good for you," he replies, feigning disinterest.

"It is good. For me," I tease.

"I'll be back. Keep your hands on the steering wheel."

"Yes, officer."

He returns to his squad car, but I'm pretty sure he's doing absolutely nothing. Except copying my address.

I roll my window up and send Chase a quick text. He'd sent me three question marks while I was sleeping. Suddenly I notice Cliff's presence right outside the car.

"How long you been out?" he asks when I roll my window back down.

"I don't know. An hour?"

"Think you can make it home?"

"Sure."

"Well, you're relatively safe here, but you'd be safer at home." He hands back my license and registration. "Drive safe, if you can manage it. You're free to go, Miss Forrester."

"I'm what?"

"You can go."

"You don't wanna... search me?"

"Search you for what?"

"I don't know. Weapons."

"Do you have any weapons?" he smirks.

"Does my ass count?" I ask. He smiles.

"Go home, Bria. I don't like you on the side of the road."

"...Cliff, you have to do me right now."

"Officer Novak," he corrects me. *Oh*my God.

"Officer Novak, you have to do me right now," I whine, hanging on the driver side window.

He looks off in the distance at the patch of highway around us, and I can tell he's formulating a plan. A plan that he looks to have very little faith in.

"You can wait a few hours," he decides.

"Wait, wait, wait. It's all you ever say now. I'm starting to take it personally," I say, reaching for his crotch. He backs away.

"What are you doing?"

"Show me your cock, officer."

"Ma'am if you keep being unruly, I'm gonna have to ask you to step out of the car."

"Yessss," I open the door and start to step out.

"I didn't say 'get out of the car,' Bria. Jesus," he reprimands me.

"Sorry."

"Haven't you ever been pulled over before?"

"Were you for real scared?" I laugh. He send me an unamused look and I retreat back in the car sheepishly.

"First rule of getting pulled over by a cop: listen. Second rule: obey."

"Ooh," I grin.

"You just earned yourself a frisking. You wanna be frisked?"

"Yes."

"Step out of the car to the hood of the vehicle."

I try to be seductive while being exhausted with just my undershirt and jeans on with a pair of white Keds.

"Your ass looks like it was poured into your jeans like a clay mold. Ma'am."

"Thank you, officer."

"I've got no idea how to make frisking sexy, by the way."

"I believe in you, officer," I say as I feel his hands on me from behind. His touch lights up my brain, but it feels different. I feel different. It jars my memories.

He lied about not knowing how to make frisking sexy. Or perhaps he's just now learning. His touch goes from routine to exploratory. Lingering. Worshipful. Both of us turn eerily quiet.

A lone car passes in the night as his hands meander back up my hips and around my middle. He doesn't seem to notice.

Now I'm worrying that I've convinced him to compromise his job. My heart pounds with a swirl of lust and guilt.

"Does this dash cam have audio?" I ask.

"...It does," he answers.

"So people can hear what I'm saying to you right now?"

"Faintly. It's more for me than for you."

"Oh."

I seize as his hands touch my bare skin under my shirt. His lips graze my ear.

"*Večeras ću te pojesti živog,*" he says, slowly. Menacingly, like a villain. I don't need to know what it means to know I'm in the best kind of trouble.

"No fair," I said.

"Do I have permission to search your back seat?"

I tilt my head with a smile. "...Is that code for something?"

"Yes and no."

I shrug one shoulder, not sure where this is going. "Um... sure."

"You have to say yes," he says with a veiled expression.

Hmm....

227

"Yes."

He takes my hand and moves me to the passenger side, likely where the dashcam is out of sight.

"Are the uh, lights necessary?"

"With you on the side of the road, it draws even more attention when they're off."

"Ah."

"This can only work one way," he says, "so you have to listen, alright?"

"Okay."

He opens up my backdoor and makes a few search-like movements before he gets in and lays flat on his back.

"*Skini svoje hlače,*" he says. My eyes narrow at the phrase.

Sly dog.

"Do you remember?" he asks.

"Yes."

"Ball's in your court," he says.

I smile, looking around the deserted stretch of highway.

I can't believe this is his actual job. I'm confused, and yet I love it.

I start to peel off my size ten jeans, with astonishingly little reservation. Didn't quite have the courage to take off the underwear.

"What do I do um... after this?"

"*Sjedni mi na lice,*" he said. Another dirty command I committed to memory. Always sounded like Italian to me.

"Which way? Officer."

He said, "*šezdeset i devet*" and my mouth watered.

"Should I keep my head down?"

"As low as possible."

I crawled on top of him and he gave my mouth a slow, muted

kiss before putting a finger to his lips in a "shhh" motion. I turned around and showed him my ass which he squeezed in gratitude. I found his zipper with ease and released his rock hard member.

"This gun's not gonna go off is it?"

"Not if you don't touch it."

"Are we talking about the same thing?"

"...I don't think we are."

I want to laugh, but my lips touch his cock and the only thing I can do is go to town.

I let a few moans escape, but he's in no state to shush me. I can feel his grip on my body become tight and I only feel air down below, which means he's totally gone right now. Probably slack jawed and already close to coming.

"How long's it been baby," I ask in a low voice. No answer, just his labored breath.

I want him to do me too, as he descends into ecstasy I want to feel his tongue on me.

But I don't ask it of him. I just use my need to move my mouth further and further down his shaft.

It takes me a moment to register that he's doing just what I wished for, as though reading my mind.

"Mm-hm," I hum an affirmation with my mouth full of cock, my head bobbing up and down and a slight ache in my neck forming. But I don't stop. And I don't waver on what I'm doing. Neither does he. That's what I love, when we're so fucking in sync that our bodies just become each other's pleasure machines and I can't believe I ever fucking thought that I'd be able to give chemistry like this up once it came back to me...

The arousal starts to become unbearable. I need release. My hums become groanings as my hips undulate just above his tongue. I give my neck a break and spit into my hand, putting my full concentration onto the climax that's heating up hard and fast inside me as I stroke him.

"Shit, I'm coming already," I lament as I lazily grit my teeth. Slowly my eyes roll, my body arches uncontrollably, quietly but probably in full view of that dash cam. Whoops.*f*

I muffle the sounds of my grateful satisfaction with my mouth on his cock, sucking him like a pacifier as I come down off my high.

I can hear his unrest, his climax on the heels of mine. His body stiffens. I brace for the warm spray to hit the back of my throat, squint my eyes and let my mouth fall slack as it all pools down and around my fist still holding him. I spit, powering through the salty, metal taste to lick the tip and reap the moans of a job well done. The air of sex is causing delirium. I keep licking and moaning and kissing. Every lick makes him wince, but I won't stop unless he tells me to.

"*Dosta*," he finally pants.

I didn't turn the car back on so we're covered in sweat, my windows are foggy. And no one has any regrets.

I find a random something in the back to clean up with. I pick my pants up off the floorboards, put my legs into them and step out of the car to ease them on and zip them up.

"Am I free to go now?" I ask, once he's righted himself and stands close to me.

"You're beautiful," he replies, gazing into my eyes. He grabs me caveman style, with one arm around my waist, the other at his side. He leans in and we taste each other's climax as we kiss. He saunters around the back of both our cars to get to the driver side of his.

"You got that address?" I check.

"I do. You're not that far from me."

"Small world, huh?" I say as I get back into my car. I guess he can't leave until I do.

"Drive safe," he says with a grin.

"Don't dawdle," I warn him. I start my car and pull off onto the highway, now wide awake on the short trek home.

20

Cliff

I arrive at Bria's house and ring the doorbell.

The house is an impressive size, but such is Texas. The area's safe, middle class and mostly families. In Novak money she's slumming it. In Forrester money as well, for that matter. I could probably afford this house on just what they pay me.

All this time and she was ten minutes away.

Our tryst on the side of the highway made the last 2.5 hours of my shift bearable, but electric. I'm wide awake now, my erratic breath the only sound in the dark quiet as I see Bria's shadowy frame through the slender glass panes on either side of the door. She makes her way down the dark corridor to the front door and I hear the flick of the porch light as it comes on.

Should I rush inside and ravish her right there on the floor? Lift her in my arms and carry me to the closest room with a bed in it?

The knob turns, and the door creaks open. I settle on doing nothing as we look at each other nervously.

She slowly grabs my hand and leads me inside. I shut the

door behind me and she doesn't tell me to lock it. Either she's forgotten or doesn't care. My squad car is parked outside, so I'm not worried.

We make it past the open living and dining rooms. Bria walks backward as she slowly leads me across the house. I give myself a quick eye tour before she lets go of my hand in the hallway to take off her shirt as we keep walking.

I come out of my shoes, untuck my shirt and unbutton it before we get to the room at the end of the hallway, a master bedroom with vaulted ceilings. She turns to face me and starts on my belt buckle, then the zipper.

I feel a tap on my brain and I seize, feeling a plague of anxiety. *Not now, not now...*

"I have to tell you something," I whisper.

"Okay..."

I swallow, shutting my eyes tight. "I... sometimes have nightmares. Bad ones."

"Okay," she repeats patiently.

"It may be nothing it's just... my medication's at home. It's kind of a long story—"

"Is it... because of... the accident?"

I don't answer, but my eyes open. I see the knowing all over her face.

"You didn't think I would look you up?" she quietly wonders, gazing up at me, "Clifford Novak Jr. the highway patrolman from Chicago, Illinois? Actually my mom did all the work, she just sent me the link."

"Your mom?"

"Yeah, when I was telling her about you, after Austin happened. She looked you up online."

I blink nervously and lower my head with a furrowed brow.

233

Shit.

I was going to tell her. After.

I just wanted to get to this point. On my own. As Cliff, and not as Luke.

"It said that you... got hit by a bus," she says.

She didn't know in Dallas, but she knew in Austin.

No wonder she looked at me the way she did.

"Ancient history," I dismiss.

"A coma? Surgeries? Amnesia??"

"Temporary, obviously. I'm fully recovered now."

She lets out an exasperated sigh of a laugh. "Of course, you would shrug off a coma."

"I'm not shrugging it off."

"Just when did you plan on telling me?"

"Honestly, I hadn't thought about it."

"Cliff..."

"Really. I didn't think much farther than laying eyes on you again. And everything after that's sort of been a blur..."

She shakes her head soberly. "You let me go on and on in that hotel room. Like a crazy person..."

"You had every right to be angry," I tell her again.

"I thought all this time you were just... is that why it took you so long? You were recovering that whole time?"

"...Recovering from a few things. From being me. And living with that," I say. There's no way I'm gonna be able to get her off the subject.

"Was it an accident or did you really—"

"Is this the only reason you're taking me back?" I blurt out.

"What?"

"Because you saw some article and had pity on me?"

"Um... *yeah.*"

"Bria, that's not what I want."

"No. Let me finish, okay?" she huffs, grabbing hold of my unbuttoned shirt. She's still not wearing one at all. The swoop of her breasts cause my pants to tighten.

"Seeing that article just made me wonder why you felt like you couldn't tell me. And then... the more I wondered the more I started to see your pain instead of mine, for the first time. So I just... stayed quiet. When we walked to your car and I told you it was okay... and you fucking *cried*, I felt like a fucking monster. I was so caught up in my own... shit, that I couldn't see that you were hurting. Like... *really* hurting."

I watch her beautiful face as she tries to come up with the right word and I want to grab her and kiss her, before I wake up from this dream.

But she hates when I interrupt her, even with something good. I don't know why I even do it, I don't think I interrupt anyone else. I think she just makes me more excited than most people.

At Halcyon, she once threatened to cut my throat if I interrupted her one more time.

I just walked away from her and called her irrational. We were five months in.

"If I'm being honest, the instant I saw you I wanted you back," she confesses. "I was gonna take you right back. Because that's just... who I am. But I was afraid to trust that. I didn't want to be a sucker. And I'm... sorry."

I sigh and my brow wrinkles. I try to give her the explanation I owe her without having to uproot the darkest period of my buried life.

"It was another lifetime ago. Felix was the first cop on the scene. He's the reason I became a cop. He saved my life.

"Walking away from that life we made, from what I'd done.

235

To you. To myself. It hit me all at once. About a year later. All at once, and I couldn't handle it."

"Oh my God," she quietly sighs in empathy.

"It's not something that I like to dwell on. It happened. I've got a few scars now... but I'm better for it."

"I'm so sorry."

"It was entirely about me. None of it was your fault."

"You went through all that alone," she says in a whisper as she takes my face in her small hands. She looks at me, and tries to get me to look up. But I won't.

I take one of her hands to my lips and kiss it. "But I didn't," I confess, finally confronting her gaze.

"No wonder you look so..." she trails off, unable to find a word to describe the six year difference in me.

She, however, is pretty much the same and I'm glad of that. To the point of arousal. I look down at her bare chest, suddenly reminded of her toplessness.

"We're here now. Like you said," I say as I sway her in my arms. I feel like an asshole, but putting my arms all the way around Lyric's waist for the first time, nearly twice, is getting me hot enough to lose my mind.

My grip on her tightens and her breath audibly abandons her. It's starting.

Finally, our lips meet again. I don't close my eyes and neither does she. My gaze intensifies. It's been six years and I know my eyes are going to bore a hole in hers straight down to the floor.

"Luke," she gasps without a second thought.

"Lyric...*prasice*..." I whisper between kisses to her eyes, face, neck.

I kiss her everywhere, and I don't know where the next one will land or how long I'll linger there. I kiss her like dry land after months at sea and I don't know which way is up.

Suddenly we tumble on the bed behind us and the kisses continue, moving lower and slower and to unlikely places. The top of her breast, along her rib cage.

I slip her pajama bottoms off. She reaches for her underwear and chases them off too. I rush out of the rest of my unbuttoned uniform and undershirt before perusing her body fully with my eyes and hands, the way I wanted to on the hood of her car.

I study her and she studies me back, looking for traces of awe at her transformed body. I hope she can see it, as the curves of her new body formulate my strategy.

I don't want to just say, "you're beautiful" as if she wasn't before. Even though she is. She knows "*lijepa si*" in Croatian. I decide to forego words.

I lay down next to her on my side and trace her body from her neck and down with my fingers. I place a hand on her stomach as I stare, move it around her navel. She's so quiet, like the very first time, as if inside she's screaming, wanting to savor every moment.

My erection slaps against my middle as I take off my boxer briefs. She stares and stares at it as if hypnotized as I hover over her. I nudge her legs open with a knee to nestle between them and look in her eyes. She looks in mine.

Both of us settle, calm and revisiting each other's features with our fingers. Her lips, my hair. We're locked in and waking up from a six-year long dream.

Her gorgeous brown thighs draw me in like a tractor beam and I find myself enamored with the sight that I once took for granted, and even loathed:

"*I can either go down on you or rub it.*"

"*You can't come up with like, anything else?*"

"You can't just be happy that I'm going down on you?"

"You don't want to do it, and I don't want it done."

"Fucking forget it, Jesus..."

"Oh God," her whispers force me to the present.

"Fuck," I moan. Because we're not in the back of a car and she doesn't have to be quiet and neither do I.

"Don't stop, I'm gonna come so hard," she's already panting and it makes me grunt uncontrollably like an animal until she's clutching the pillows on either side of her and her body slowly sickles.

"Oh, fuck yes fuck yesfuck yess..." she cries, her orgasm washing over her like smooth waves. I lick until she's gushing, until it becomes too much and she has to curl herself into a ball as soon as I move my mouth away. She shivers as her thighs clench over and over, and my throbbing erection won't let her revel there.

I pry her knees apart, slowly positioning myself inside and locks my eyes on hers. I slide in slowly and with ease, willing myself to go slow but it's no use. Bria's got golden ticket pussy and I haven't had sex in two years.

I get in a few more thrusts from tip to base before I'm pulling out and icing her belly and cleavage with cum. Soft gasps escape my lips on a slight delay. Bria's cursing and moaning with delight, not unlike our pre-first time first time. I push her back against the headboard so that I can climb all the way on top of her until we're nose to nose.

"You didn't have to do that," she says to me, a drop of jizz on her lip. Her tongue reaches for it.

"What?"

"Pull out."

"I wanted to," I pant, looking down at her from my kneeling

position on the bed. I reach for my discarded shirt at the edge of the bed and use it to clean up the mess.

"Don't do it again," she commands me.

"I won't," I assure her.

"You're gorgeous," she says, right before I cover her with my body and kiss her.

I don't answer as my hardness nudges her at her opening again. Her leg cranes up to accommodate me and I'm ready to ravish her.

I hike her leg over one arm and the sensation of her warmth on my still erect, post-orgasm cock makes me wince for a moment. I look down to see her watching my every move, feeling my every move, biting her lip as my pace quickens.

Finally her head goes back and forth in ecstasy and awe, stoking my hunger. She mumbles all kinds of nonsense about never having been fucked like this, my ego stories high. I silences her lips with my tongue.

I let myself get lost in this maze of lust, quick and pounding one moment to slow and penetrating strokes the next. I feel Bria's hands on my back, misty with sweat, words lodged in my throat. I withdraw and get on my back, and she knows instantly what it means.

It's one of my favorite positions, the one I want to die in, and the one I want to fuck Bria in right now until I come. She hurriedly climbs on top and hangs on to the headboard as I thrust her again and again.

"*Teze tata*," she says to me, in the naughty Croatian that she wanted to learn.

"*Sjećate se onoga što sam vas naučio*," I reply in a low rumble. She loves Croatian dirty talk, and I, of course, love that she loves it. She came to me counting to one hundred once.

"Oh my God, more," she demands, like a needy pervert. A shiver runs through me.

"*Jesi li ga koristio na njemu? Hm?*" I ask tenderly, the grip on her hips tightening.

She starts to grind on me and I can tell she's going to come again, which is the exact thing I want to see right now.

I link one arm around her and her hands go to the side of my head to steady herself. I hold onto her for dear life, fucking her hard and fast. I can't see, I can't breathe, I'm just trying to hold back until I can at least make it to the beginning of her end.

"Don't hold back anymore baby," she pleads.

"Bria," I pant.

"I want to hear you fuckin' come while I explode," she growls.

"*Fuck,*" I yell, as my orgasm soars like a rocket, higher and higher as the headboard beats against the wall. Bria's uncontrollable cries resonate in my ears as she spasms all over me, my eyes roll without effort as Bria sends me into signature eye-rolling raptures at the end.

I swear I didn't even know I could come like that until her. Her body keeps shivering as my vision returns to see her doubled over and watching me.

"Holy fucking shit," she says. She rolls next to me.

"I'm never letting you go," I whisper.

21

Luke

The day the evaluation results were slipped under the door, we hadn't even noticed.

It was a weekend, and there was a bottle of wine in with our box meal to commemorate the day. The halfway mark.

With no excuse to leave the room, we lit the place up with candles after dinner and made love until the following morning.

"Well I'll be damned," Lyric said from the living room the next morning.

She walked back to the doorway in her loosely fastened white silk robe, the manila envelope held up in one hand.

"Shall I do the honors?"

"Don't open it," I said, when she laid next to me on the bed. She scoffed.

"Are you really worried?" she smiled sweetly.

"I just know how my mind is. If it turns out I was right—"

"Then they would be in here escorting us out, not slipping

241

your results under the door," Lyric rolled her eyes. She pinched the tabs at the top of the manila envelope.

"I hope you understand how long you'll have to go down on me, after this thing says what I know it says," she muttered.

"Then I can't wait."

She pulled out the documents and perused them quietly. She sat up, pretending to be jarred by what she was reading.

"What is it?"

She turned the jumbled stats towards me, where our names were paired at the bottom with a small graph and the words "confirmed match" near our percentages, 96% and 98% respectively.

"Hope you like a muff," she said.

"You're so gross."

Two Months Left

We woke up in the morning and stared at each other in bed. Lyric seemed a little sad, but she never said a word as I took her hand in mine and watched her back. She played with a few strands of my hair and sighed. Something was on her mind.

"What?"

She faintly shook her head and grinned, focused on me. The distraction left her gorgeous eyes.

"You're my human," she said to me.

"You're my human," I said back.

After we banged in the shower, I sat on the toilet seat while Lyric performed her morning routine with her hair, because there's literally nothing else to do. Luckily, it's pretty fascinating.

I watched as Lyric combed her hair with a hot device that would absolutely be mistaken for an instrument of torture if it wasn't pink.

She sang along to her headache-inducing playlist emanating from her speaker. I wasn't super into most things on it, but it made her happier to have it on. She patiently transformed her impossibly curly-textured hair into a long, thick, flaxen cascade.

"You should wear it like that."

"Pffff....I look like a lion," she giggled.

"You look like you're from the future," I said. She cracked up laughing, reaching for another hot, torturous-looking instrument, ready to transform it further to its familar straightened appearance.

"Can I touch it?"

"If you must," she sighed.

I stood up and gathered her surprisingly soft hair in a bundle with my fist. I brushed it all over my face like one of those makeup brushes. She laughed.

"I wanna rub this on my cock."

"Ew, get *outta* here, you perv," she elbowed me.

Later that day was my solo session with Dr. Payton. It took me about twenty minutes to start.

"I don't want to hurt her feelings. I know she's sensitive about her weight. I want her to be healthy. But I know she exercises. I know for a fact she eats healthy, because we eat the same things. I don't want to say it's not her fault, but I do feel for her. I wish I could say that I love her because of her weight, but I don't. I love her despite it."

"But you do love her," he pounced on my choice of words.

"Yes."

"A recent discovery?"

243

"Very. Just now, maybe."

"So, you've never told her."

"No."

"Have you broached the subject at all with her?"

"Absolutely not," I replied.

"Out of fear?"

"Out of respect. I mean what, like she doesn't know? She's not here to talk about that."

Dr. Payton shifted in his chair. "Is it a health concern, or something more?"

"...Both. I mean... if she never loses the weight could I be with her? I don't know how I could," I confess. "But at the same time...."

"Yes?"

"I don't wanna say. 'Cause it's horrible."

"Must be, if you're afraid to tell me," he quietly marveled.

"I'm just thinking.... once she loses the weight she'll be... well, perfect. And then... what's to keep her from leaving me?"

"You're describing a conundrum of trust that all relationships confront."

"Maybe so, but... this is like deja vu for me. Meet a beautiful woman that doesn't know she's beautiful, I convince her that she is, she believes it, she moves on."

Dr. Payton's wall clock became deafening as he waited for me to continue, rather than interject. Which meant he hated me. I sympathized.

"I guess I have an advantage in that I'm her first," I reasoned. "But how long would it realistically take for her to put two and two together about my average-sized dick?"

"You're suggesting enabling Lyric's insecurities so that you can sleep better at night?"

"I'm not talking about feeding her a fucking pizza every night I'm just... airing my thoughts and fears right now. The anxiety that she could come to me at any point and say, 'I'm moving on,' I mean... it's not crippling. Yet. I just can't see myself living through that again."

"You should definitely have a talk about your expectations. We can bring it up in your joint session, when you're ready."

Yeah, no. That's not gonna happen.

"Let me sleep on it, Doc."

"Very well."

Two Months Left

"Luke, I gotta be honest here," Lyric sighed.

"By all means."

"I just don't see myself living in Chicago."

At some point we got a little more specific about our lives, including our family trees and where we lived.

"Well, my parents would probably die if I moved," I said.

"Same."

"Well, shit."

We laid naked in the big bed, our legs intertwined as we spoke in the dark.

"Is this our first fight?" she smiled.

"No. We'll figure it out."

"Well, we should probably figure it out before we leave here."

"We're only half way through. Plenty of time for us to fall back out of love."

"Are we in love?" I asked, lowering my head and slowly tonguing one of her nipples.

"...We're not *not* in love."

"I love how heavy your boobs are."

"You really wanna move in together as soon as we leave here?"

I lifted my head to confront her skeptical stare. "My parents are expecting me to emerge from this thing with a wife."

"Right..."

"You getting cold feet?" I smirked.

"No, it's just... practically speaking, I just realized I never thought past getting here. We don't even know where we're going to live."

"Let's go someplace neutral. Somewhere in the middle."

"Everywhere in the middle is too cold."

"Texas?"

"Mm... maybe. I have a sister that lives there. Houston."

"I've always wanted to go to Florida."

"Too hot."

"Sounds like Texas it is, then."

"I still have to finish school, I mean... you don't have anything going on, right?"

"No."

"What's your degree in again?"

"I uh... didn't finish."

"Oh. Well what were you studying?"

"Finance."

"That's right," she remembered. "Maybe you could transfer to USC. I only have two semesters left but—

"School wasn't really for me."

"Okay, so... what do you want to do?"

"Listen, can we talk about something else?"

She was politely silent for a moment. A clear indication she wanted to keep talking. But she conceded.

"Sure, but... this stuff's sorta important. We can't really put it off for too long, you know?"

"Yeah."

"Bored?" she asks, her hand in my hair.

"Yeah."

"Wanna read something?"

She meant her lady porn, as I call it. I shake my head. "We've read everything like, three times."

"We can go back through the ones you didn't finish. They might surprise you."

"No, I can't. I don't want to hear anymore stories about white women with the heart of a fucking lion."

"What are you talking about?" she laughed.

"You don't notice that? They're fucking always blushing and saying 'how dare you' and flailing around giving people ultimatums and shit. And they're only flaw is that they care too much. They're not even secret psychopaths, they're just open ones. There, on the surface."

"I feel like some projection is happening right now."

One Month Left

"So, I know you don't wanna talk about the wedding—"

"I never said I didn't want to talk about the wedding."

"You don't have to. I think we should wait until I finish school. And maybe longer."

"To get married?" I asked.

"To have a wedding."

"Okay."

I leaned against the kitchen counter while Lyric pulled out leftovers to heat them up.

She was wearing these stretchy shorts she felt bold enough to parade around in a few months back.

"I think we should travel. I mean, we've gotten to know each other being cooped up here, but traveling is a different animal."

"Aren't you done challenging our relationship?"

"I just want you to be sure."

"I'm sure there's not another woman in the world that can put up with me the way you can," I confessed.

She tilted her head adorably and failed to stifle a smile. "Luke, I'm blushing," she deadpanned.

"Honestly, the first thing I wanna do when we get outta here is go to the movies."

"We can go to Catalina," her dark eyes brightened. "They've got a cute little vintage movie theater there. Honestly, I can't believe you've never been."

"You mean, once we leave here?"

"Yeah, you know just for a few days. Without telling anyone that we're out. Just you and me."

I stayed quiet.

"Because things are gonna be crazy once we get back to reality."

"Why would they be crazy?"

"Um, it's just sort of how we roll. In my family. You're going to be passed around, and that's all I'm saying," she said, opening the oven. "It sounds sexual, but it's not."

"I'm down for Catalina, but... after that... what's say we go our separate ways for a while?"

"What do you mean?" she said in her way. That always began quiet but never ended that way.

"I mean, we've been couped up here for six months. You threw a cup at my head yesterday."

"...That wasn't yesterday."

"It was. I think the first thing we should do is get away from each other."

She walked away and disappeared into our room for a full minute before she responded. "That is... not what I want."

"I haven't heard anything in your plan about going to Chicago. When am I supposed to go home, exactly?"

"We can go together," she shrugged.

"I just think it's wise for us to have a hiatus."

"You think it's *wise*?"

"Yeah. Go our separate ways, call each other on the phone and talk about how we miss each other. Don't you wanna miss me?"

She looked at me soberly and then finally glared.

"....What the fuck are you talking about?"

"Never mind. Obviously this is triggering you."

"No, like... why do you wanna *miss* me?"

"Forget it."

"Dude, if you don't want to do this, tell me now," she said with her arms raised, a familiar refrain, worded slightly differently.

"Forget I fuckin' said it, alright?"

"You know what, you can opt out. Then you can miss me for the rest of your life."

I grin a little. Such a sassy gal.

"I'm not gonna do that."

"You're not?"

"No, I'd die without your pussy."

She chuckled a little about that, grabbing hot tin foil pans from the oven.

"You'd die without my pussy?" she teased, in her beautiful speaking voice. God, that is so hot to me.

"Yes."

"Is that the only thing you'd die without?"

"Pretty much."

"You bastard," she laughed as she shook her head.

She walked up to me and put my arms on her sides.

"You're in this. With me. Aren't you?"

"I am."

"That's good, 'cause... you're my human," she hummed, looking into my eyes. I kissed her on hers.

"And you're mine."

"Okay then. I guess... we can talk about time apart. Once we checkout," she conceded.

"That's all I ask."

"I know. And it's reasonable."

"I love you," I said.

We agreed not to say it at all. It hardly meant anything while we're forced to interact, she reasoned.

Her face lit up against her will and she lowered her head. My heart thumped and I wanted to take a picture. What were the odds of us ever finding each other outside of these walls?

"I love you," she admitted with a smile. She slipped out of my grasp as she walked away to set the table for dinner, an original melody from her lips perfuming the air.

Present Day

I have no idea what time it is when I finally wake up. The sound of the shower cuts through my sleep and I try to sleep through it.

A moment later I hear Bria singing and further sleeping is now impossible.

I smile, immediately hopping out of bed and following the sound of Bria's voice. The deja vu is so acute that for a moment I'm disoriented.

It doesn't take long for her to sense my naked presence in the big bathroom. I can't help noticing the separate shower/tub layout that wasn't unlike the one we shared at Halcyon.

"Hey you," she smiles as she opens the shower door and bids me entry. I'm still adjusting to her beautiful body, but her eyes are still as mesmerizing as they ever were.

"This bathroom is eerily similar," I say.

"I know. When I saw it, I just cracked up. My realtor thought I was crazy."

"It didn't freak you out?"

"No, it was comforting. To have a piece of it."

I give her a forehead kiss. "I appreciate the wake-up call."

"I thought you would," she smiled, her hands on my chest as she reaches up for a real kiss. The taste of her soft full lips mingles with the hot shower water.

"Is this real?" I ask.

She doesn't respond. She takes her washcloth and begins to wash me down below. She gets down on her knees where she's eye to eye with my growing erection.

"This is definitely real," she says, rinsing me off. She grabbed my length with one hand and held the tip on her tongue, the same temperature as the water.

We made breakfast. Together. Wordless.

We ate it in the same peace. Even though I had a million things to tell her. But then, I always did. And it always hardly mattered.

"Work tonight?" she asks.

"Yes. You?"

She shook her head. "I'm not looking at anything band related

251

for a week."

"Aren't you also the manager or something?"

"Not anymore. I fired myself. Or the band did."

"You didn't like it?"

"I loved it. Some parts. But I can't do both jobs."

"I'm really fucking proud of you Lyric, if that means any-thing."

"It does. Of course it does. *Luke.*"

"Should we stop using the names, or what?" I propose.

"I don't know. It's gonna take some getting used to."

"Wonder how long it took Darren to stop calling her Jem."

Bria laughs, hearing the names.

"So... what should we do?" I ask.

"Maybe just use them as our super-secret pet names."

"No, I mean... with our lives," I say.

"Oh," she realizes, as if startled by the dilemma. "Maybe let's just... focus on today. You know, for now."

I smile. Lyric has indeed changed. I'm impressed.

"We could go to a movie. To the zoo..." I reminisce. She loved to talk about the first thing we would do together when we got out.

"Or maybe just... stay in?" she wrinkled her nose with a smile.

You'd think after spending the length of our relationship inside a dating service compound, it would be the last thing we want to do. Turns out it's the first.

"Play cards?" I tease her.

"Or read," she teases me back with a smile.

"Got any more of those romance novels?" I ask between a sip of coffee. She laughs and then raises one eyebrow.

"Oh, Luke. You have no idea," she shakes her head.

22

Bria

Present Day— Two Years Later

S tanding in front of the presidential suite mirror, my mother and sister stand behind me. April and Chelsea keep me company and agreed to run interference against Skye.

I can't do it, because it's my wedding day, so I won't. And my mother can't do it, because as far as she's concerned we're still 8 and 15 years old.

I expected her to be a lot more of a problem after rehearsal, where she called Chase a bitter loser, which was pretty rich. And then told embarrassing stories about me to any in-law who would listen, like the time I broke a chair at an outdoor restaurant and the paparazzi laughed themselves silly.

The Novaks are unfamiliar with my sister's antics. But she's doing a lot better today.

Farrah, Felix's wife, is chatting up Aunt Pat. She's adorable. Apparently, she was Cliff's only outlet while we were separated.

She knew more about Cliff and me than I did. When we met, she practically burst into tears.

Cliff's sister Claudia is also here, newly graduated from college and the bridge between Cliff's family and mine.

They've been very nice, all of them, don't get me wrong. But they're a bit stuffy. Compared to Cliff's, my parents may as well be peasants.

We certainly act that way when we get out, like when Cliff's dad took us all to Africa for a safari.

"Is this some racist bullshit?" My dad asked.

"Daddy, the entire continent can't be off-limits."

I grew up with everything, but my parents' poverty-stricken memories never let them go a day without gratitude for the life they lead. The Novaks haven't known poverty for generations.

Except for my mother-in-law Nadia who apparently grew up poor in Croatia, and was eager to enter the poverty Olympics with my parents when they first met, comparing stories. But only Claudia feels removed enough from her classical upbringing to be herself around us.

Aunt Pat has removed the last roller from my hair and suddenly it takes an army to put a wedding dress on.

I can feel as the zipper on my princess A-line satin wedding dress with the extra long train makes the journey from just above my backside to between my shoulder blades. The journey is smooth, simple and comfortable. I lower my arms, look at myself in the mirror and take a breath as my hair falls down my back in soft ringlets.

You, Bria Forrester… you are wearing a size six wedding dress, bitch. How's it feel biaaaaaaatch!!!

My mom looks at me with tears in her eyes. She purposely saved the makeup for last, but I didn't, so I have to keep it together. The dress was the last step. Well, the next to last after the veil.

"Bria, you look *sick*. Mom *look* at this!" Skye grabs my clavicle bone. My mom quickly comes out of the tender moment. Way to be unintentionally helpful, Skye.

"Skye, I don't know why you always gotta instigate!"

"Size six was always the goal," I reply, blinking away any traces of water and examining my mascara in the mirror.

"How does Cliff feel about his wife wasting away?"

"He supports me no matter what."

"I hear that, but you gotta keep him happy, Bri. I don't see how another extreme is the answer."

"Skye, I'm the same size as you, how is that extreme?"

"It's not the size, it's the mindset, Bria. You've become one of the worse fat shamers out there. And that's really alarming. You should really hear yourself."

"Cliff's at the door y'all," Aunt Pat comes to the rescue with her exasperated sounding announcement.

"What does he want?"

"I just wanna talk—" he begins, before all the women rally around me frantically, trying to hide me from him as he enters the room.

"It's okay guys. No one here's worried about bad luck."

"Bria, you're a performer dahling you have to make an entrance," my mother insists.

"I don't want the first time I see her to be shared with everyone else," he says.

Well, no one can argue with that.

Everyone rushes out of the room to give us privacy.

"You look beautiful," he smiles in a low voice.

"Thanks, so do you," I say as he wraps his arms around me.

He was wearing a beautiful white shirt with a beige tuxedo jacket and black trousers. I picked it out and I'm obsessed.

"You look like a cloud," he says.

I laugh. "Thanks, I guess."

"It's a compliment."

"I know."

"I feel like I've waited my whole life to get here," he says, studying me as he caresses my bare shoulders.

"Me too," I quietly reply.

"And now I kinda wish it was over," he admits. I snicker.

"We have our whole lives to be together," I re-assure him.

"I know. You're right," he nods with a grin, moving his hands to mine. "I should get back. I didn't tell anyone where I was going."

"See you on the other side?" I say.

It took me a half second to realize what I'd said.

The same thing I said the day he opted out.

Cliff was instantly emotional, lowering his head as he nodded.

"Fuck, I didn't mean to say that," I laughed through tears. "Get out of here, you're gonna ruin my makeup."

He gives my hand a kiss and quietly leaves.

Halcyon: Check Out— 0 Days Left

"See you on the other side?" Lyric asks.

I huffed a little laugh as I looked at her. The two staff members on either side of her escort her out, her packed duffle bag in one hand.

She's wearing the same thing I first saw her in, with the same fear and apprehension on her face. Except this time it's about leaving my side.

I answer her with a slow kiss on her lips. It seemed to re-assure her, but I didn't want to seem non-committal.

"See you on the other side," I replied.

The three of them walked out of the now vacant room.

It's strange to think of this room as empty, since it looks just about the same as it always does. But it's not just another room to me anymore.

This room changed my life.

I take a few last looks, waiting for my turn to go through checkout.

When my escorts arrive and take me back to the main lobby, Dr. Payton is there, with another woman I faintly recognize from my evaluation. It's strange to see Dr. Payton exist outside of his office.

"As you know, before we can release you to your Match, you'll be asked a series of questions and be given the opportunity to opt-out. Should you choose that option, you'll be taken through the Halcyon exit doors, given a plane ticket free of charge to your predetermined destination, and will relinquish all information related to your Match or your time at Halcyon. Do you understand?"

"Yes."

"Perfect. Your questionnaire will remain confidential and will be unmonitored by anyone related to your case, including Dr. Payton or any of the intake staff and of course, your Match. Any questions?"

"No."

They take me to a room so unbelievably drab and average, I wonder if perhaps I've been swindled.

None of it ever happened. Or someone will suddenly appear

257

from behind the door to shoot me in the head at point blank range. Lyric's already dead. Or perhaps in on it, as part of an elaborate ruse.

There's a small ten inch tablet sitting on a two person table in front of a single chair. I sit down and follow the directions on the screen.

"On a scale of 1 to 10, how would you rate your experience with Halcyon?"

I can't imagine how they could find such a question quantifiable at all. I choose ten, out of sheer impotence.

"On a scale of 1 to 10, how would to describe your emotional attachment to your Match?"

This survey is retarded. 10 being co-dependency and 1 being I want to murder her? Honestly, what the hell, Halcyon. I pick eight, to be safe.

I can't see myself without Lyric in my life, now that she's here. My heart jolts a little thinking about seeing her beam with pride on my arm. A smile like the actual sun. For an instant, I get an image of all the bitching and blacklisting that's going to happen when we make our debut. It makes me smirk, thinking of all the uncomfortable parties we'll skip. Or maybe we'll go. I'd have fun, but Lyric wouldn't.

"Are you confident in Halcyon's selection of your long-term monogamous partner?

Thankfully this question's a yes or no. I hit 'yes,' though it hardly matters.

Ultimately it was my selection. I'm simply happy with my choice. It was an invaluable lesson.

"Do you have serious doubts in the validity of Halcyon's methods?

It stands to reason that I could do the same outside these doors, I suddenly realized. A frightening epiphany. Like being surrounded by an ocean.

This new knowledge that I'm sitting on, not just of Lyric but of myself.

Am I really going to turn my back on that? Did I give up too early?

Sure, I was unsuccessful out there, but I was looking for something that doesn't really exist.

It's a bit embarrassing to look back on. With the entire world at my disposal, would I really make the same mistake again?

I absent-mindedly answer 'yes' on the survey, my train of thought having completely jumped the track. It mindlessly moves on to the next question.

Are you satisfied with the sexual compatibility of your long-term monogamous partner?

I get another vision, this time of the gaggle of women that would inevitably throw themselves at me once I become unavailable.

Do I really possess the fortitude *not* to fuck them? Once the memories of this place fade?

I get another vision of Lyric's angelic teary face. Reminding me every day what a piece of shit I am. I've been on that hiatus for six months and this drab, unflattering room is a reminder.

No, I would never live my life without her.

But it doesn't mean I'd treat her the way she deserves.

"Do you see yourself with your long-term monogamous partner for 6 months or more?"

Maybe it's not a person at all that I'm after.

Maybe I just love the thrill that I get.

Maybe it's not love, it's just thankfulness.

Maybe I can customize this experience 1,000 more times.

Maybe I can't be hurt, but she can.

Maybe there's a woman out there that'll stop me cold in my tracks one day.

But it's not Lyric, if I'm being honest.

Three years ago it was Stacey, but I had crazy blinders on.

There just has to be a winning combination out there. If there isn't, I need to know for myself.

"Do you see yourself with your long-term monogamous partner for 5 years or more?"

I start to shiver as I stare at the question with alarm.

Shit. *Shit...*

I'm not going to fucking do this, am I?

The wedding's not happening.

Catalina's not happening. None of it's happening.

My body shakes, because I don't understand.

I want Lyric in my life. I can't see my life without her.

But somehow I know I won't go through with this. Tears of confusion blur my eyes.

"Your final evaluation is complete. If you choose to opt-in, proceed to the door on your right, if not, choose opt-out."

You owe it to her to see her on the other side of that door.

You owe her at least that.

Break up with her, cheat on her, whatever.

But you can't do it like this.

You'll kill her. You'll kill that thing in her.

But I'm no good. And this proves it.

And this way she'll know. She'll know without having every good memory dissolve away into nothing.

It's going to hurt like shit, but now she can do so much better than this.

I won't waste her time. I won't waste any woman's time, ever again.

My heart seizes as the opt-out button turns red underneath my shaky finger.

"You have chosen to opt out. This decision is final and cannot be changed."

She'll do so much better than me, I keep chanting in my head. It keeps me from having a panic attack for about 30 seconds at a time.

"Your Match has chosen to opt-in and will be briefed at Checkout in your absence. Would you like to leave your Match an optional message?"

The room is getting smaller and I have to get out of here.

I leave it blank and bang on the door for someone to let me out. Two male staff members emerge from behind the opposite door.

"Mr. Novak?"

I'm jarred by the sudden use of my real name.

"Please answer the final question to complete the process of opt-out."

I was right. None of this was real.

This drab room, this is the real Halcyon.

A drab room with two dudes hiding behind glass. It's all a test.

Either I'm the only man that's ever failed, or the only man that's ever passed.

I still feel a bit like Alice out of the rabbit hole as a calm comes over me. I hit the final confirmation button on table and it fades into a Halcyon home screen.

"This way please."

Two grown men walk stoically next to me while they walk me back across the same entrance that I used when I arrived, alone again. For the first time in six months. Alone the same way I came.

I sob like I've lost a loved one.

I have. I really have. The movie reel of the last six months starts up.

This. This does not feel good.

When does the relief come?

This is for the best.

The first thing I'm doing when I get out of here is getting white boy wasted. I understand not wanting to serve booze, Halcyon, but for fuck's sake.

I'm going go to a bar and look at every woman I see on the way. And I mean, really look at them.

I'm going to Stacey's wedding in the fall, with my head held high. And with Lyric gone I can bang a chick during the ceremony.

I'm going to re-evaluate my social circle. With new eyes.

Wait a minute... is this magical combination of woman *also* going to be willing to put up with me?

This is for the best.

It's not guaranteed to be chosen back.

But that's not really the root of it, it's... actually I don't know if I remember the root of it.

But I know that walking out of here is the most I've felt like myself in months.

You're never going to see Lyric again. You're never going to know her real name, or who she really was, or who she's going to become outside these walls.

You won't travel together, you won't grow together. You won't see her shine.

You may have really fucked yourself this time, Cliff.

This is for the best.

A car picks me up and takes me to the airport. Stoically I get in with my bag in my lap, anxious to leave the scene.

What just happened?

Is this what murderers feel like?

I'm pretty sure this is what murderers go through. A murderer's refrain passes through my mind like a recording: *"Just don't think about it. It's done, you did it. This is your life."*

This is for the best.

I crane my neck to watch the Halcyon compound disappear in the distance and I face forward, feeling nauseous.

This is for the best.

"Look at you, you're a piece of shit. Look what you're capable of. You didn't even know you could be this shitty. Did you? You did her a favor."

This is for the best.

"This is for the best," I say aloud.

The voices quiet. For now.

The only sound is that of my hiccupping sobs.

This is for the best. This is for the best.

This is for the best.

23

Epilogue

Cliff

I watch from the crowd as Bria's face lights up while she's on stage even after all these years.

The stage is only a small fraction of the stages she used to perform on, of course. This stage is in the airport lounge.

And the crowd is me at a small cocktail table while we wait for our flight back home to LA.

The piano player plays the opening bars of "Concord Queen," a modest hit Bria had with the band before the kids were born.

The last time they toured was about eight years ago, when she felt the kids were old enough to leave at home, since they didn't want to be pulled out of school to go on the road. Seeing her now, I have a feeling she'll be calling Chase out of the blue again.

She sits down after the room gives her a prolonged note of applause. Afterwards, the entire band comes over and gushes. Bria maintains her gracious air as I hang back like the proud husband I am.

"This is my husband, Cliff," she defers.

"So nice to meet you," they smile.

"Congratulations on retirement," one of them says to me.

"Thank you," I say, genuinely surprised that strangers know these things. And a little freaked out.

It was more of a semi-retirement. A show of respect from the department.

Basically I up and quit because I felt like everyone just tolerated me playing dress up.

There were some young guys in the department coming up that I watched grow into great officers, and I was in their way. Too many would-be leaders with families to take care of.

They didn't have to do anything for me, but it was nice to feel appreciated.

We just got back from visiting my mother in Chicago. It was partly a birthday excursion for Bria's 50th, partly a covert operation to convince Mom to move to California with us.

Bria convinced me to move 12 years ago and with my father gone, my mother could use the distraction of grandkids and the year long sunshine.

We sit waiting at the gate before our plane arrives. Bria doesn't like flying private if we're not leaving the country, or if it's just us. I tend to agree.

In another lifetime I wouldn't have cared. But it's embarrassing being the Deputy of Police and complaining to anyone about flying first class.

Bria's phone vibrates on the table and she picks it up.

"Well, well, look who it is," she grins.

She shows me the name on the phone. "Jem."

Jem's real name is Barroness Alaina Monopolous.

Not long after we got married, she caught wind of us and

reached out. Her husband Niko is the Greek heir of a family fortune that deals in raw goods and pharmaceuticals.

Naturally, we refuse to refer to them as anything but Jem and Darren. Which helps with anonymity on the outside as well.

"Hey you... on our way to Cali, you should meet us," Bria says on the phone.

We're meeting the kids at their grandfather's house.

Bria's father has been having health problems, so it was serendipitous that they both chose to stay in California for school.

I have a suspicion that their grandmother had a hand in that little bargain. Or they could genuinely be that kind-hearted. They get that from Mom.

"What?!?!" Bria sits upright in her seat. My heart beats a little faster as we lock eyes, wondering if this shade of shock on her face is that of grief, surprise, anger, or happiness.

It's a draw. But Jem is rarely the source of bad news, or any news really. I can't imagine it's related to us.

Or is it?

"I gotta go I gotta call you back," Bria says, searching her phone for corroboration of whatever Jem's told her.

So this is about world events. That are apparently very, very, shocking?

"Clifford..." she says, daring me not to believe what she's about to say next.

"I'm dying over here," I grin.

"So... Jem is saying there's a documentary on Halcyon that's coming out, and... turns out the entire Halcyon program is bullshit."

I give her an eyeroll.

Every few years it seems there's someone crying foul on the

Halcyon program, that closed its doors ten years ago, 16 years after we entered it.

It's hard to take any of them seriously.

After our reunion, their perfect record appeared to be intact. A lot of industries tried to compete and failed.

Many more had everything to lose with content, monogamous love breaking out all over the place, so it was hard to see the accusations as anything but sabotage.

How this is different from every other attack on Halcyon, I have no idea.

"Jem has the inside scoop, does she?"

"Apparently the founding scientist has died, and the son is spilling *all* the beans."

"Now that *is* interesting," I nod my head. "So what's the story?"

Bria doesn't answer. She searches a little longer on her phone and resumes talking when she's still unable to find what she's looking for.

"Jem says the BBC is doing a big story on it and they called her for comment."

"They know who's been in it?"

She shakes her head. "She volunteered in exchange for maintaining her anonymity. But there's a lot of couples that went in after us that are going on record."

Her phone dings and it's a text from Jem. An article. She clicks on it.

"'How Halcyon defrauded the rich for 25 years,'" she reads aloud. She looks at me with a face full of priceless shock that I find hilarious.

It's intriguing, I can't lie.

"Oh my God!!!" she says as she reads.

"Read it outloud."

"The program's efficacy is purported to come from a system of low-concentration DNA matching, rather than psychological study, which behavioral biologist Dr. Lerger says could account for perhaps some of the familiarity and attachment that couples still experience, even after being confronted with the evidence of Halcyon's fraudulent methods.'"

"So what, we're like... distant cousins or something?" I say with a squint. She continues.

"'The institution of aliases and the option for candidates to quote "opt out" was to ensure Halcyon's inviolability'....They're saying it was a fluke and they basically experimented on us... Oh...my....God," she says as she keeps reading. "'The average couple shares up to 0.2% DNA in common, among a stationary population, whereas Halcyon couples who took voluntary blood tests that revealed a percentage of as much as SIX PERCENT.'"

"So they paired rich people up with their cousins," I conclude.

Bria dissolved into laughter that got progressively more intense.

"You're handling this very well for someone who believed in the program," I grin.

"Well I mean... *fuck*," she raises her arms in the air in smiling resignation. "What can we do about it now?"

"Wanna sue?" I ask.

"Why are *you* so calm? You were right from the beginning."

"Bri, I didn't marry you just because of some program. I went after you because of who you are. I liked you. And I made a choice."

"You 'liked' me?"

I nodded. "Best decision I ever made."

"Fuck that, I thought you were my soul mate," she whines.

268

"You had the hots for your cousin."

She gave me her signature smile-glare.

"'Have' the hots. And so do you, by the way," she says with an eyebrow raise.

She gives me a little lip bite as she nods and I laugh. She keeps reading but doesn't share anymore of her findings. She seems lost in thought.

"What's wrong?" I ask after a moment. She just groans in response.

"Come here," I gesture with my arms wide open. She slowly gathers herself into my lap.

"Does it bother you that we're not soul mates?"

"*Noooo*," she whines, unconvincingly. "I just... some of that shit that we... I just have a real hard time believing it was all placebo and... our own... whatevers."

I sweep a piece of hair from her eyes. "I never could quite shake the feeling that I didn't deserve you."

"And now you know why," she grins, slightly accusatory.

Her response makes me smile. I'm feeling genuinely proud of myself as I take in the sight of her ageless beauty.

"You smug bastard," she smiles into my ear. "My poor soul mate's out there twisting in the wind."

"Fuck 'em," I say with a shrug and a kiss on her neck. She laughs.

She looks into my eyes as if studying me for authenticity, the six years of our separation dwarfed by the next 24 together. The six months of the program still etched in our fabric.

"You're still my human," she says.

Looking at her makes it hard to know what to truly believe. Not even the creators themselves could tarnish the legacy of Halcyon. We all came out with something that we didn't have before, and that was each other.

Perhaps they didn't mean well, but we did. And as much as they were able come away with, I still think we came away with that much more.

"I call dibs on the window seat," she says.

She always calls dibs on the window seat, as though it were necessary.

I nuzzle her forehead with my chin as I whisper. "It's yours."

Join the C.L. Donley Mailing List!

Get mailing list exclusives, bonus content, and news on upcoming releases! No spam, just updates!

https://www.subscribepage.com/CLDMLLanding

Books by C.L. Donley

Want to read more? Check out the full back catalog at
cldonley.com.

About the Author

C.L. Donley lives in Texas with her husband and three small children. She spends her days daydreaming, reading, perusing social media, watching YouTube and/or Netflix, and occasionally writes books in between.

You can connect with me on:
- https://cldonley.com
- https://twitter.com/C_L_Donley
- https://facebook.com/amarascalling
- https://bookbub.com/authors/c-l-donley

Subscribe to my newsletter:
- https://www.subscribepage.com/CLDMLLanding